# MEAN MOMS

Also by Emma Rosenblum

*Very Bad Company*

*Bad Summer People*

# MEAN MOMS

*A Novel*

## Emma Rosenblum

FLATIRON
BOOKS
NEW YORK

MEAN MOMS. Copyright © 2025 by Emma Rosenblum. All rights reserved. Printed in the United States of America. For information, address Flatiron Books, 120 Broadway, New York, NY 10271. EU Representative: Macmillan Publishers Ireland Ltd., 1st Floor, The Liffey Trust Centre, 117–126 Sheriff Street Upper, Dublin 1, D01 YC43.

www.flatironbooks.com

Illustration by ZadorArt/Shutterstock

Emoji art by Carboxylase/Shutterstock.com

Designed by Donna Sinisgalli Noetzel

Library of Congress Cataloging-in-Publication Data

Names: Rosenblum, Emma, author.
Title: Mean moms : a novel / Emma Rosenblum.
Description: First edition. | New York : Flatiron Books, 2025.
Identifiers: LCCN 2024061204 | ISBN 9781250364203
   (hardcover) | ISBN 9781250364210 (ebook)
Subjects: LCGFT: Thrillers (Fiction). | Novels.
Classification: LCC PS3618.O8338 M43 2025 |
   DDC 813/.6—dc23/eng/20241220
LC record available at https://lccn.loc.gov/2024061204

Our books may be purchased in bulk for specialty retail/wholesale, literacy, corporate/premium, educational, and subscription box use. Please contact MacmillanSpecialMarkets@macmillan.com.

First Edition: 2025

10   9   8   7   6   5   4   3   2   1

*For my mom, Barbara*

# Prologue

=

Every wealthy mom in New York City, from uptown Manhattan to down, from Brooklyn Heights to Cobble Hill to Park Slope, had heard about what happened at Atherton Academy. They'd read the panicked WhatsApp missives from the safety of their penthouses and town homes, huddled under cashmere blankets, clutching glasses of cabernet. An incident at Atherton's annual benefit, something terrible, beyond words. Someone was behind it all, but no one knew who. Accusations were flying. A mom. It was definitely a mom. A real psycho. A possible murderer in their midst, wearing the same designers that they did, getting a blowout at their same salon, possibly even sharing the same dermatologist.

Maybe it was the selfless mom, the one who always volunteered, who collected money for gifts, who chaperoned the school trips.

Maybe it was the popular mom, the one everyone worshipped, the prettiest and richest and coolest.

Maybe it was the working mom, the one who missed the parent get-togethers, who rarely came to pickup, who was always racing off to a Zoom.

Maybe it was the flirty mom, the one who leaned into the dads at cocktail parties, who showed too much cleavage, who made eyes at the hot male teachers.

Maybe it was the messy mom, the one who arrived ten minutes late, who forgot to buy school supplies, who never read the important emails.

Maybe it was the sporty mom, the one whose kids played lacrosse, hockey, *and* football, who had coaches on speed-dial, who wore her tennis outfit all day long.

Maybe it was the know-it-all mom, the one who spewed the latest parenting research, who knew exactly what the surgeon general recommended, who could cite stats about the dangers of screen time.

Maybe it was the anxious mom, the one who still cut her middle schooler's grapes, who'd tracked her children since pre-K.

Maybe it was, maybe it was, maybe it was.

A sociopath standing alongside them at pickup, listening in as they chatted about weekend plans and moms' nights out. One of their own. But who could it be?

# PART I

## Fall

# WhatsApp Chat

*Atherton Lower School Moms*
*94 Participants*

**Dre Finlay**

Good morning, Atherton moms! This chat is for general announcements and info, but is not, I repeat, is *not*, the official channel for school communication. Dr. Broker and your class moms will send emails for that purpose. Please forward me contact info for any moms I missed—only I can add them as admin. Happy first day of school!

**Jennifer Smyth**

Hi all! I was wondering about after-school sign-ups. I want to get Jordy into chess on Wednesdays but can't find where to register.

**Armena Justice**

Jennifer, registration closed last week. Email Mrs. Pegaru to see if there's any room left.

**Jennifer Smyth**

How is it closed already? I never got a notification.

**Armena Justice**

Maybe check your spam folder? I definitely got a notification. Does anyone know when school picture day is? Hermenia's photos were horrendous last year, the wonky color correction made her blond hair look orange, like a mini Donald Trump. Shudder. ☺

**Caroline Press**

It's on the 19th. They're using the same company this year—it's actually my company.

**Armena Justice**

OMG, I had no idea! I was only kidding—it was Hermenia's fault for being born with that hair, not the photographer's . . .

**Kim Berns**

Hi, ladies! We're no longer at Atherton. We will miss everyone but felt that Liam needed to be in a more structured environment. Dre, can you please take me off the chat?

**Jessica Hillton**

Remember to save the date—October 3rd—for kindergarten moms' night out!

**Valerie Greg**

Why aren't the dads on this chain?

**Dre Finlay**

Valerie, we had all the dads on the chain last year, but they never participated, so we felt it best not to inundate their WhatsApp messages ;) But if you'd like to include your husband, feel free to send me his info.

**Valerie Greg**

I'm a lesbian.

**Kim Berns**

I'm still receiving these messages . . . Dre, can you take me off the chat?

## Chapter 1

# The First Day of School!

—

Belle Redness lived for the first day of Atherton drop-off. She loved getting back into the swing of her New York City life. She enjoyed the Hamptons, but by August she was hot and bored and sick of the pool, the garden parties, and the bugs. Especially the bugs. This summer, they'd been dealing with a nightmarish infestation of lanternflies, inch-long monsters with spotted brown wings that laid shiny eggs all over her beautiful trees. They'd soar around her yard, creating a horrible, biblical scene on her pristine East Hampton estate. She'd gotten used to the sensation of squashing them, hard, crushing their shells into the grass with her strappy sandals. For nearly the entirety of August, Belle had stopped entertaining, so distressed by the idea that her friends would notice the insect carcasses littering her lawn. Bugs, apparently, didn't care how much money you had. It was the worst thing about them, worse than the bites.

So she'd been happy to get back to the city last week, away from the vermin plague, settling into their four-thousand-square-foot floor-through penthouse on Leonard Street, their "Tribeca Gem," as *Architectural Digest* had put it. Belle and her husband, Jeff, had gutted the apartment over two years, living in the Greenwich Hotel with their daughter, Hildy, and their son, Miles, while their architect and designer, a husband-husband duo who called themselves "the Davids," went to town. In *AD*, Belle had described their time at the hotel as Hildy's "Madeline in the City moment," which she'd thought was a charming way of putting it. In reality, all of them, particularly Belle, had nearly gone crazy, packed into a two-room suite with no kitchen and just one and a half baths. But they'd survived.

The apartment, after all that, turned out perfectly, exactly how Belle had imagined it. It opened with a gallery-style foyer, ideal for displaying their growing art collection, including pieces by Marilyn Minter and Jeff Koons. The entry led to a living-library space, separated from the rest of the apartment with a sliding door, which the Davids had covered in bright purple felt. (The project, which ended up costing $8 million, was funded entirely by Belle's father, the former CEO of J.P. Morgan, as was everything else in Belle's lucky life.) Aesthetics were very important to Belle, who was a fashion designer. Well, she wasn't *quite* a designer yet. But soon. Very soon.

This morning, the first morning of school, Belle sat in her kitchen, sipping a latte that their live-in housekeeper, Ivanna, had made for her. She stared out the big bay windows, with their clear southern-facing views of One World Trade. It was 7:30 a.m., the downtown sun was bright, and Belle felt rested and ready to jump into fall. Later this year, she was set to launch her first company, Pippins Cottage Home, a small clothing-slash-lifestyle brand. It was debuting with just one item: a flowy linen dress that resembled the nightgowns Belle wore as a child. She'd named it "The Dress."

Hildy came in, wearing sweats and a hoodie that hung on her

thin frame. Belle winced at Hildy's outfit but said nothing. Miles followed, in colorful Flow Society shorts and hideous blue Crocs, the pride of every fourth-grade boy. He gave Belle a hug, twirling her long hair playfully as he did. When Belle was young, she'd grown her thick, chestnut hair to her midback, and she'd kept it that length into adulthood. She felt that it gave her a girlish charm and loved that it had become her signature look, topping it with ribbons and bows and the odd headband.

Hildy stayed far away. The family's white Ragdoll cats, Duke and Sky, came slinking in together, each rubbing on one of Hildy's legs.

"Mom, come on, let's go," said Hildy, bending down to pet Duke. Hildy was in the seventh grade. Both the Redness children attended Atherton Academy, on Sixteenth Street near Stuyvesant Square Park. Atherton was the top private school in downtown Manhattan, catering to children of tech CEOs and creative empires rather than the private-equity crowd that lived uptown. It was eminently more fashionable to have your kid at Atherton than, say, Trinity or Dalton or St. Bernard's, and Belle was all about being fashionable.

Belle's only gripe about the school was that it didn't have a uniform. Some nonsense about the importance of self-expression. Every morning was a war, with Hildy refusing to wear any of the overtly feminine items Belle had bought for her at LoveShackFancy. Hildy had no interest in looking "cute," as she put it with a grimace. She rightly pointed out that these clothes were Belle's style, not her own. Instead, Hildy bought her sweats exclusively from Champion.

"Just because you and the other moms are bitchy fembots who dress and look alike doesn't mean that I have to be like that," Hildy explained to her matter-of-factly, after Belle had offered to take her school shopping. Belle had nodded and kept her mouth shut. Her therapist had told her that the more she pressured Hildy to look a certain way, the more she would resist, and so Belle had been working on holding her tongue. If this was the worst thing about Hildy, so be it. Hildy already had a couple "theys" in her grade at Atherton, as well as one boy who was transitioning. Hildy had assured Belle that her fashion choices were just that; she liked boys, she didn't want to *be* one. But the dread that one day Hildy would change her mind, come home, and tell them to call her "Henry" lingered.

Was this what it felt like during the 1950s, when no one knew which child would come down with polio? Belle wondered. She understood that questioning your gender didn't equal possible paralysis or even death, but there was something strange about New York City lately, something mysterious and sinister, that was spiking her anxiety. The lanternflies everywhere. Dog poop decorating the sidewalks. Slugs after rainstorms. The uptick in subway slashings, which Belle kept hearing whispered about at cocktail parties. Everything suddenly felt like a threat.

Belle shivered as she and Hildy and Miles approached the main building of Atherton, a gorgeous rust-red structure with proud white columns. They'd had their driver, Fred, drop them off a couple of blocks away from the school, as the area became clogged with SUVs and Ubers and even the occasional Rolls-Royce. The September air was warm and heavy. They passed a sleeping figure on the sidewalk, covered in ratty black blankets, and the pungent, sour smell of unwashed human hit Belle's nose. She held her breath and grabbed her children's hands. Hildy shook her off as if Belle was a stranger.

Belle, stung, recovered in time to put on a big smile for the drop-off crowd gathered in front of the school entrance, the moms with fresh chops, waving goodbye, taking pictures of their little ones with signs like NOAH'S FIRST DAY OF FIRST GRADE! ☺ and CONGRATS TO FIFI ON KINDERGARTEN! OUR STAR! All the moms went to the first day of drop-off. It was where you reconnected with people you hadn't seen over the summer, who'd been living on Shelter Island or Martha's Vineyard or Fire Island instead of the Hamptons. Everyone dressed up, showing off their tasteful tans and new wardrobes. Belle was in a variation of her standard uniform: a silk cream minidress from Khaite with a dainty scalloped collar, with Manolo Blahnik polka-dot Mary Janes. She'd tied her hair with a large pink bow.

There were no nannies in sight, which would surely change tomorrow, when the sidewalk would be filled with women of different sizes and ethnicities. But today was for the parents. To preen. To chat. To remind each other they existed.

"I can go by myself now, drop-off is for the lower school babies like Miles," Hildy scoffed. "Suck it, Hildy," said Miles, who then raced off to find his friends, leaving Hildy and Belle standing together miserably.

"Belle! Hi! Gertrude already went in!" Belle saw Morgan Chary walking toward them through the perfumed throng, her thin arms outstretched. Morgan was the wife of Art Chary, the founder of the billion-dollar sneaker startup Welly, the one that sold trendy shoes for $100. Morgan was in her postworkout best—Beyond Yoga everything, including some sort of Lycra turtleneck situation, her blond hair pulled back in a high ponytail, her feet clad in her favorite Loewe sneakers. "Excuse my outfit," said Morgan, as if she'd be wearing anything other than overpriced spandex. Morgan was the workout queen. "I'm just coming from a class with Tracy Anderson—she's the best."

Belle and Morgan and their other closest friend, Frost Trevor, had known each other since the first day of pre-K at Atherton. The women had become an inseparable troop, gravitating toward one another, as some moms inevitably did, lured by a commonality of style, money, and circumstance. They were a powerful bunch, both the wealthiest and the prettiest moms in the lower school, which was saying something, as most of the Atherton moms were wealthy and pretty. If you weren't, well, why not?

A minute later, Frost appeared, wearing a sleeveless pinstripe vest and swingy wide-legged pants, which Belle assumed were some prized vintage find. "Oh, thank God you're both here, I didn't want to have to speak to anyone else," Frost said conspiratorially. She was glowing from her summer vacation abroad. Belle noticed that the other mothers, particularly the newer ones, were looking their way, admiring their group as you would celebrities—at a distance, with reverence and not a little jealousy.

"Uh, Mom, I'm still here," said Hildy with an eye roll. She was standing to the side, slumped a little, and Belle inwardly cringed at her disheveled appearance.

"Hildy, darling, how was your summer?" asked Frost, giving Hildy a big, warm hug. Though Morgan was the super-mom, Frost was the most maternal of the bunch, though you wouldn't guess it from her avant-garde clothes and intimidating beauty.

"Yeah, fine, sleepaway was good, Mom and Dad didn't drive me *too* crazy when I got back," Hildy said. "Actually, maybe Mom did." Frost laughed. Belle didn't. "I'm going into the building now, but nice to see you both," said Hildy.

"You too, sweetie," said Morgan. Hildy slunk away, putting her hoodie over her head as she walked inside.

"Maybe you'll see the boys at lunch," Frost shouted after her. Frost's twin sons, Alfred and King, were also in the seventh grade, along with Morgan's only daughter, Gertrude. Belle watched as Hildy disappeared into the building, a moody twelve-year-old weight off Belle's shoulders. Then she turned back to her friends, lighter. She saw Miles from afar. He waved at her and blew her a kiss, then headed into school, following King and Alfred like a puppy.

"So . . ." said Morgan, leaning closer to Belle and Frost. "Have you heard about this new woman? Sofia or something?" Morgan always knew everything first; gossip found her, nourishing her body in place of the food she barely ate.

"A new mom, apparently very . . . attractive," continued Morgan, her voice low, her eyes darting around to make sure they weren't being overheard. Belle wondered how attractive this woman could possibly be. Weren't they all "very attractive"?

"Her kids are starting in second and fourth; no one has any idea how she got them in. That's basically impossible," said Morgan. A blonde and brunette, arms linked, both in crisp white midi dresses, walked by. Belle recognized them as third-grade moms and remembered that they both had four children each, that classic New York City rich-family flex (four private school tuitions plus a five-bedroom apartment equals fuck-off money). Morgan waved as they passed. "Hi, Armena! Hi, Kendra!"

Morgan knew everything and everyone. In between her barre classes and marathon training, Morgan was on every school committee, did copious research about how to live your best life, and made it her job to dole out useful information. Need to find an after-school art class? Ask Morgan. Need a weekend nanny? Ask Morgan. Looking for a contractor to combine two apartments? Ask Morgan! They joked that she should start her own "Ask Morgan" Substack, and that every mom below Twenty-Third Street would subscribe.

"Ohhh, tell us more about this Sofia person," encouraged Frost, a small smile on her red lips. "She sounds fab. Maybe she's, like, a princess or something. You know Atherton loves a royal. Remember when Princess Anne's grandkids went here for a year? Such tiny snobs." Frost laughed, shaking her glossy red hair, the envy of every Atherton mom. Frost was the daughter of a prominent art dealer and famous literary agent, and she'd been an It Girl in the early 2000s.

Out of the mob appeared a strikingly pale woman in a black leather skirt, ankle boots, and an oversize black cashmere turtleneck, somehow not melting in the September heat. It was Ava Leo, one of Atherton's most famous parents.

"Ladies! Hello!" said Ava, running her hand through her sharp bob. Belle admired Ava's blunt bangs, cutting a perfectly straight line across her forehead. Ava had a huge, amorphous job at Pinterest, and she was as out-and-about as they come—in the front row of every fashion show, at galas, fundraisers, even the Oscars, somehow. Her husband, David Chung, was the chef/owner of the hottest restaurant group in New York, BaoFuku, and they had a combined social following of four million. Their girls were in kindergarten and fourth grade.

"What's happening, Ava? All set for the big to-do?" asked Frost.

A few years ago, Frost had thrown a legendary Valentine's Day bash at her and her husband Tim's home, a Gramercy town house overlooking the park. "It's like a Wes Anderson movie set; it's just layers upon colors upon symmetry," Frost had said in a feature about it in *Architectural Digest* (the story was written by the same journalist who'd profiled Belle, and it was, much to Belle's frustration, two pages longer than her feature). Frost had thought it'd be a riot to go full-on theme party, so she'd dubbed the shindig "Love-a-Palooza" and hired a high-end wedding planner to execute. They'd painted the outside of her house red and paid the company that owns Conversation Hearts to make life-size candy hearts, with cheeky sayings like TAKE MY HUSBAND and KEY PARTY PARTICIPANT, which were placed around her home like sculptures. And she'd mandated a dress code of "Sexy V-Day Getups." The Atherton crowd had gone all out. Belle had paid a Broadway costume designer $20,000 to create a Swarovski crystal bodysuit for her and a three-piece red suit for Jeff.

The party was such a smash that it got written up in the *New York Times* Styles section—"Parents Gone Wild! The New Trend Among Wealthy Breeders: Theme Party Mania."

Since then, over-the-top theme parties had become an Atherton tradition, with different couples doing the honors. The small school's already impressive clout had increased as a result. Everyone in Manhattan wanted to send their children to Atherton because everyone wanted to go to these events. Admissions had become even more competitive in recent years, locking out some of the richest and most prominent. (Which is why when someone said there was a "new mom," particularly one whose children were starting in a nonentry year, an interesting story was certain to follow.)

Ava and David were next up to host. They were calling the party "A Bouquet of Newly Sharpened Pencils," after a line from *You've Got Mail*, referring to the magic of New York City in the fall. Guests had been tasked with dressing up like "autumn in New York," whatever that meant.

"Ugh, we are totally not ready," said Ava. "There's still so much left to plan, and it's coming up in two weeks. We have the menu set, at least—David is being obsessive about the food, no surprise.

He's having the BaoFuku staff re-create iconic NYC dishes—Russ & Daughters' bagels with lox and cream cheese; shooters of Manhattan clam chowder from Grand Central Oyster Bar; Dominique Ansel's Cronut. I need to figure out the decor, but I think we'll pull it off in the end."

"I can't wait!" said Belle, who meant it. She loved the theme parties and particularly loved picking her looks for them. And she wouldn't mind the face time with Ava, who could potentially help with PR when The Dress debuted. Belle had been gearing up to ask Ava if she could post a picture of herself wearing The Dress in her Instagram feed. She'd sent a sample over to Ava and hadn't heard back from her yet. She knew Ava was inundated with these kinds of requests, but Belle was hoping that their Atherton connection would put her at the top of the pile. "I bet it's going to be one of the best parties ever," added Belle, laying it on thick. She glanced over at Frost, who was looking at her skeptically.

Their conversation was interrupted by Gabby Mahler, Ava's best friend and one half of Atherton's fanciest lesbian couple. Gabby's family had some sort of real estate fortune and at one point had simultaneously owned the Chrysler Building *and* the Empire State. Gabby's white-blond hair was cropped short, and she was wearing almost comically oversize black frame glasses.

"I trust everyone had a faaaabulous summer? At your faaaaabulous Hamptons homes?" Gabby continued mockingly. Gabby was *allowed* to be funny because Gabby was a lesbian. The rest of them had to be nice, and to take each other very seriously. Those were the rules.

"I have to run," said Ava. "I'm meeting with one of the set designers of *When Harry Met Sally*, to see how we can infuse that vibe into the party."

"Well, that wasn't in my top ten things I thought you'd say next, Ava," said Gabby. "But impressive! Can't wait for it. Margo and I are thinking of dressing up like Richard Gere and Winona Ryder, from *Autumn in New York*. I'm Richard Gere, with the hair. Margo's going to be the Winona Ryder character." Gabby's wife, Margo, rarely made appearances at school drop-off or mom get-togethers. Margo had carried all three of the couple's sons, Howie, Sully, and Mac, and there was some gossipy debate over whose eggs went with which kid.

"Doesn't Winona Ryder die in that movie?" asked Frost.

There was a quick moment of awkward silence before Ava air-kissed them all and ran off, a flash of black leather. They were then joined by Clara Cain, whose son, Ozzie, was in Hildy's grade. Clara was a high-powered lawyer, defending wealthy men who'd been accused of sexual assault.

"Hi, how is everyone?" Clara said with a gummy smile. She was in a skirt suit and had news anchor hair, overly blown out. "I've been so busy with work; I can barely come up for air." Clara constantly spoke about how much she was working, always in a mildly condescending tone, as if saying to the others, *And what the hell are you doing with your time?*

"Miladies, it's been a blast seeing you all, but I'm taking off as well," said Gabby with a quick bow. "Let's schedule drinks soonest." She hurried away, likely hastened by Clara glomming on to the group.

"Oh my God, look," Clara said in a loud whisper, turning everyone's attention toward a woman and her two children, a boy and a girl, walking toward Atherton's main entrance. She was in a form-fitting yellow dress, the color of a banana the minute before it turns brown, showing off a voluptuous, Kardashian-esque figure.

Her face, framed by glossy caramel waves, was hidden by large black sunglasses. The beautiful little girl was in a smocked blue romper, and the boy resembled a Ralph Lauren model in khakis and a white polo. This must be the woman Morgan had told them about: Sofia. Belle had never seen anything like her. Not in Manhattan, at least. Not at Atherton, certainly. Belle crossed her arms around her body, her straight, small-breasted shape, so fashionable in New York City, suddenly feeling boyish and unattractive.

"Holy shit," said Frost in a whisper, her eyes glued to Sofia. "She's amazing looking."

"That's definitely her," said Morgan. "I heard she's from Miami. It's got to be."

The other moms, in their Toteme flats, their The Row pants, their Rachel Comey jumpsuits, stared at the colorful zoo animal in their midst.

"Should we say hi to her? Be friendly?" asked Frost.

Clara had taken off, leaving the three friends standing alone. Sofia and her children walked up the school steps, stopping in front of Atherton's headmaster, Dr. Broker, who was greeting students as they entered for their first day. Dr. Broker was in a worn plaid shirt and Levi's that hugged his fit behind. He had springy, salt-and-pepper hair, and bore a distinct resemblance to Patrick Dempsey. He was unmarried, though definitely not gay—Belle had heard a rumor that he was dating a downtown actress—and he spoke to the moms with a combination of adoration, appeasement, and control that drove them all mad with lust. Frost liked to joke that Dr. Broker should put himself up on the auction block at the annual school fundraiser, generously fucking the mom who paid the most for the privilege. The scholarship tuitions would be covered for years.

Sofia said something to Dr. Broker and then handed her kids off to him, kissing their heads and hugging them into her body before they disappeared into the grand building. She slowly wound down the stairs, careful not to trip in her high heels, lifting her sunglasses and rubbing her eyes briefly, a gesture that could only mean she was wiping away tears. Belle couldn't remember the last time she'd cried when saying goodbye to Miles and Hildy.

Then Sofia was right in front of them. She paused, taking her phone out of her Gucci logo bag, checking something or other. Or maybe she was just stalling, without anywhere to go.

"Hi! I'm Morgan Chary!" Morgan extended her hand brightly, and, for a second, Sofia looked at it like it was a hot pan she didn't want to touch. Then she seemed to remember herself, taking Morgan's fingers in her own.

"I'm Sofia, it's so nice to meet you. Are you all Atherton mamas?" Her voice was deep, with a hint of a South American accent.

"Yes!" they all said in unison.

Sofia took off her sunglasses. Her eyes were dark, with surprising yellow rings around her pupils that reflected golden in the light.

"My son is in fourth grade, and my daughter is in second. We've just moved from Florida. I'm so happy to have them at such a wonderful school. I'm a little nervous for them, being new."

"Atherton is great at acclimating new kids," said Morgan reassuringly. "I'm sure they'll fit in just fine."

Sofia smiled and a mysteriously creepy feeling came over Belle, her stomach dropping as if she were on a roller coaster. She had the bizarre sense that her head was lighter. Had someone cut off her hair? She reached back and felt its comforting weight.

"I'm Belle and this is Frost," said Belle, trying to shake it off. "We'd love to get coffee soon and get to know you! We've been at the school since pre-K. It's the best. It's like this little safe haven in the middle of Manhattan."

Their attention was then directed to a commotion at the entrance, some sort of scuffle. Belle couldn't see exactly what was happening, but it looked as though people had started to run in the other direction. Someone let out a frightened squeal, and before the women could move, the homeless man, the one whom Belle and Hildy and Miles had passed by, was standing directly in their sight line. Belle could have touched him, he was that close. He was in a ripped black shirt and hospital scrubs, and was shoeless, his feet swollen and bloody. His barnyard smell made Belle feel ill. Should Belle run? Would he chase her? She momentarily made eye contact with him, breaking that cardinal New York City rule, unable to look away. He winked at her. He winked! Then he made a strange gargling sound, deep in his chest, and abruptly coughed out a white ball of phlegm. The spit went flying straight into Belle's wide-open mouth, like a dart hitting its human bull's-eye.

Belle stood there, stunned, trying not to swallow but feeling the slime slip down her throat. The man lurched toward her. She didn't know what to do other than cover her face with her hands, closing her eyes in panic, hoping he somehow wouldn't reach her.

"*Ayuda! Ayuda!*" Belle heard someone shout. There was a thud and then Belle felt herself wrapped tightly in an embrace. "*Te tengo,*" the voice said into her ear. "I've got you."

Belle, relieved to be alive, opened her eyes to see she was entwined with Sofia, Sofia's face so close to Belle's that it felt like they were about to kiss. The man had vanished, leaving behind a pack of petrified women in sweaty designer clothing.

Frost joined them, taking Belle's hands in hers. "Belle, Sofia whacked that crazy guy with her purse and then he took off running." Sofia looked down at the ground shyly.

Dr. Broker arrived, taking in the scene. He put his hand on Belle's shoulder and looked at her with deep concern.

"Are you hurt?" he asked. She shook her head, making sure her hair swung sexily as she did. It was an old trick she used when she wanted male attention.

"I've called the police," Dr. Broker said. Belle noticed, with interest, that Dr. Broker's wrists were thick, before remembering that she'd nearly been mowed down by a vagrant. Dr. Broker assured the parents that their children were safe, and that this would be taken care of. "Atherton is on it," he kept repeating to concerned sighs.

"Sofia, let us take you out for a drink sometime, it's the least we can do," said Frost.

"I'd love that," said Sofia gratefully.

"Our hero!" said Frost.

"Our hero," echoed Belle. She still felt a little trembly. What a disastrous first day of Atherton drop-off. On cue, a lanternfly landed on the sidewalk in front of the women. Belle squashed it with her Manolos, feeling it die beneath her Mary Janes with a satisfying crunch.

**Chapter 2**

# A New Friend!

≡

Y ou are *bad*, Frost," breathed Art Chary into Frost Trevor's neck. Frost kept going, grinding down on her friend's husband, as if trying to rub a stain out with her entire body. She did it over and over, until she felt her pelvis start to tingle and her legs begin to shake. Then she seized, her hair flying forward, her breasts swinging, her nipples catching in Art's mouth. She collapsed on top of him, gently nibbling his shoulder as she allowed herself to relax. "Bad girl," he said again, his face nuzzled into her neck.

Frost lay like that for a few minutes, inhaling Art's scent. Then she rolled to his side, staring at his defined chest, almond colored with barely any hair, rising with slow breaths. His left hand was placed gently on top of it, his gold wedding band dulled by time. Frost knew that its inside was inscribed HONEYDEW FOREVER, matching the inside of Morgan's ring. It was a private joke between the two of them: the name of the dive bar in Cambridge where they'd met, when Art was getting an MBA at Harvard and Morgan had been studying for her master's in nutrition from Tufts. Morgan, her high-heeled boots still covered in snow, had slipped on spilled beer, crashing into the bar and cutting her forehead on its edge. Art, who'd been premed at Yale before deciding to switch to econ, had rushed to her aid, whisking her away to the emergency room with a supportive arm around her shoulder.

Out of all of them, Frost thought as she gently licked Art's salty skin, Morgan loved her husband the most. And she didn't blame her. He was the most handsome dad at school and one of the most successful. Art was also charismatic and kind; though he'd made a killing on Welly, the company's mission included charity as part of its ethos. For every pair of sneakers purchased, Welly gifted another to a person in need. Morgan seemed to absolutely adore Art—she was always touching the dramatic swoop of his hair, giving him kisses on the cheek, banging into him like a fly to a zapper—which wasn't something Frost could say about her own husband, Tim.

Frost looked at her phone. It was already two forty-five, and she needed to be at Atherton for pickup by three thirty. King and Alfred had tennis lessons at the John McEnroe Tennis Academy at Randall's Island, and they were excited to show their coach how much progress they'd made over the summer. The family had brought along a private pro to Europe, the boys training on dusty clay courts in Spain and France while Frost had watched them, plying herself with white wine.

Though a summer abroad had sounded glamorous, and all her friends had proclaimed jealousy from the comfort of their Hamptons mansions, the trip hadn't been a success. The *idea* of it—as a cozy family escape, and a marriage kick-in-the-butt for Tim and Frost—had been better than the reality. Tim, a movie producer, had been working the whole time, trying to get a project out of development hell, a midbudget drama about a dysfunctional family of circus performers called *Ladies and Gentlemen, The Flying Wallendars!* Who would ever pay to see something with that stupid title? But when Frost had said that to Tim, he'd totally snapped, accusing her of being dismissive of his work. So Frost, bored and restless and pissed, drank too much while King and Alfred fought constantly.

She gently shook Art's arm. He always fell asleep after sex, no matter the time of day. Frost found it endearing. It reminded her of her sons, who could nap anywhere—at the dinner table, on a cold, hard floor, their beautiful eyes with that telltale hooded look, and then . . . bam. Art fluttered awake. He looked up at her and smiled.

"Well, that was nice," he said, taking her hand and kissing it. Frost nodded.

"I have to go get the boys and you have to get out of here," she said, playfully dragging him across the bed, made up in Frost's favorite white silk sheets. They were in her apartment, her own private space. She and Tim had bought it last year, after she'd said she wanted somewhere to make her art, somewhere that was just hers. Tim had thought it was unnecessary—"Frost, come on, we have an entire house at your disposal, can't you just designate a room to be your studio? Can't you fit these"—he'd pointed at the mixed-media collages Frost had been working on, lying vulnerably on their Vern + Vera dining table—"in the basement?"

Frost shook her head. She couldn't work in her home. There were too many distractions. She needed somewhere empty, somewhere spare and clean. She'd kept at it, bothering Tim until he'd begrudgingly agreed to purchase this one-bedroom condo for $2,200,000 in cash in a new building on Twenty-Second near Park, a few blocks from their home in Gramercy. She'd converted the living space to a studio, filling it with easels and materials, ranging from colored paper to wax to small objects she'd found on the street: coins, receipts, a solo leather glove.

The apartment was now her favorite place on earth. She'd come here after drop-off and spend the morning hours tinkering with her current project—a photo collage portfolio of It Girls through the years, from Ali MacGraw to Chloë Sevigny to a picture of herself, Frost Trevor, at sixteen, staring blankly at the camera, alone in a banquette at a nameless club. She'd layer materials over each photograph, obscuring the location, altering each girl's face with paper. One she gave a large blue eye, cut out from a magazine, on another she glued a picture of a pit bull over naked breasts. It was meant as a commentary on the worth of a certain type of woman, their sad disposability after a period of intense societal worship.

Frost didn't really consider herself an artist, though she was desperate to be one, a desire she'd only newly admitted to herself. She'd grown up in the world. Her mother was a trailblazing female art dealer, and she owned an imposing seven-story, Norman Foster–designed gallery on the Lower East Side. Her father was an uber-successful literary agent, working with the likes of David Foster Wallace and Philip Roth, among other male luminaries. Frost had been the only child in a stunning apartment on Fifth Avenue and Seventy-Sixth Street; her bedroom had one of Andy Warhol's *Jackie* prints hanging on the wall.

Frost had also been lucky enough to have been born beautiful, with copper-red hair and sparkly brown eyes. She was a bright, aimless kid, attending Chapin, one of the best girls' schools in Manhattan, but never putting her heart into it. By the time she was twelve, she was sneaking into clubs with her older friends, drinking vodka sodas, smoking Marlboros, and staying out till all hours. She'd given her first blow job when she was thirteen, to an NYU student she'd met at a party at Bowlmor Lanes on University. She gave many more after that. Page Six would frequently publish pictures of her and her semi-famous friends, photographers trailing them on nights out. Her parents, though kind, were absentee, always at events, traveling the world for their jobs. Frost had wanted their attention, but it had never appeared.

Frost toweled off after her shower, glancing in the mirror and pinching her cheeks before going back into the bedroom. Art was sitting on her desk chair and checking his phone. They never spoke of Morgan or Tim, never even mentioned their names. They'd been seeing each other sporadically for over a year, since last July, the night of the "Zoo-ly Fourth" theme party at Trina and Bud Cunningham's East Hampton house, right on the ocean. The outdoor space had been transformed into a fantastical zoo, including a bird barn and a polar area with penguins (an industrial-grade meat locker company came to facilitate). The pièce de résistance was a trio of live zebras that the Cunninghams had shipped from an exotic animal farm in Texas.

The gossip that night had revolved around: A. if a group of zebras was called a "zeal" or a "dazzle"; B. the legality of converting a Hamptons estate into a zoo; and C. the fact that Caroline Morehouse's husband, Dave, had brought what looked to be a nasal spray for allergies, but in fact contained ketamine, which partygoers were spraying into their noses and getting high, high, high. Frost had done K before, back when it was a club drug referred to as Special K, but not for a while—she was now strictly a booze-and-gummy kind of gal, having given up the hard stuff after the twins were born.

By that point, more than ten years in, she and Tim had been in a precarious place in their union. Their wedding had been a buzzy affair, the joining of an It Girl and her indie-movie prince, a New York City fairy tale. Tim had just produced his one (and only) big hit, *Daylight*, about a young Latino man in Spanish Harlem explor-ing his sexuality, which had been nominated for two Oscars. Frost had been working as a photographer's assistant, trying to figure out what she wanted to do while her parents paid for her lifestyle. She and Tim had met at a book party for a mutual writer friend. "You're Frost Trevor, right?" he'd said to her as an opener. "You're even more beautiful in person than in the *Post*!" It had delighted her. Tim was kinder than the men Frost usually went for. He was also driven, wanting to make a career of his own though he didn't need to; he was the heir to a pharmaceutical fortune. They both liked what the other did for their social standing. They just kind of fit, and that was enough. A gorgeous couple who had a gorgeous wedding at the top of the gorgeous Gramercy Park Hotel, worthy of an entire spread in the Styles section.

Afterward, it had been more of the same—parties, luxurious va-cations, followed by Frost's pregnancy, which started out perfectly but soon turned harrowing. She'd nearly lost both twins at five months; she'd been at brunch at Balthazar, eating a burger, and felt something cold on her leg. She'd looked down to see blood everywhere, smeared all over the red leather booth, pouring onto the floor, the fairy tale turned nightmare. The bleeding eventually stopped, but she'd been on bed rest for the duration, spending months alone in their Chelsea loft while Tim flew off to be on the set of his next film, a flop about a drug-addicted dolphin trainer.

Frost had been worried that motherhood would wreck her. Everything in her life before that had been in pursuit of being "cool," and turning into a mom of screaming babies certainly wasn't it. But then the opposite had happened. She'd adored it. She'd loved them so much, her precious boys, with their tiny fists and their wailing cries and their deep, insatiable need for her. She'd vowed to be the opposite of her own mother—warm and coddling instead of imperious and distant. And she'd done it. King and Alfred were wonderful.

Her marriage, however, was not. Tim's career stalled, and he'd spent years spinning his wheels with nothing to show for it. Frost felt for him, but she'd been focused on the kids at the expense of her own creativity as well. Tim had started to take his frustrations out on her, criticizing her and criticizing her, like she could never do anything right. Why was she spending so much time on her artwork? Why was she throwing so many parties? She shouldn't let the boys watch TV, he'd said, she shouldn't feed them sweets, he'd said, she shouldn't let them sleep with her, he'd said, she shouldn't, she shouldn't, she shouldn't.

So at Zoo-ly Fourth, when Dave Morehouse handed her the ketamine nasal spray with a wink, she'd placed it up her nose and inhaled strongly. For about fifteen minutes, she hadn't felt anything and thought perhaps Dave had been duping them all. She'd lost Tim ages ago, and so she'd gone over to chat with some moms. Ava Leo had been talking shit about someone Frost didn't know—"and she *never* brings birthday gifts to parties, it's the weirdest thing. Like, we all pay for Atherton, you can afford to buy a gift for a seven-year-old."

"Maybe it's an environmental thing," Trina had offered up with a shrug.

And then suddenly Frost was floating outside of her body, watching herself from above, admiring her sharp shoulders, the curve of her butt in the formfitting leopard-print dress. She'd felt happy in a way she hadn't in years, relaxation flowing through her limbs. She'd walked into the bird barn. Tropical parrots clucked and sang, the sounds overwhelmingly vivid. And then Art had arrived, looking at her with interest. She'd seen him with the nasal spray earlier, so she knew he felt as wonderful as Frost, beyond description, just warmth and joy and light. He was dressed as a wolf, a furry snout covering his nose, in a sleek gray suit, his eyes shining black.

They'd snuck off to the beach, made love, high on illegal substances and on each other, as their spouses mingled, unaware. Had she always been attracted to Art? Or had the drugs made her see him anew?

"I've got to go," she said now to Art, shaking off her memories and guilt and motioning for him to follow her. They took the elevator down together—no one in the building knew her, and so she and Art used the place as if they were a couple. They nodded to the doorman at the entrance (doormen were paid to be vaults; no worry there), and Art gave her a brief kiss on the lips at the door before exiting first.

Frost stepped out not a second later, the searing heat hitting her like a wall. Autumn in the city could be hot, but this felt different, like it was a permanent shift into another dimension. The sidewalks, the buildings, the cars of New York weren't built for this; they absorbed and absorbed and absorbed until swollen with warmth. Frost, eyes closed against the bright sun, smashed into a woman standing directly in front of her, causing them both to drop their bags, sending lipsticks, mints, phones, and pens scattering to the pavement.

"Ay!" the woman yelled as Frost reeled backward from the impact.

"I'm so sorry," Frost said, picking up her things, clumsily bumping heads with the woman, who was doing the same thing. "Ouch!" they both said at the same time. Frost stood up to face her and was struck by the woman's beauty, her perfect body under a pink skirt, which hit well above the knee. Was she an actress? Frost thought, before her brain clicked and she realized she actually knew this person.

"Oh, hello, you!" said Frost to Sofia. "Nice to run into you, though I apologize about *literally* running into you," she continued.

"No problem at all! I'd know you anywhere, with those gorgeous eyes and hair," said Sofia.

Frost, who retained a lifelong pride in her looks, blushed. "I'm going to get King and Alfred now. Are you headed to pickup? If so, let's walk together."

Sofia nodded, and they started down the street, walking toward Irving Place. Frost noticed that Sofia was wobbling and saw that her towering stilettos kept getting stuck in the sidewalk crags. "Do you live around here?" Sofia said, walking slower than Frost, a lifelong New Yorker, who was used to running everywhere.

"I have a place in the building I was coming out of," said Frost. "I use it as my office. Well, actually, that's where I make my art." Frost's therapist had been encouraging her to openly embrace this part of her life, but it was proving tough to do so. Frost's mother had never taken her seriously as an artist, and so Frost hadn't taken herself seriously, either.

"You're an artist? How wonderful," said Sofia.

"Just for pleasure," said Frost automatically. Then remembered herself. "Though I do hope one day to turn it into more than a hobby."

"How cool. I'm not an artist myself, but I love going to museums," said Sofia. There was something guileless about her that Frost liked, a kind of childlike enthusiasm that was missing from the "over it" attitudes of most of the moms Frost knew. "I was in this neighborhood getting a facial. My skin in this city! Horrible! The dirt is seeping into my pores," Sofia said.

"But I must say, even though you all are being so kind to me, I'm having a hard time with it all," she went on, babbling now in an endearing way, clearly starved for company. "New York is so different than Miami. Everyone here is so intimidating to me, so accomplished and stylish." Frost watched her as she spoke, struck by the way her lips were the shape of a perfect bow.

"I thought I'd come here, and it would be like *Sex and the City*. I'd find a group of friends, we'd have cocktails and chat about men, wear nice clothes, go shopping together." Frost laughed to herself at Sofia's naivete. Could she possibly be . . . genuine?

"Instead," Sofia went on, "I'm alone all day, getting facials and manicures and watching junk TV. At least there's a good Barry's Bootcamp near my house. It's the only place that feels a little bit like home."

They'd made their way down Irving, crossing on Seventeenth Street and walking toward Third Avenue, a few blocks from Atherton. Frost felt for Sofia. She couldn't imagine having to relocate with her children without Tim, moving to a city in which she knew no one.

"That sounds difficult," said Frost, patting Sofia's arm. "Atherton's great, but the moms can be kind of cliquey. And I'm sure many of them are intimidated by you, even if you think the opposite."

"By me?!" said Sofia, laughing. "I have no friends, I'm divorced, and no one told me that in New York you're supposed to wear expensive sacks instead of, like, nice clothes." Sofia's voice was loud and direct, with an inflection that exaggerated some words—"diiiiivorced," "liiiike." Sofia gestured to her own outfit and then fingered Frost's loose cotton dress, sticking out her tongue. Frost laughed. She liked this lady.

"You can be friends with us," said Frost, remembering that they'd already promised to take Sofia to drinks. Frost linked her arm with Sofia's. "You've already proved you're good in an emergency!" They'd arrived at the school, surrounded by mini groups of moms and nannies, chatting, looking at their phones, waiting for their charges to exit. As Frost and Sofia approached the lower school entrance, heads turned to watch them go, a new alliance formed.

Frost caught sight of Morgan and Belle and Jeff. Belle, in her usual minidress, this one covered in great big sunflowers, saw them and waved. Belle was set to launch a capsule clothing line called Pippins Cottage Home this winter, something she'd been talking about doing since Frost had met her. Frost knew this was Belle's "passion," but as a true fashion person, someone who still occasionally got invited to sit front row, it was hard for Frost to ignore: Belle's sense of style was the pits. She dressed the way little girls did in the 1980s, with the frills and the bows and the Laura Ashley of it all. It was all so infantilizing and, frankly, weird. And that hair . . . Belle would look so much chicer with a bob, in Frost's opinion. Funnily enough, it was Hildy, in her carefully curated hoodies, who had the sartorial spark Belle lacked.

"Belle, I see you've brought your bodyguard," said Frost, motioning to Jeff, who didn't look up from his phone to hear the joke. The incident with the homeless man had spread through downtown society like wildfire, scaring the bejeezus out of everyone with an Amex Black Card. The police were still looking for him; Frost wasn't sure what was taking so long, though she supposed in a city riddled with crime, this wasn't exactly a top priority.

Parents had taken the issue into their own hands, forming committees, including one called Atherton Parents Against Persons

Experiencing Homelessness. Dr. Broker and the board had added extra security out front, nearly barricading the entire block, reminding Frost of that time just after 9/11, when city schools and temples and churches had armed guards stationed at the doors.

"Hi, hi!" said Morgan, pulling Frost in for a kiss on the cheek, her perfume washing over them. Morgan's unending energy was both her best and most grating trait. She was in another of her many workout outfits, this time a cropped mock neck, her toned abs exposed. Frost couldn't imagine how Art could want Frost after wanting . . . that. They were so different. But people changed, she supposed. Frost knew it was marginally insane that she was able to maintain a close friendship with the woman whose husband she was sleeping with. But Frost had the ability to be two people at once. Most women did, she thought.

"And so nice to see you, Sofia," continued Morgan, kissing her, too, which Sofia seemed grateful for.

"Sofia and I ran into each other on the street on the way here," said Frost, squeezing Sofia's arm. "I told her we'd be her friends." Sofia laughed, a sparkly lilt.

"Of course we will!" said Belle gamely. "I am in debt to you forever, Sofia. That man might have killed me if you hadn't stepped in."

Sofia shook her head, pleased by the attention.

"Belle, Jeff, what are you guys even doing here? Since when do you pick up the kids?" asked Frost.

"Hildy has an orthodontist appointment after school, to tighten those horrible train tracks of hers," said Belle with a shudder.

"Dr. Ta? At Tribeca North?" said Morgan.

"You were the one who told me to go to her. Ask Morgan! Duh," said Belle. Morgan smiled sheepishly. "And Jeff and I just had a meeting with a marketing firm about Pippins Cottage Home, so he decided to tag along." Jeff finally looked up from his phone at the mention of his name, clocking Sofia for the first time, his eyes bulging out of his head appreciatively. He was in the typical uniform of the Tribeca dad: a beard, a backward baseball cap, and limited edition Air Force 1's. Jeff was the kind of guy who constantly talked about their place "out East," and the best butcher for dry-aged meat, and cited stats from his Oura ring, like his resting heart rate and his "readiness" for the day. He loved to say "we'll bake it into the model" when referring to the high cost of life in New York City. Sleepaway camp? "We'll bake it into the model." Private lacrosse lessons for Miles? "We'll bake it into the model." A bat mitzvah for Hildy at the Rainbow Room? "We'll bake it into the model." (Good thing for Jeff that "the model" was funded by Belle's dad.) Jeff turned back to his phone and the women turned to each other.

"I have something to tell you all," said Morgan. "And it's a life decision that you might be surprised by." Morgan's voice had a strange timbre, and Frost's breath went shallow. Was it something to do with Morgan's marriage? Could she have somehow found out about Frost and Art? Frost swallowed hard, her throat suddenly dry. Frost wasn't in love with Art, but she loved that he made her feel young and wanted. Yes, Frost was still beautiful, and men still turned their heads when she entered a room. But, at forty-two, she could sense her inevitable, middle-aged invisibility stalking her like a drunk guy at a club. Frost hated the idea that she might have peaked too early in life. She didn't want to be a has-been, a "former" anything. At least Art looked at her like she was *someone*. Tim certainly didn't anymore.

"I'm going to open a sound bath spa!" Morgan announced, to

Frost's relief. "I'm calling it Thyme & Time." A sound bath spa was better than a divorce, even if Frost had no idea what Morgan was talking about.

"What?" said Belle. "Why?" She sounded offended.

"What do you mean, 'Why'?" said Morgan. Belle, caught, shifted her scowl into a supportive smile.

"Sorry, I'm just confused," said Belle. "You've never said anything about wanting to open a spa. When did you decide to do that? Why not just go back to being a nutritionist?" Frost glanced at Sofia, who was quietly listening to the exchange.

"It's something I've been thinking about for a while," said Morgan. "I had a sound bath when we went to LA last year—they're all the rage there—and noticed there was a hole in the downtown market here. So I thought: I should be the one to open one! Gertrude's getting older, and you know I like to have new goals." Belle raised an eyebrow suspiciously.

"Forgive me," interrupted Sofia. "And I'm probably just stupid. But what's a sound bath?"

"A sound bath is a meditative experience," said Morgan. "You enter a small room, either alone or with others, and you're bathed in sounds. It's very cleansing, and you emerge feeling refreshed and energized."

"I see," said Sofia. "So, like, classical music, or wind chimes, or something?"

Morgan clarified that the sounds could range from things like gongs to crystal singing bowls to tuning forks to screaming human voices.

"Screaming human voices? Sounds relaxing," Frost heard Jeff mutter, still not looking up from his phone. Frost stifled a laugh.

"So what neighborhoods are you looking at? And what's the

overhead?" Belle asked, probing. Before she'd had children, Belle had worked briefly at Deutsche Bank, and she never let any of them forget it. Belle had been talking about launching her own company forever, so Frost had to imagine that if Morgan, who'd never expressed interest in such things, got there first, it would certainly sting.

"We already found a small space in Tribeca, next to the Jacadi on Reade Street. We're opening in a few weeks!"

Belle's face fell. She looked off to the side, and Frost could tell she was fuming.

"Congrats!" said Sofia.

The children had started to file out of the school, down the staircase, comprised of eight large stone steps. Up top stood Dr. Broker, chatting with the kids as they left.

"Ms. Perez!" Dr. Broker called down, motioning to Sofia to come join him. Sofia, somewhat alarmed to have been singled out, raised her eyebrows at the women and then trudged up the stairs, stepping around children to get to Dr. Broker, who gave her a vigorous handshake and then said something into her ear. Sofia grimaced. Right then, Gabby Mahler and Ava Leo walked up, their eyes on Sofia.

"I wonder what they're talking about," said Gabby, tipping down her black framed glasses, as if that would let her see the situation better instead of blurrier.

"Maybe he's saying that she's the hottest woman he's ever seen, and he *has* to have her right now, or he'll die," said Ava with a wicked smile.

"I don't think there have ever been boobs like that on an Atherton mom," said Gabby, joining her friend in the fun-making.

"He's got to be salivating. Hell, I'm salivating." She and Ava tittered.

"And look at her shoes," said Ava with a sneer. "It's like Louboutin-meets-lady-of-the-night."

"Guys, stop being bitches," said Frost sharply. "She's nice and lonely and we're going to befriend her," she continued, feeling protective for some reason. Gabby put up her hands, as if to say "you do you."

"Right, right, she's your *hero*, I forgot," said Ava with a smirk. Sofia looked pained as she and Dr. Broker spoke. He gave her a final handshake and sent her on her way.

Students were streaming out of the building, skipping across the steps, glancing left and right in search of their grown-ups. Sofia gingerly made her way down, searching fruitlessly for a banister. She got caught in the mix of yelling, teasing youth, her tall, impossibly pointy high heels causing her to walk like an elderly woman afraid of rebreaking her hip. Even Jeff was torn away from his phone, rapt.

Dr. Broker, witnessing the impending calamity, bounded down to try to help her, reaching for Sofia's hand. But instead of helping, he somehow sent her flying forward, her heel catching on a stone edge. She careened into a group of young girls, sending them right into a growing line of little ones, who all began to fall, slowly then fast fast fast, an entire school tumbling onto the pavement. Cries of agony could be heard as the students hit the hard ground. "My knee!" "Mommy, my arm!" "Ow!" and so on, until what felt like the whole block was filled with whimpering children. Frost couldn't believe what she was witnessing, as child after child went down, like a gory scene out of *Chicka Chicka Boom Boom*.

Then out of the pile rose Sofia, a phoenix in a sexy pink skirt, her hair a little mussed but otherwise looking pretty damn incredible. She took in the chaos, swiveling her head this way and that, her chest heaving. Frost had the impulse to comfort her, before realizing that no, Sofia wasn't crying. She was laughing. A great, loud, attractive laugh.

"I told you she was my hero," said Frost, in awe. They all shook their heads in disbelief at the alien among them.

## Chapter 3

# Girls' Drinks!

≡

Morgan Chary was tired of being so fucking cheerful. She'd been cheerful her whole life. Why did some women always have to be cheerful? She'd been the cheerful kid, the middle daughter of three, the one who always had a happy face on while her two sisters got to be total sticks in the mud. She was the cheerful friend, the one who pepped everyone up when they were low, who brought cupcakes when they were sick, with herbal remedies and recommendations for the best acupuncturists. She was the cheerful mom, never yelling at Gertrude, always gentle parenting, letting her feel her feelings. Sometimes Morgan just wanted to shout at her, "I know you don't want to go to swimming today, but sometimes we HAVE TO DO THINGS WE DON'T WANT TO DO! That's fucking life!" But she kept it in. She always kept it in. And she was also the cheerful wife, supporting Art in his career, keeping everything perfect at home with a smile, her one cheek dimple in overuse, sunny and positive.

She'd been cheerful for forty-one years. That was a long time to be smiling. She looked in the mirror in the bathroom of Thyme &

Time, the walls a pale shade of moss, the sink an attractive block of gray marble with a hanging gold faucet. She studied her jutting cheekbones, giving her all-American appearance an alluring angularity. Her face had changed shape as she'd aged, hollowing out in a way she liked. She'd just gotten her hair colored with Jacob Schmidt at Sally Hershberger, the best (Ask Morgan!), toning down her summer blond into a lovely fall honey. She looked good, all things considered.

Perimenopause had recently hit Morgan like a ton of hormonal bricks. Drenching night sweats, her wickedly sharp brain always in a fog. Her body chemistry felt altered. Some days she was Morgan, some days she was a stranger with a temper and a pounding headache. The worst part had been weight gain, a padding around her middle that her entire adult life she'd worked so hard to avoid. No amount of Tracy Anderson seemed to matter, it was just . . . there . . . like an unwanted guest at a cocktail party. Morgan rubbed the scar on her forehead, the one she'd gotten the day she and Art met, just a faint line at this point. She frowned, her mouth curving downward, her face muscles unused to such an expression.

Morgan then reached into her purse, a dainty green Bottega Bucket Bag, and unzipped the side pocket. There, alongside her Chanel lipstick, was a thin blue container that looked like a cross between a tampon and a pen, plus a clear plastic packet. She took both out and opened the top of the larger one, revealing a vial of clear liquid. Then she unwrapped the second piece, a needle, a silver sliver of metal. She inserted it into the vial, then pulled down her high-waisted leggings, all the way to the top of her pubic bone. She stuck the instrument into the flesh right above her underwear, just to the left of her C-section scar, and held it there for a count of six, until the medicine had entirely drained into her body. She pulled her leggings up and put the mechanism back in her bag—she'd dispose of it later in a New York City trash can.

Morgan felt a jolt of exhilaration, the semaglutides coursing through her veins. Her weekly Wegovy shot was her little secret, not even Art knew. It was none of anyone's business how she remained so fit, and she loved the way it made her life so much easier, not having to worry about food, not having to exert all that self-control. She was now as thin as she'd ever been, perimenopause be damned. For years, Morgan had felt almost nothing; a black hole wrapped in an Alo Yoga matching set. She'd been hiding in plain sight. Now her appetite was suppressed, but her true self had been unleashed. She felt free. She felt angry. She felt everything lately. It was a new Morgan.

Next up, she had early drinks with the girls—Belle, Frost, and Sofia—whom they'd been seeing quite a lot of lately. Morgan stripped out of her workout garb and into a crisp white shirtdress, its collar popped up, walking out through Thyme & Time, which officially opened later that week. She'd had an architecture firm, Ronan Lev, known for designing the Goop offices, outfit the three-thousand-square-foot space. The granite shelving was filled with gorgeous books with titles like *Chakras, Enchantments*, and *Art in the Age of Anxiety*, interspersed with essential oils, sleekly designed gut supplements, and clean skincare, all available for purchase.

Morgan walked the two short blocks to the Odeon to meet her friends. It had been Frost's choice for cocktails, because "it makes me nostalgic for my youth," she'd written to their group text, followed by a slew of Old Woman emojis. The restaurant was full at the early hour, mostly with polished thirty- and fortysomethings, all of whom likely had the same idea as the Atherton moms. Morgan spotted Sofia in a booth toward the back, radiant in a printed silk tank, which dipped low in the front and displayed the tops of Sofia's bouncy, possibly fake breasts. A handful of delicate gold chains hung around her neck, and her lips were covered in a striking matte red. Morgan felt self-conscious, as if she were dressed for a PA meeting while Sofia was off to a fabulous evening event.

Sofia was sipping a large martini and already had a plate of french fries in front of her, dragging each one through ketchup the color of blood. Morgan felt nauseated at the sight of them.

She slid in next to Sofia, not quite sure what to say to her.

"Nice to see you," enthused Sofia, looking at her intently. "How are you doing? How's the spa?" The rings around Sofia's pupils were nearly glowing.

"All set for opening," said Morgan. "We already have bookings through the month, which is a great start."

"Have you always wanted to open a spa?" asked Sofia. "Belle told me she'd been dreaming of launching a company for her entire life, so I wanted to know if you felt the same way. You women up here are so smart and focused. In Miami, we just like to work out and shop." She giggled.

They were interrupted by Belle and Frost, who'd come into the restaurant together. After hugs and hellos and drinks delivered to the table (another vodka martini for Sofia, who'd polished off her first in a jiffy; a champagne for Frost; a chardonnay for Belle; and a room-temperature water, no ice, with lemon, for Morgan), the ladies settled into a chat. The three originals had known each other forever, so this was more about Sofia, as most of their meetings had been lately.

"Please, we're all dying to know: How did you choose Atherton?" Frost asked. Frost's red hair was pulled back into a bun, and she was wearing a blousy shirt in that boho style she liked. Her face was tastefully expressive, with soft lines around her eyes. The current trend was to age gracefully, which meant targeted Botox use instead of vials and vials, and lots of facials, lasers, and expensive serums instead of filler. Puffy and frozen was so five years ago. Sofia seemed to be getting the memo; in the short time she'd been at Atherton, her face had gone from plumped to natural, and she was even prettier for it, like a mannequin that had suddenly come to life.

"I'm going through a divorce, as you all know." All the women murmured "I'm so sorry" at once. "And I just had to get away from Miami. It was too hard to be around my old life there; I needed to be on my own. Our split was mutual. No hard feelings, no scandal, we just shouldn't have been married in the first place. We ended up being friends, you know what I mean?" (They nodded, though they didn't know what she meant.) "New York is going to be *our* place—me and Carlos and Lucia, together. I was worried about uprooting them right as Mommy and Daddy were separating, but children are resilient. My father grew up in Colombia, with gangs and drugs and poverty. He survived, providing me with the opportunity to do better. I plan to not only survive this ordeal but to thrive here in New York."

"Wow," said Belle. "That's really brave of you."

Belle was wearing the prototype of her own The Dress, a nude-colored caftan thing that reminded Morgan of the hospital gown her grandmother had worn when she was dying.

"And I know you're all wondering how I got the kids into Atherton," continued Sofia. No one said a word. This was the gossip they'd been waiting for. Morgan's heart quickened in anticipation. "I fucked that gorgeous man, Dr. Broker. He could barely handle me, but it was worth it for admission." They all laughed out loud at her bawdy joke.

"What was Dr. Broker talking to you about the day you, er, fell down the stairs, if you don't mind me asking," said Frost. Sofia looked away, clearing her throat a little, before turning back to the group with a slight frown.

"Ah, he told me that he wanted to do a little ceremony at the school honoring *me*," said Sofia. "For what happened to you, Belle, with that homeless man. He said there's something called an Atherton Altruist award that goes to parents and students who do good, or something like that. But I said no way."

"Oh my god, the Altruist award! That's amazing!" said Morgan. Belle and Frost clapped.

"I know it sounds silly, but it's a big deal at the school," Morgan continued. "They only give out a couple a year, and everyone goes to the ceremonies—last year, they gave the award to Julie Klein for funding the Atherton Diversity and Inclusion wing."

"Is that where they hide the other Colombian kids?" said Sofia, deadpan. No one laughed that time. "Anyway, I don't like being the center of attention," she continued. "He mentioned that we could organize it for later in the fall, and I told him I'd consider it. And then I went flying down the stairs! I haven't really thought about it since."

"Well, I think you should do it," said Belle. "We'd all come to support you. And the kids of the award winner get to sit up onstage with them, so that might be nice for Carlos and Lucia."

Sofia mmmmed. She took a large sip of her martini.

"Ugh, did you all get the lice email?" said Frost, changing the subject. Everyone moaned in unison. Atherton periodically endured lice epidemics, the bugs spreading through classrooms and grades and sometimes, God forbid, to parents, too. There was something insulting about these infestations, a feeling that they all paid too much for it to happen, that the vermin should stay in their place in the public schools. The emails they received from the nurse about it sparked a flurry of WhatsApp chatter speculating as to whose dirty kid was patient zero.

The women eventually finished their drinks and parted ways, Belle and Frost and Morgan splitting the check, treating Sofia, cheek kissing with lots of promises to do it again soon. Morgan was planning to walk home, so she convinced Frost to go with her, despite the heat and Frost's protests that her feet were already feeling swollen in her sandals. The two women turned onto Hudson and went up from there, waving goodbyes to Belle, who was heading off to a dinner, and Sofia, who said she needed to get back to her kids.

"Dude, slow down, I can't keep up," said Frost, laughing and hurrying to catch Morgan. "I walk fast, but you're a speed demon! Save it for the marathon."

Though you wouldn't know it by looking at her, all bones and sharp edges, Morgan was a true athlete. When she was little, a blond cherub, she'd chosen gymnastics, a sport where cheerfulness was not only embraced but required. She'd been particularly talented at tumbling. She'd loved to throw her body around, higher and higher, to soar in the air. At one point, it seemed there might be a chance she'd go all the way, or at least halfway, with a shot at the Junior Olympics in sight. She'd just been a slip of a thing, muscles but no fat, a straight line up and down. But early into her preteen years, puberty had taken hold, and she'd been betrayed by her hips and breasts and that fucking added weight. So much added weight. She'd just wanted to fly.

Morgan now thought of Gertrude, her poor Gertrude. Her generous stomach, her sturdy legs. The weight stalked Gertrude as it had Morgan, but it had come even earlier for her little girl. Gertrude was constantly teased about it at school, by ruthless boys who somehow avoided getting caught by any teachers, calling her "Gir-thy Gertrude," snorting like a pig when she walked by in the hallway. Morgan had tried go through the proper channels, get the bullies ex-pelled from Atherton, but none of the teachers could confirm what was happening. Were they blind? When she'd wanted to elevate the issue to the school's board, Gertrude hadn't let her, begging her, weeping, to please not get involved, saying that Morgan would only make it worse. It haunted Morgan, this idea that she couldn't help her child, that the proper punishment wasn't being meted out.

"I wonder what's really going on with Sofia," said Frost as they walked. "Like, how did she *actually* get into the school? I really like her, but she's kind of cagey about some things. Maybe one of your PA friends knows . . ." Morgan felt a buzz in her bag. They were standing on Spring and Hudson, a nondescript block on the edge of SoHo. It was still light out. An e-bike whizzed past, going way too fast; if she'd stepped a foot to her right, she'd have been mowed down. New York was so dangerous lately. Muggings. Stabbings. Pe-destrian deaths.

Morgan checked her phone. It was 6:33. She saw she had one voicemail from an unknown number. She'd save that for later.

While Frost was telling her some story about King and Alfred's tennis group, an uber-competitive mom she hated, blah, blah, Morgan's mind ticked through all she had to get done for the spa opening. Make sure the bookings were set, stock the minifridge out front with La Croix, triple-check the confirmed hours with each practitioner, and test the sound system before the first appointment.

They'd made it up to Hudson and Morton, crossing from Green-wich Village into the West Village, where Morgan lived. "So then she came up to me and said, 'How many private lessons are you doing? Because Henry's doing three a week, and we were thinking of going up to four,'" continued Frost. Morgan found her mind wandering, as it often had been lately.

She thought back to yesterday. She'd skipped dinner, then gotten woozy heading up to her bedroom—the Wegovy at work. She'd had to sit down on the stairs to regain her sense of balance. Gertrude had found her there.

"Mom, are you okay?" Gertrude had asked, plopping down next to Morgan on the wooden step.

"I'm fine, honey, just a little tired," Morgan had said, rubbing Gertrude's back. Gertrude was wearing a crop top, the current, and, in Morgan's opinion, cruel uniform of tween girls in New York City. Gertrude's exposed stomach was pushing out over her bottoms, and Morgan had the urge to tuck her sweet child's flesh back into her pants. She looked just like Morgan; there was barely any sign of Art in her at all. In Morgan's darker moments, she sometimes thought Art might be relieved by this.

They'd sat there in silence, Morgan listening to Gertrude's breath. Morgan had suffered through her pregnancy with Gertrude, never feeling quite right. She'd hated the heaviness of carrying a baby in her body, the scale ticking up, the feeling of being out of control.

"Mom, I don't want to go back to school tomorrow," Gertrude had said. She'd turned to Morgan with tears in her round eyes, her lips shaking. "It's Miles Redness. He's just so mean."

"I know, sweetie," Morgan had said with a sigh. "I know." Gertrude had put her head in Morgan's lap, and Morgan stroked her hair, still soft like a baby's. "I'm taking care of everything," she'd assured her precious daughter. She'd felt like punching a wall.

It was now 6:37. Morgan and Frost were at a grungy intersection, with a nail place, a cannabis shop, and a pizza parlor on each corner. Though Morgan felt sticky and soured, she was still light on her feet. "Let's cross," Morgan said, hopping off the sidewalk onto the street. She looked to the right to make sure no cars were coming, and took two steps forward, fast, Frost following behind. There was a loud whiz and then a crack, and Morgan turned to see her friend Frost flying up in the air, her blousy top rippling in the wind, the whole thing happening as if in slow motion. For a split second, Morgan was reminded of what it felt like to do a tumbling pass on the mat, a back handspring into a back tuck, her head facing down before she'd miraculously land, boom, right side up. Instead, Frost crashed, scraping her cheek along the hot asphalt as she came to a rest a few steps from where she'd been knocked off the ground.

Morgan ran to Frost, hauling her to sitting as she yelped in pain, inspecting Frost's face, blood trickling down Frost's pale cheek. She looked at Morgan with shocked, glassy eyes, not quite registering what had happened. Her left arm was sitting at an angle that an arm really shouldn't be sitting at. Beside them was a guy in Nikes, a blue baseball cap pulled low on his head and an N95 mask covering most of his face. He was crouching next to his electric scooter, checking it for damage. He glanced at the two of them and then swiftly stood up, got back on his scooter, and zoomed off down Hudson Street, weaving in and out of traffic as he went.

A few pedestrians were now surrounding them, including two older women, expressing concern.

"Are you okay, sweetheart? Your face is bleeding. Maybe you should call an ambulance?" one of them asked. "Can we help you two up?" Frost hadn't said anything yet, though she was quietly crying. Her hair had escaped the bun and she had dirt and scrapes on her hands and knees. Morgan, with the women's assistance, pulled Frost to standing, careful not to touch her injured arm. Frost wobbled a bit but found her footing.

"Is it bad?" Frost asked. One of the women handed Frost a napkin, and she held it to her face, pulling it away to look at her own blood. The bleeding was minimal. It was mostly surface scratches, though it looked nasty.

"I think you're okay, but you probably need an X-ray for your arm. Let's get you to my house and call a doctor," said Morgan.

"Did you see the guy on the scooter?" Frost asked. "Where did he go?"

Morgan shook her head. "Not really. He drove away before I could really get a good look at him or say anything. What an asshole."

"I saw the whole thing," one of the women interjected. "It looked like he headed directly for you. On purpose!"

"What a maniac," said Morgan. "New York is filled with them."

Feeling light-headed, Morgan closed her eyes. Fucking Wegovy. A blackness came over her, and then she was falling, falling, falling, back to the pavement.

"*Dios mio*, Morgan, are you awake?" she heard someone say into her ear a few seconds later, helping her up with a strong arm around her back.

"I fainted," said Morgan. Her eyes readjusted to see Sofia standing next to Frost. The two older women had left, likely not wanting the curse to spread to them.

"Frost got hit by an e-scooter, which was totally out of control, and then I went down," said Morgan. "It must have been the sight of all that blood." Sofia patted Morgan's arm sympathetically. She handed Frost another tissue to put on her face, and Frost dabbed her cheek, wincing in pain.

"Everyone's crashing and bleeding and falling and getting spit on," said Sofia, chuckling darkly. "Why are all these things happening? I hope I didn't bring bad luck to you all."

Sofia guided Morgan and Frost across the street, one arm locked in each of theirs.

"What are you doing here?" said Morgan. "I thought you lived in Tribeca and were going straight home."

"I do," said Sofia, "but I like to walk around after I have drinks. I find it helps take the edge off the alcohol and allows me to sleep better." Morgan hadn't had a drink in months, since she'd started on the weight-loss drugs. It was as if the chemicals had erased that desire entirely. She'd heard that they messed with the pleasure center of your brain, and in addition to alcohol, people who took them reported that they lost interest in sex, too. Luckily, Morgan had had no such side effect.

"You should definitely see a doctor," said Sofia to Frost.

"Yeah, my arm is really starting to hurt," said Frost, cringing.

"And you, too." Sofia motioned to Morgan. "Morgan, have you eaten anything today? Maybe that's why you fainted." Morgan didn't reply. They were nearing Morgan and Art's place on Grove Street, between Bedford and Bleecker, a lovely block filled with leafy trees and historic town houses. Outside of their home was Art, climbing the steps to the door. He glanced back and saw them. His face registered confusion and then alarm, and he hurried down to meet the women. Morgan was struck, as she often was, by her husband's handsomeness; he'd only gotten better-looking as they'd aged, his jawline cut with masculinity, his full head of dark hair reflecting the late summer light.

"What happened?" he said, breathless, taking in Frost's face and arm and his wife's disheveled state.

"Someone hit me with a scooter," Frost said shyly, looking down. A single tear slid from her face onto the pavement.

"Who?" said Art, his voice full of rage. Frost shrugged.

"We didn't see. He was in a mask. Then he just took off," said Morgan. "And then I fainted." Art scrunched up his mouth, the way he did when something wasn't making sense.

"I texted Tim, he'll be here in a minute," said Frost. "He'll take me to the hospital—we have a friend who's a doctor at Mount Sinai, so I can cut the line at the ER there."

Sofia cleared her throat.

"I'm sorry: Art, this is Sofia," said Morgan. "We had drinks earlier, then she found us on the sidewalk and helped us home."

A car pulled up and Tim jumped out, in ratty shorts and a JOHN'S OF BLEECKER STREET T-shirt. Tim was good-looking in a scruffy, artsy way, always in narrow jeans and a vintage T-shirt. Earlier in their lives, they would have referred to him as a "hipster," but Morgan didn't think that term existed anymore. "Holy shit," Tim said, giving Frost a gentle hug, careful not to squeeze her injury. "Thanks for taking care of her." He took Frost's right hand to lead her to the car, and for a second Frost hesitated before following him.

"Thank you so much, Sofia," said Morgan now, wanting to shoo her away without actually shooing her away. "I can't wait to see you at the Thyme & Time opening party!"

"Same here," said Sofia with a smile. "You get a good night's rest and remember to eat something!"

Morgan waved goodbye as Sofia swished away. Morgan noticed she'd swapped out her heels for fashionable, flat gladiator sandals. It gave Morgan comfort that Sofia was too beautiful to possibly be very smart.

When they were inside, Art tried to interrogate Morgan about what had happened, but she waved him off, blaming nerves and trauma and the need for silence. Later that night, after Gertrude was asleep, Morgan's personal doctor, Dr. Bossidy, a kind man in his sixties, came and checked her out.

"Wegovy doesn't agree with everyone, and fainting can be dangerous," Dr. Bossidy said after Art was out of earshot. "You don't *need* it, Morgan. This is ridiculous."

"Oh, please, I bet half the moms at Atherton are on it," she replied. "It's not going to kill me, right?" He shook his head, knowing she planned to ignore his advice.

Morgan was now snuggled into her bed, alone, scrolling through Instagram. The Charys' house was a masterpiece of function and design, and Morgan particularly loved her bedroom, with its harmonious textiles and a 1930s Venetian chandelier. Art was in his home office, working.

Morgan pulled up Sofia's profile, which she often did, noticing she hadn't added anything new since arriving in New York. There were pictures of the kids in Miami, swimming in a pool at an enormous home, shots of Sofia wearing tight designer dresses, standing next to an unremarkable man who Morgan assumed was her ex-husband, JP. She zoomed into Sofia's face, studying its symmetrical shape, Sofia's smooth skin, small waist, and exaggerated hips.

Morgan then flipped back to her text messages, shooting off responses to some of the typical mom questions she got nearly every day. Ask Morgan was on the case.

Tribeca Pediatrics isn't for everyone—they're very stingy with antibiotics.

The Bulldog baseball league meets on Saturday mornings at Asphalt Green. I'll send you the names of the best coaches.

No, that's not poison ivy, that's fifth disease. After the rash
appears, it's not contagious anymore.

Go to Dr. Shafer for Botox, he is the absolute best. Don't
even think about anyone else.

That done, it was time for Morgan's nightly presleep meditation.
She put down her phone and closed her eyes, repeating her mantra
over and over—"I'm a monster on the hill," her favorite Taylor
Swift lyric. She zoned out for her allotted fifteen minutes, feeling
peaceful and calm. She opened her eyes, and images butted into her
brain. The shape of Frost's body outlined against the Manhattan
sky, about to smash into the sidewalk. Gertrude's tearstained face as
she recounted being bullied. Sofia tumbling down Atherton's stairs.
Morgan stabbing Frost with a knife. Bashing Belle's head in with a
hammer. But then Morgan pushed the intrusive thoughts away, using a trick she'd learned from a prominent mind-body practitioner,
visualizing them being swept under a rug, a pile of dirt no longer
in her sightline.

She turned off her light and pulled the covers over her head. She
put her phone to her ear and pressed play on her voicemail.

"I'm in my apartment, thinking about you," a raspy male voice
said. "I'm thinking about your face. About your body. About your
lovely neck. Your mouth. Thinking about the next time I'll get to
see you. I can't wait to touch you everywhere. To feel you. To
squeeze you until I can't." There was the sound of ruffling, then
unzipping, and then a few loud breaths followed by moaning.
Morgan listened to it again and again, pressing her cute, pink,
egg-shaped vibrator against herself as she did. She fell asleep easily
after that.

## Chapter 4

## An Opening Party!

===

Unlike her new friends, Sofia Perez wasn't rich. To clarify: She *used* to be rich. But now Sofia Perez was poor. Not quite as poor as she'd been when she was growing up, the child of Colombian immigrants, her mother a cleaning lady for Miami office buildings, her father a mechanic at a garage in Coconut Grove. But close. On top of that, Sofia hadn't voluntarily left Miami for New York, this run-down city, with its rodents and robberies and smells of trash and piss. No, she'd been banished, ruined, nearly penniless.

Atherton had been her lifeline, though she still wasn't exactly sure why she was here. A couple of months prior, living in a furnished apartment in South Beach while she figured out her next move, she'd received a mysterious call from Dr. Broker, saying he'd heard of her predicament (how?) and could offer two nonentry spots at Atherton to her children. Sofia was familiar with the ways of the wealthy—her ex-husband, JP, was one of the richest men in Miami, and she'd been in that world since they'd married a decade ago. But she'd been surprised by this call. Had a friend of a friend emailed Dr. Broker? Someone she knew socially in Miami who also had a place in Manhattan? And if so, why keep their identity a secret?

She'd rolled with it, though, as she'd needed an out—there was no way she could have survived in Miami, among her husband's friends and allies. JP was basically Miami royalty, traveling in a rarefied social set, a group of land barons and kingpins and Donald Trump's annoying kids. JP's father, Jorge, had also come to America from Colombia. But instead of fixing cars like Sofia's papá, Jorge made it big by building high-rise condos all over the southern United States.

Sofia felt like Jorge had always disapproved of her. She didn't have "class." JP hadn't seemed to care when he'd first met her. She was in community college then and had tagged along with a girlfriend to a gala, excited to see how the other half lived. Sofia was beautiful. She was clever, too, but her looks were outstanding. JP had swept her off her feet, taking her to dinners, flying her to exotic locations, buying her jewelry. He told her he'd take care of her forever. She never *loved* loved him (JP was five foot eight, with a mushy face and the charm of an iguana). But they'd had a gorgeous beach wedding at Casa de Campo in the Dominican Republic. Marc Anthony had played at the reception. Who needed love when you had Marc Anthony?

Sofia thought about her situation as she walked briskly to Morgan's Thyme & Time opening party, a few blocks from her Tribeca loft. Her heels clicked over the uneven terrain. She'd walked more in the short time since arriving in New York than she'd walked in her entire life, combined. What had her legs been doing this entire time? She'd exercised, done miles and miles on treadmills. But had she ever really walked? She hadn't needed to.

She even still had her chauffeur, Rodrick, but he was only there to shepherd the children around the city—he had a direct line to JP, who tracked their movements. JP was covering the private school fees, the kids' expenses, and he'd secured the apartment in his name. Otherwise, Sofia was only getting a small stipend, $2,000 a month, which was about the amount that she used to spend on her hair and nails. So Sofia was playing rich, lying about getting facials and taking expensive exercise classes while existing on the largesse of her new Atherton acquaintances, who didn't seem to notice—and were too wealthy to care—that she never paid for anything. "Do you have Venmo?" Morgan had asked after they all grabbed a coffee the other day, to which Sofia had feigned technological ignorance. The matter was soon dropped.

When anyone asked what happened with her marriage, she said that it had dissolved amicably, two old friends drifting apart. In fact, it had ended with a bang, literally, when JP had found out that Sofia had been sleeping with her trainer, Michael. Ah, Michael, the reason she was now in dirty old Tribeca instead of sunny, gorgeous South Beach. Sofia's heel caught on a crag in the cobblestone on Harrison Street, taking her shoe along with it. She was learning, slowly, that as easy as Carrie Bradshaw had made it look, it was nearly impossible to walk in Manhattan in stilettos. She hopped back to her Louboutin and slid her foot in, remembering how Michael had massaged her feet after every workout, getting into the joint of each toe, deeply, painfully, pleasurably. She shook her head again at her own stupidity. It had been so unlike Sofia, street-smart and resourceful, eyes always on the prize, to have made that mistake. She should have known better. But she'd been blinded by love, as embarrassing as that was now to admit.

She focused on her new mission as she entered Thyme & Time, already filled with perfectly chic women dressed in strappy, expensive-looking tanks. Sofia was starting to appreciate the New York look, so different from Miami, where skin, boobs, and augmentation reigned. Tonight, she was wearing her most demure outfit, a sleek pantsuit she'd purchased for JP's grandmother's memorial last year. For budget reasons, she'd cut back on dermatology needs, letting her lips deflate to their natural state. Not being able to afford filler was a blessing in disguise: she didn't like standing out, and she'd noticed the other moms staring at her face judgmentally.

"Sofia! You made it!" Morgan grabbed her and gave her a quick hug. She was in a high-necked sheath dress, her blond hair swept to the side. Morgan was a ball of energy, with endless friendliness and pep. She was exhausting to speak with, always punctuating her sentences with "amazing!" and "awesome!" and "I love that."

Morgan's eyes roamed the room, finally settling on Sofia with a vaguely anxious twitch. "This place is *amazing*," Sofia said, trying to make Morgan feel better by parroting Morgan's own language. Sofia wasn't sure what, exactly, Morgan had to be worried about. She knew that Morgan's husband, Art, was totally loaded, and that he and his company were bankrolling this Thyme & Time thing. Even Sofia had heard of Welly. What was the worst that could happen? Sofia surveyed the gathering, the women chatting in small groups and saying how fabulous it all was. She wondered what surprises they were concealing beneath their air kisses and no-makeup-makeup.

Sofia had broken her marriage vows for the first time after an early afternoon workout session at her home gym. It had been the culmination of months of hot, building tension, Michael's hands on her thighs, on her abs, creeping up to her breasts. Michael had come recommended by a mom-friend, Andrea. ("He has the body of a model and the soul of a poet," Andrea had texted her, alongside a laughing emoji and a fire emoji.) Sofia had hired him right away, intrigued, and he'd shown up the next day, chiseled and perfect, like a character out of the romance novels Sofia was so fond of.

Three times a week, they'd stretch, work out, and then stretch again, all while chatting about their lives, getting more and more personal as time went on. Michael's background was similar to Sofia's. He'd pulled himself out of poverty, building his business with no safety net, and found a lucrative niche as the trainer-to-Miami-housewives. He had a nice apartment in Wynwood—he'd shown Sofia pictures—and he loved cooking and his dog.

In another life, Sofia might have married Michael. He was kind, he was funny, he was smart. He got her in a way that JP never had, appreciating her intelligence and sense of humor instead of just her face and body. Sofia hadn't realized that men could be like that. And it didn't hurt that he was so, so hot. Sofia came to crave his scent, his touch, the way he encouraged her to run a little faster, lift a little more, dig a little deeper.

They'd started to text on the side, and messages about Sofia's workouts turned into inside jokes, heart emojis, selfies that showed a liiiiiittle too much of their bodies. Sofia in a towel, which had fallen to reveal the tops of her breasts. Michael's hand sliding down his chest toward his pants. Sofia knew they were playing with fire. JP, regardless of what *he* was up to on the side, wouldn't stand to have a wife who cheated on him. No sirree. *Nunca, nunca.* Sofia knew this. But she was a woman obsessed. Maybe even in love. She'd never been in love before.

Then, one fateful day, Sofia, not knowing (but knowing) where it would lead, invited Michael to stay while she'd hopped in her sauna. "You can cool down while I steam," she'd said to him offhandedly, the danger of the situation making her body tingle. She'd undressed swiftly, leaving her sweaty clothes in a pile on the floor, and stepped into the steamy box, waiting on the damp wooden bench, already near orgasm from the anticipation of it all. Thirty seconds later, the door opened, and Michael had entered, naked, floating toward Sofia in the red-cedar room, his mouth flexed into an amused, sexy smile. She went to him, not thinking about the consequences of her actions, but rather *pleasure, pleasure, pleasure.*

They'd settled into a pattern. Training three days a week, sex afterward in the sauna. Rinse and repeat. Sofia hadn't been actively worried about JP—he worked during the day and had never come home once unexpectedly during their ten-year marriage. He left her to it. But instead of JP, she should have been concerned about Michael. She'd thought he'd known the deal. She'd thought he'd known the boundaries. This couldn't be real, as much as they both fantasized about it. She'd figured that, at some point, they'd have to stop. Maybe Michael would meet someone else. Maybe Sofia would get bored. Maybe she'd get frustrated that she wasn't able to go out to dinner with the man she adored. But they'd kept going, unable to face reality.

"Oh, thank you! The space still needs a few last-minute touches, but we're excited to start welcoming customers," said Morgan now. Sofia clicked back to earth, remembering where she was and this weird woman she was talking to. Morgan was weird, right? No one else seemed to think so. Sofia felt a million miles away from Michael, and for a quick moment her heart ached thinking about him.

"You must come to the spa soon, I'll comp you a free sound bath."

"Please, I'll pay," said Sofia, lying. Morgan went off to greet other partygoers. Sofia noticed Morgan's daughter, Gertrude, sitting alone on a small sofa, scrolling on her phone. She looked like a heavier, younger version of Morgan, with that same blond hair and dimple. But instead of cheerful like her mom she seemed miserable, her mouth set in a grim scowl.

Sofia, on motherly impulse, approached Gertrude, laying a hand on her shoulder, startling her away from whatever messages a twelve-year-old would send.

"Hi, sweetie, you okay? I'm your mom's new friend, Sofia," said Sofia. Gertrude stared at her warily.

"I'm fine," she said flatly, turning back to her phone. What an unpleasant child, Sofia thought, then quickly felt bad for her ungenerous take. She was probably just bored, or annoyed to be dragged to this adult event.

Sofia then made her way to the bar, which was set up next to the front desk. She picked up a champagne and perused the product display, sniffing a particularly pretty-looking rose oil. She looked to her right and saw Ava Leo, alone, standing by a shelf full of creams and crystals. Ava didn't notice her. Sofia watched as Ava stealthily picked up a face serum and slipped it into her black Chanel handbag. Sofia was confused. Were the products free? They didn't appear to be. But why on earth would Ava steal a serum? Sofia, not wanting to be seen, speed-walked to the other side of the room, hiding behind a trio of influencers, decked out in full glam and designer crop tops.

"Sofia!" She felt a hand on her neck and jumped, but it was only Frost, in an amazing vintage slip dress that looked straight out of a 1998 *Vogue*. She had a bandage across her face from the scooter accident, and her left arm was in a sling. Somehow, she still looked glamorous. "How's my favorite new mom-friend?" Frost purred. Sofia liked Frost the best of all of them. She'd considered telling Frost the truth about her marriage but couldn't yet bring herself to do it. First, it was just too humiliating. What was Frost going to say to that? "Sorry you're broke"? Second, part of the deal with JP was that Sofia wasn't supposed to tell anyone anything. He'd pay for the apartment and their groceries and allow her to have just enough to keep up the charade if she kept her mouth shut.

After Sofia's infidelity had come to light, JP's family had banded together to protect him. Sofia, feeling intimidated and out of her depth, agreed to a have one mediator instead of separate divorce lawyers. She'd figured that because she was the one who cheated, she'd just have to swallow it. She knew she could have asked for more, fought a little, but she didn't know how to. Sofia's parents were both dead—her dad when she was a teen and her mom just a few years ago, from cervical cancer that had gone undetected. Sofia was an only child. She had no one.

"How's your arm, Frost?" said Sofia. Frost smiled distractedly.

"It still hurts, but it's only a sprain, not broken. And now Tim is on a mission to find the guy who hit me, so we've hired someone to look into it," said Frost. "Ask Morgan to the rescue again! She researched for me and found a great private detective." Morgan, deep in conversation with Clara Cain, looked over at them as if she'd heard what they were saying.

Sofia saw Ava out of the corner of her eye, taking selfies against the white script Thyme & Time logo on the wall, likely posting to her million Instagram followers. Should she tell Frost she'd seen her pocketing a serum?

"Hey, ladies, thanks for coming." It was Art, Morgan's dashing husband, in a deep blue suit and his signature white Welly sneakers.

He put a hand on Frost's shoulder, and Frost blushed and batted her eyes charmingly.

"It's so great of you to come and support Morgan," said Art.

Sofia was struck with the feeling that she'd seen him somewhere before. Somewhere outside of the context of Morgan.

"How *is* Morgan?" asked Frost. "This is such a lovely event. I hope she's soaking it all in." They all turned to look at Morgan, still chatting with Clara.

"She's great," said Art with a doting smile. "You know Morgan: the best at everything she tries." Sofia noticed that Frost couldn't take her eyes off him. "Though perhaps she needs saving from Clara."

He walked toward his wife, and the two women were joined by Gabby Mahler, stylish in a black jumpsuit, her short hair spiked up dramatically. Ava approached, linking arms with Gabby, her Chanel bag full of contraband dangling from her other limb.

"Who's going to take a sound bath with me?!" said Gabby mischievously. "Let's get naked, sit in a padded room, and listen to 'My Heart Will Go On' on repeat," she said. Ava giggled.

Sofia saw that Morgan had moved on to another mom, Becky Oranga, mother of a third grader named Jesse. Sofia had chatted with her at a few of the Atherton meet and greets. Becky had the startled look of a surprised deer and a habit of referring to her son as "my Jesse," as if all of them also didn't have children that were theirs.

"Ava, I can't wait for the party next weekend. Are you totally ready?" said Frost.

"Everything but my outfit, which unfortunately is the most important part," said Ava.

Sofia had been invited to Ava's Bouquet of Newly Sharpened Pencils event along with the rest of Atherton. She'd heard that everyone put lots of effort—and money—into their costumes, and that most coordinated with their husbands. Sofia was fearing an evening of being the odd woman out, particularly because she couldn't afford to buy anything new.

"Guys, let's do a selfie," said Ava, holding her phone up and out. The women gathered around her, making sure to get their most flattering angles.

"Has anyone seen Belle?" asked Frost. They all shook their heads.

"Maybe she's boycotting because Morgan opened her business first," said Gabby, doing air quotes at "business."

"You're such a bitch, Gabby," said Ava good-naturedly.

A glass clanked loudly, and the room, now at capacity with beauty editors, wellness influencers, and Morgan's mom-friends, quieted. Art and Morgan stood together near the entrance, Gertrude hovering awkwardly nearby. Art was holding a glass of wine and a microphone. Sofia noticed all the women ogling him—good-looking, wealthy, kind to his wife. Even Sofia was taken in, thinking about how unimpressive JP was compared to this model husband. Morgan's face was pinched into a smile. She was holding a glass of sparkling water so tightly that Sofia feared it might burst.

"We are so happy you've all made it to the opening of Thyme & Time," said Art to applause.

"Morgan is a *force*," he said to the sound of the audience's muffled, knowing chuckles. "She is always on the go, making things happen, with good cheer and positive energy. You know the drill—ask Morgan! And she runs our life flawlessly. She's also a very fast runner. She finished the New York City marathon in three hours and thirty minutes!—and is the best mom and wife." Sofia felt Frost stiffen next to her.

"So, when she told me she wanted a business to call her own, I knew that whatever it was, Welly and I would gladly step in with our support. Morgan has always been passionate about spas and sound baths—"

Behind her, Sofia could hear Gabby softly humming "My Heart Will Go On" and Ava silently convulsing, trying to hold it together.

Art went on in this way, and Sofia tuned out, spiraling down a dark path in her mind that she lately couldn't stop herself from: the idea that JP would take her children from her. Was he setting the stage for a full-custody play? He wouldn't do it until he was remarried; JP paid about as little attention to Carlos and Lucia as he had to Sofia. But he *would* get remarried, and then he might try to take her children back to Miami, saying that their lying, cheating mother didn't have the resources to give them the life they deserved. Sofia flicked the thought away.

"Let's raise our glasses to Morgan, and to Thyme & Time, and to getting the word out about this wonderful place!" They all clinked their drinks and cheered. Art then handed the mic to Morgan, who was looking paler and tenser by the second.

"Friends, thank you so much for supporting our dream of creating a sound bath spa in the heart of Tribeca! It's an amazing honor to have you all here." Morgan's voice was strained.

"We wanted to give you all a little preview of our offerings, so I'd love to introduce one of our expert practitioners, who'll give a quick demonstration."

A pretty, light-skinned Black woman in beige yoga pants and a matching top stepped to the front of the room. She was followed by three young women, each hauling a crystal bowl, one small, one medium, and one large. They set the bowls in front of the practitioner, who kneeled behind them. She was holding smooth ceramic sticks in each hand, the length and thickness of a tennis racket handle.

"I'm Tilly," she said, her voice like smooth cream. "Today I will be using crystal singing bowls to help you experience relaxation. Now close your eyes and enjoy the sound bath."

"What the fuck is a singing bowl?" Gabby cough-laughed into Sofia's neck. No one closed their eyes. Tilly hit the middle bowl lightly with her stick, creating an echoey church-bell tone, then proceeded to swirl the stick along the bowl's perimeter, making a sound like blowing air into a beer bottle. She did this to each bowl, producing different notes, swaying as she went. Gabby was creating trouble by singing along—"laaaaa, laaaa, laaa"—and Ava was shaking with swallowed laughter.

In the middle of it all, Frost leaned into Sofia. "I wonder where Belle is," she whispered into her ear. "Something must be wrong for her to miss it. Though she has been kind of bitchy about this whole thing—" Frost gestured around the spa. "So maybe she was just too jealous to make it." For a bunch of women who were supposedly best friends, Sofia was struck by how easily they all fell into shit-talking one another.

Sofia's last real friends were from childhood, her true *amigas*, girls she'd grown up with in Miami whose parents hung with hers. She'd lost touch with them when she'd married JP, falling instead into a circle of fake acquaintances, their relationships based on money and looks and the fact that all their children had gone to the same private school, Gulliver. No one had even said goodbye to her when she'd moved, when she'd sent out a cryptic group text explaining that the kids wouldn't be back in the fall (true), and that she'd loved getting to know them all (lie). Andrea had been the only one to reply, with a crying emoji plus a heart emoji. Then a follow-up: "Michael?" Sofia had never responded.

Tilly finally wrapped. "You may now take a deep breath before opening your eyes." She said. They all shut their eyes, pretending they'd been obeying her directive the whole time.

"Everyone, arms out!" Sofia heard someone shout. She opened her eyes to see a large man in a black ski mask standing before the group. He had a silver gun, which he was pointing at the horrified crowd. Frost grabbed Sofia's hand and squeezed it, making frightened eye contact with her.

"Put your arms out, I said!" demanded the man, demonstrating clumsily, the gun briefly hanging upside down as he did. Art and Morgan were standing in front of Gertrude protectively, and the Thyme & Time employees were unsuccessfully trying to hide behind their crystal bowls. Tilly was closest to the man, still holding her ceramic sticks, silent tears rolling down her lovely cheeks.

Sofia lifted her arms away from her body, all the guests doing the same, no one saying a word. Frost lifted her one arm up, her other trapped still in its sling. Sofia had read about this happening before—there had been a series of downtown robberies targeting wealthy people in restaurants and stores; it had been all over the *New York Post*. And so Sofia was nervous, but not majorly. She felt a thrill being part of such a dramatic scene. She'd lived in rough-enough neighborhoods to know that it wouldn't end in violence unless someone totally fucked up. The man had just playacted a zombie, for crying out loud.

"I'm going to take your watches and bracelets. Don't move," he said, somewhat shakily. He put the gun in his pocket and, one by one, stopped in front of each of guest, removing her jewelry and putting it into a black sack. It reminded Sofia of trick-or-treating with the kids, only instead of Skittles and Kit Kats the man was collecting Rolexes, Tiffany, and Van Cleef & Arpels.

"It's, uh, you have to snap the safety latch first," said Gabby, haltingly, when it was her turn. He slipped off her tennis bracelet, a strand of stunning diamonds that Sofia was sure was worth upward of $100,000. Sofia had a thought—should *she* be getting into this game? It seemed easy and lucrative, and she always knew where the Atherton crowd would be.

"You. Now," the man said. He was right in front of Sofia, and she looked into his eyes, the only part of him exposed, as he unhooked her gold Cartier tank watch, a gift from JP for their fifth wedding anniversary, and slipped it into his bag. He glanced down to avoid her gaze.

"I'm sorry," said Sofia softly. "But do I know you?" Something about his voice sounded so familiar. Was Sofia going crazy?

At that, the criminal froze. Then he quickly sprinted out the door, leaving it ajar. Sofia saw him zooming off on a moped down Reade Street, the black sack of jewelry sitting on the pavement, left behind. The room erupted into pandemonium, people pulling out their phones and excitedly calling friends and family to recount the story.

"There was a guy with a gun! No, I don't know what his race was; he had a ski mask on. No, I didn't look at his hands! I was trying to stay alive!"

"I'm fine, but he stole my Rolex, that asshole."

"We all almost died. We have *children*. No, they wouldn't be better off living with the nanny. Fuck you, Jason, that's not funny. I'm freaking out here."

Sofia had a better idea. She navigated the mayhem and walked outside, picking up the abandoned bag from the sidewalk, clutching it to her chest, feeling the comforting weight of all that money. She was probably holding more than a million dollars' worth of jewelry. She fished her Cartier out of the sack before returning to her friends, standing in a semicircle near the reception desk.

"The robber's loot!" said Gabby happily. "It's like out of a cartoon or something. Can I get my tennis bracelet back, por favor?" Sofia handed her the bag, glad to be rid of it. It was too tempting given her current situation.

Gabby plucked out her strand of diamonds, and then passed the sack along like a hot potato, each person retrieving her own piece.

"Well, at least it all ended okay," said Ava. "Should I delete my Instagram story? Is it in poor taste now?"

"Absolutely don't delete it," said Frost firmly. "Morgan won't want this to detract from the party. If anything, post more happy pictures, make the space look great."

"I think Morgan left," said Ava. "She must have taken Gertrude home." The door of the spa opened, and the women saw Art reenter, sent to do damage control, chatting and assuring, until he landed next to them. Sofia was now certain she'd seen him before the day of Frost's accident—but where? He smelled like a mix of stress sweat and Tom Ford cologne.

"Morgan took an Uber home with Gertrude. They're pretty shaken up but will be fine," said Art. "Since all the jewelry has been recovered, I'm not even sure if it's worth us filing a police report."

"He had a gun!" said Gabby.

"I called NYPD just now, and the officer I spoke with said that lots of times these guys have fake weapons," said Art. "Someone recently got robbed outside Carbone—he lost an Audemars Piguet—and it turned out the man who did it was holding up a water gun that he'd painted black. We don't know if this guy had a *real* gun. Plus, Morgan is concerned about the negative publicity—will people come to the spa if they know that something like this could happen?"

"Let us know how we can help," said Frost. The other women all nodded earnestly. "And tell Morgan we're sorry and we're thinking of her."

"Okay, gals, I've got other people to chat with," he said. "Finish your drinks and please, please don't make this a big story at drop-off tomorrow. Morgan is counting on you to be in her corner."

Gabby gave him a thumbs-up.

"I need a real drink after that, not a glass of shitty white wine. Who wants to come with me?" said Ava. Gabby raised her hand. So did Frost. Sofia knew she should go—she needed to forge relationships with these women, not just for herself, but also for her kids and their future.

But all she really wanted to do was walk around the city alone. Perhaps find someone interesting to trail. It was something she'd been doing to various people—other moms, men she found attractive, women who were particularly stylish—since she'd arrived in New York. She'd walk about a block behind her target, careful not to get too close: Sofia, with her TV-star good looks, was certainly noticeable. Then she'd track them until she got tired, sometimes for just a few minutes, and sometimes for longer. She particularly liked to follow her new friends, which is how she'd come upon Frost and Morgan after the scooter accident. It made her feel closer to them, in a strange way, to shadow them unknowingly. Sofia hadn't realized how much of her time previously had been taken up by spending money.

"Barry's Bootcamp calls! I have to get up super early for a workout," Sofia said now. "But next time."

"I love that dedication to your hot bod," said Gabby, Sofia hanging back as they left, waving goodbye. Frost gave Sofia the "call me" sign, and Sofia felt her cheeks warm with the glow of a burgeoning friendship.

Then there was a hand on her shoulder, and Sofia turned to see Art, his forehead shiny. His face was very close to hers and she could feel his breath, which was warm and wine-y.

"Did everyone else leave?" he asked.

"Yes, they just did," said Sofia. A piece of his hair fell over his eye, and Sofia had the satisfying feeling, not unlike an orgasm or sneeze, of having reached a thing she'd been grasping for.

She'd trailed Frost home during the first week of school, or at least to where she'd thought was Frost's home, to a new-looking building on Twenty-Second Street near Park Avenue. She'd googled Frost beforehand and had been impressed with all she'd found: she'd been an It Girl with famous parents. She was exactly the type of person who could introduce Sofia to the other wealthy women of New York. So later that day, Sofia had waited outside Frost's building before pickup, hoping to run into her, which she had.

Looking again at Art, the straight line of his nose, his full, sensual lips, it all clicked. Right before Frost had exited her building that afternoon, a well-dressed Indian man had come out, passing Sofia, who'd turned her back toward the street so as not to attract his attention. She'd only gotten a glimpse of him, of his profile and the back of his head, but she was sure that the same man was now standing right in front of her—Art, Morgan's husband.

"I'd better go home, I have to put the kids to bed," Sofia said pleasantly to Art. He smiled at her, but not with his eyes. "I hope Morgan feels better and that Gertrude is okay. I'm glad we got our jewelry back." He nodded and patted her back, his hand lingering for just a split second too long before moving on to a group of nubile young beauty editors.

What had Art and Frost been up to? Nothing good, clearly. Sofia knew about the risks of extramarital affairs, and she hoped it didn't blow up in Frost's face the way that it had in hers. She thought back to that Saturday, six months after she'd started sleeping with Michael. The kids were already out of the house, Carlos at soccer, Lucia at a birthday party. Sofia had been sitting in her bedroom, just out of the shower, thinking about Michael, as she often did. What was he up to? Was he missing her? JP and his father, Jorge, had been downstairs, about to leave for their weekly golf game at La Gorce. All seemed calm and normal. And then she'd heard JP yell her name. Then yell it again. "SOFIA," he'd roared. She'd sat for just a moment longer, her heart sinking, sensing that everything was about to change. She'd walked down the stairs to the front foyer, to find JP in his best Nike Golf outfit, wearing those stupid Oakley sunglasses that she hated, holding a piece of paper. Next to him was Jorge, glaring, the wrinkles on his forehead almost comedically furrowed. JP threw the paper at her, passing her coldly on his way out, Jorge whispering "*puta*" as he slammed the front door in Sofia's face. She'd read the note, her hands shaking.

"Sofia. I love you. You are my everything. I want to be with you. Love, Michael." She'd blinked back tears, seeing her pink Birkin open on the console. Sofia still kept the note in her wallet, next to her two faded sonograms, a sad reminder that someone out there had once cared deeply for her.

Sofia went out to Reade Street now, wondering if Michael was thinking about her. They didn't speak; one of the conditions of her pathetic alimony was that she cut off communication with him. The last time she saw him, right before she'd moved, he'd offered to come with them, to build his business in New York, to make a life together. But she'd been scared that JP would use Michael as an excuse to take away the kids, so she'd said no, sobbing. He'd understood. But Sofia second-guessed that choice every single day.

It was still hot outside, though the sun was setting. Her mind wandered to the man with the gun, and she reached back into her memories, trying to pull his voice out of everything that was jumbled up inside. But there was nothing. She stopped in front of the Jacadi next door, pretending to window-shop for tiny blazers while using the glass reflection to size up potential targets. A well-dressed Asian couple passed by. They were around Sofia's age, likely Tribeca locals heading out to a date night. Boring. Next came two teen girls, their long straight hair swinging, in matching baggy pants and tops that ended way above their belly buttons. Sofia shuddered to think of Lucia in such an outfit, but also knew that times had changed since she was a girl, when her father would send her upstairs to change if her bra strap was poking out of her tank top. "*Puta*," Jorge had called her. Whore.

Sofia let the girls walk by. Then she saw two twentysomething women in evening gowns, their makeup carefully done, chatting with each other about something juicy. Perfect. They continued toward the subway stop at West Broadway. Sofia teetered off after them, careful to stay out of view.

## Chapter 5

# A Bouquet of Newly Sharpened Pencils!

═══

Belle Redness had just had the worst week of her life. The whole family had gotten lice—lice! It had started with Miles, predictably, with that shaggy Alpaca hairstyle he refused to get trimmed. Belle had noticed him scratching his head after school, the telltale sign, and had forced Ivanna to search his scalp thoroughly as Belle held the flashlight, bracing herself. They'd seen the tiny insects crawling everywhere, not even trying to hide, flaunting the fact that they'd taken up residence in her son's hair like a crew of uncooperative squatters. Belle swallowed a scream, trying her best not to scare the shit out of Miles. First came the lanternflies, then came the lice. Was God punishing her for something?

"Mom, what's happening?" Miles had said. He was cradling Belle's phone, checking NFL scores.

"Does he have *lice*?" said Hildy with disgust. She'd walked in, her hoodie pulled over her head. "Your turn, sweetie," Belle said, her stomach roiling with queasiness. Hildy had looked at her mother with alarm.

After finding nits in Hildy's hair, Ivanna had checked Belle, combing through Belle's thick, heavy mane. It felt good, like getting a wash at the salon. But then Ivanna squeaked, stopping the search midcomb.

"I'm sorry, Miss Belle," said Ivanna quietly. "I see them. Lots of them." Her head hadn't felt itchy beforehand, but at that moment Belle's scalp had felt like it was on fire. She'd had to sit on her hands not to scratch, for fear of drawing blood.

Belle had immediately called Licenders, the premier delousing service (Ask Morgan!). They'd arrived that evening, a pair of competent middle-aged women in vaguely medical-looking uniforms and full face and hair masks. First, they'd checked the rest of the family—Jeff and Ivanna had nits, as well—and then treated them all with a onetime hair mask. The duo spent the rest of the night, the night of Morgan's Thyme & Time opening party, delousing the house, washing all the sheets, pillows, towels, and Hildy's old stuffed animals in superstrong chemicals, Belle following them around as they worked, encouraging them to do more, more, more. The price for the treatments plus the house extermination was an even $3,000, though Belle would have literally paid half a million if they'd asked.

The worst part was, she'd had to alert Atherton—school policy dictated it. She'd had the thought to just . . . not. Mainly because she didn't want Dr. Broker to know that she had lice, as silly as that was. But she'd be in deep trouble with the administration if someone found out. She'd reluctantly emailed that night, a long, wine-fueled note about their "lice journey" that she knew Nurse Weiss, a jokester who loved to dress up as viruses for Halloween, would find funny.

The next morning, an alert went out to both Miles's and Hildy's grades, letting the other parents know to be on the lookout for lice, but not who the afflicted family was. Belle instructed Hildy and Miles to keep it quiet, bribing them with unlimited screen time. She didn't want to be associated with lice! Belle's hair was her *thing*. No, no, no. So far, so good. No one had found out, not even her friends—she'd told Morgan that she couldn't come to her opening party because of a childcare issue and was peeved. She'd missed all the drama. She secretly hoped that the robbery might ruin Thyme & Time's chances for success. It annoyed Belle when her inexperienced, frankly unqualified friends launched companies with their husbands' money. (Yes, sure, Belle was using her father's money for Pippins Cottage Home, but that was different.) It was happening more often. Dre Finlay with her girly, low-calorie Tequila brand, Titas. Elisa Brown with Explosions of Cute, a high-end baby clothing rental company that had launched and shuttered within six months after it became clear there wasn't a market for vomit-stained mini-Burberry. Couldn't they all just add on a few more hours of volunteering? Shouldn't Morgan just stick with "Ask Morgan"? She was very good at that.

At least Belle was now lice-free, and on her way to Ava's theme party, stuck in traffic on Sixth Avenue on their way to University Place. Belle had planned to leave their apartment earlier, but her makeup artist had taken her time, and now they were late, and it was making Belle crazy. She really didn't want to offend Ava, whose support for Pippins Cottage Home she was still banking on. Lately, Belle had been letting herself daydream about the possibilities for The Dress. She had fantasies of the line selling out on the first day, of walking down the street in Tribeca and seeing woman after woman wearing her design. Maybe she'd land a profile in *Vogue*! Maybe Meghan Markle would be photographed wearing it! "Belle Redness, fashion entrepreneur." It had such a nice ring to it.

"Can you drive *faster*, please," Belle pleaded with Fred.

"Sorry, Mrs. Redness, there's nothing I can do. It's Friday night and everywhere in Manhattan is clogged. I think the subway would probably be faster." Jeff, his face illuminated by the glow of his phone, laughed lightly under his breath.

Belle switched her phone to camera and looked at herself. She and Jeff were dressed as "Hudson River Foliage," and her face was a mix of bright red, orange, and yellow gems, meticulously applied in leaf patterns. She had fake eyelashes that resembled small branches, and her long hair—with the help of even longer extensions—was swept up in a tall tower, a trunk wrapped in faux vines. The structure was so high she'd barely been able to fit it into the car; she was sitting with her head tilted to the side, her hair steeple obstructing Jeff's view, developing a large crick in her neck. She looked down at her dress, a deep amber creation from Jason Wu's latest collection, that she'd bought at Bergdorf's for the bargain price of $3,895. They only had the size down—0 instead of 2—but Belle had been able to squeeze into it with deep breaths and Skims. The stars of her outfit were her jewels; Tiffany's yellow diamond studs, her necklace a stunning chain of rubies from Bulgari. In all, her look cost upward of $600,000. The 1 train wasn't exactly an option.

The car crawled along on Sixth, stopping at a red light. They were at Bleecker Street now, and Belle looked out the window to see a scuffle taking place on the sidewalk, two young men shouting at each other. One started waving a glass beer bottle at the other. Then, to Belle's shock, he threw it right at him, hitting him directly in the face. That's when the light changed to green, letting Fred move nearly an entire block. Belle strained backward, but she'd lost her view.

"Did you see that?" she asked Jeff. He was in a bright yellow suit from Tokyo James. On his head, he was wearing a crown of leaves, fashioned by Philip Treacy himself.

"What?" he said, not looking up.

"A fight," she said. "New York is going down the tubes. I still can't believe Frost was the victim of a hit-and-run. And right after I was attacked! Plus, the robbery at Morgan's party. I worry about the kids walking around the city." She wanted to say more, but she could tell he wasn't paying attention to her.

They finally pulled up to the front of Ava and David's building. The Leo-Chungs owned a penthouse triplex, spare and minimalist, and Belle and Jeff entered the apartment to see that Ava had entirely reimagined the space for the event. It felt as though they were walking into Central Park on a glorious fall day. The air smelled like crisp leaves and roasting chestnuts, and the lighting had just the right golden hour glow. An attendant swooped in to take their coats, and a server handed them, in his words, "The Tree House, made with rye whiskey and aged rum. David took inspiration for the cocktail menu from classic New York City bars—this is the signature fall drink at the Clover Club."

Belle took a sip and was instantly transported to an autumn in her twenties when she and Jeff were still just dating. She'd been working at Deutsche Bank and at the same time hatching plans to launch her first company, a wedding registry app—for men—that never got off the ground. Jeff was in the middle of establishing himself at his private-equity firm, and though he was supremely busy, he'd made time for Belle nearly every day. They'd roamed Manhattan, trying new restaurants and bars, going to museums and movies and holding hands the whole time. People would do double takes—the stunning girl with the long hair canoodling with *that* guy? But Belle didn't care. Jeff was charming and sweet. He wasn't intimidated by her beauty, her background, or her dad, who'd petrified every other man she'd been with. They'd meet for nightcaps when Jeff worked late, a whiskey for each as they chatted through their day.

She looked at Jeff now and wondered if he'd been reminded of that, as well. They'd been married forever, and she loved him still. But each year she'd found herself drifting a little further away. There was nothing *wrong*, it was all just more of the same, both of them getting older, headed toward what, exactly? In a marriage with kids, was there any other way? Belle had never discussed this feeling with anyone, not even her therapist. She'd heard whispers of people finding other . . . ways of living. Of being more open. But she didn't think she could ever broach the subject with Jeff. "Hey, husband, how do you feel about letting me fuck other men? Specifically, our children's headmaster?" Hahaha, yeah right. It would never fly.

They were approached by Ava, in a red sparkly dress with matching red armbands. Her hair was slicked back, and her ears were dripping with diamonds. Belle had to restrain herself from touching her own scalp. Though the lice were gone, she still occasionally had lingering phantom itches.

"You made it!" Ava said, giving Belle a gentle hug, careful not to muss either of their outfits. "You look gorgeous. I adore the dress—and the hair is insane! How did you get it to stand up like that?"

"Extensions!" said Belle happily. She loved when Ava doted on her. "What about you? What's the story behind this fantastic red dress?" Belle asked. Jeff had already been enveloped into a group of men standing next to a tree that wound all the way up the staircase.

"This was worn by the queen of 'Autumn in New York' herself, Ella Fitzgerald! Ella wore it while she sang with Louis Armstrong.

How cool is that? I had to alter it to death," said Ava, her whole vibe a bit googly. "Ella was bigger than I am . . ." Belle, feeling supremely sober, wondered how many Tree Houses Ava had already consumed.

"Ava, or should I call you Ella?" said Belle, thinking now might be her chance. Ava looked pleased. "I was wondering if you'd received The Dress, from my new line, Pippins Cottage Home?" Belle's mouth felt parched. She took a small sip of her drink. Ava's eyes settled over Belle's shoulder, and she didn't respond. Had Ava heard Belle? Should Belle repeat herself?

"You *must* go check out the upstairs," Ava said finally. "Each floor has a different theme." Ava looked around for the next victim to arrive, and Belle took her cue to leave, heading up the stairs in search of her friends, her body tightened in embarrassment and disappointment.

She was passed by Dr. Broker, on his way down. Dr. Broker regularly made appearances at Atherton theme parties, to schmooze and push drunken parents for more donations. Belle had known he'd be here, and had been looking forward to seeing him, like he was a boy she had a crush on at school. He was in a nubby fisherman's sweater, the sleeves pushed up to reveal strong forearms, and expertly faded jeans.

"Ah, Mrs. Redness, how are you?" Dr. Broker said, pausing briefly on the rung above her. He stepped down closer before she could answer. He licked his lips.

"Great, good, happy to be here," she said nervously. She was a little warm in her dress. Something about the intensity of his gaze screamed danger.

"You look like a gorgeous tree," he said. "I've always loved your hair. You're like a real-life Rapunzel." Belle looked around to see if anyone could hear them. Was he flirting with her? Is this how he spoke to all the moms?

"Uh, thanks," she said. Belle wasn't used to getting such a high from male attention. She felt giddy.

He leaned into her, so that she could smell his leathery cologne. "I hope to see you later in the evening," he whispered into her ear. Then he walked past her, down the stairs, and Belle felt his shoulder brush against hers, the wool of his sweater press on her bare skin. She was both confused by what had just happened, and highly turned on by it. Belle kept going, thinking about Dr. Broker's mouth as she did. When was "later in the evening"? At the top step, she bumped into Clara Cain, in a bright green dress, her shoulder-length black hair dyed silver-gray.

"I'm a Granny Smith!" said Clara, delighted with her own cleverness. Belle smiled at her but tried to keep walking up alone. No luck. Clara dragged her to the top of the staircase and then, before Belle could get a good look at the place, into a shadowy side room, perhaps a home office, shutting the door behind them. In the dim light, Belle could see skeletons hanging from the ceiling, and what looked to be wax figures of witches lined up at the walls. They were alone. It was scary in there, and Belle wanted to get out.

"I have to speak to you about something," said Clara dramatically. Clara was usually glib and self-satisfied, but not dramatic—she was a lawyer; it was her job to be dull. "It's about Hildy." Belle's jaw clenched. Hildy? Hildy and Miles were home with their babysitter, watching reruns of *Friends*. What about Hildy?

"I heard something from Ozzie," said Clara, nearly spitting Belle's way. "I heard that there were some photographs going around . . . explicit photographs." Belle's chest contracted, but she tried to breathe through it.

"But not of Hildy, right?" Belle said, shaking her head. Clara just blinked, not saying anything. "Hildy doesn't even undress in front of me, let alone take naked pictures. She doesn't have a boyfriend—or girlfriend. She hasn't even gone through puberty! There's just no way. Has Ozzie seen the pictures?" Belle looked over at a wax witch, its long nose covered in warts.

"No, but he heard from a good source. I'm telling you; I think they're out there," said Clara, enjoying contradicting Belle. Could it be true? Her little Hildy? Belle really didn't think she'd be that stupid. Plus, Hildy had been in a better mood than usual lately, saying she was enjoying her new classes. Nothing about this felt right.

"All right, I'll look into it. Even if it's a rumor, thanks for letting me know," said Belle. "Now can we get out of this weird witch room?" Belle suddenly felt desperate to get home and speak to Hildy. Clear everything up over a bowl of ice cream.

They walked out and into the most stylish haunted house Belle had ever seen. The servers were dressed as movie-quality-level zombies, and things—axes, black cats, spiders—kept jumping out at Belle, scaring the crap out of her. "Ava hired the set designer from *The Walking Dead* for this floor. Apparently, the guys who did *Night of the Living Dead* were already, well, dead," said Clara. But it was hard to see anyone in the foggy, thick air, and so instead of lingering, Belle ditched Clara and went up one more flight. Her friends had to be *somewhere*. And maybe Dr. Broker would be up there, too.

She emerged onto the third and top floor, relieved that the lighting was soft and flattering. The area was styled as a replica of Grand Central Market, with ministalls filled with riffs on New York classics. The air smelled of maple, smoked nuts, and cotton candy. She passed a circle of men and women, their voices elevated by alcohol and merriment.

"Oh my god, I know, I can't keep up," said a woman in a brown dress, a small, furry tail attached to her backside. "She, he, they, it . . . I don't care what gender you are, we live in New York, after all, but my issue is: it's incorrect grammar! It hurts me to say '*they* is such a sweet kid.'" The group laughed loudly.

"I still think the teachers are encouraging it, even after this last election," said the man next to her, his voice lowered. Belle assumed he was her husband, as he was in a similar costume, but wearing a brown suit and a pair of wall-mount-worthy antlers on his head. "Where else are they getting this from?" The rest of the listeners nodded in agreement. "I think it's not as bad uptown. It feels like the schools up there are more traditional. We love Atherton, but it's getting out of control. We're thinking about touring Buckley next fall . . ."

Belle found Morgan and Frost standing next to the Cronut bar, steam rising out the tops of the delicate, golden pastries. Morgan was in a bright pink bustier and an enormously full pink skirt, a white bonnet, and a scarf around her neck. Frost, meanwhile, had gone full Halloween, in a sexy black Elvira gown, bright red lips, and a long black wig. She'd decorated the bandage on her face with sparkly spiders, and she'd switched out her white sling for a black one. The front of Frost's dress went nearly down to her navel, and her still-perky breasts were standing at attention on either side.

"Wow, wow, wow, look at you two," said Belle, remembering that she was still holding the same drink as when she'd arrived. She downed it in a gulp, the whiskey burning her windpipe.

"Wait, Morgan, who are you again? Snow White? Cinderella?" Belle asked. She hadn't meant to be rude, but she could tell it came out that way as she'd said it.

"No, I'm Katrina from *The Legend of Sleepy Hollow*—a Disney movie about fall in New York. I told you a million times," said Morgan, annoyed. "And Art is Ichabod Crane. Remember?"

"Oh, right, right," said Belle. "How's Thyme & Time doing? Great, I hope!" she said, trying to recover.

"Yes, it's doing amazingly well. We're fully booked for next week. Not reporting the robbery was the best decision."

Belle smiled but burned a little inside. "I'm hiding from Clara Cain," said Belle softly, stepping behind Frost. She saw Clara out of the corner of her eye, at the pasta station. Behind the booth, set up like a classic New York red-sauce joint, was Mario Batali himself, his face red and jolly like Santa Claus.

"I thought Batali got canceled?" said Frost. "Didn't he sexually harass his staff or something?"

"I think he did—that must be why he's here instead of at a restaurant," said Tim, who'd sidled up to them. "He's a client of Clara Cain over there." Tim was in a black suit, black shirt, and bow tie, and his still-plentiful hair was slicked back and shiny. Tim was an independent movie producer—though Belle always thought of his job in air quotes, as really, what had he produced lately? Not much. Belle knew that Tim's career, or lack thereof, was a sore spot in his and Frost's marriage, and felt for her about it. No matter how much family money you had, people needed to feel useful, like they were contributing to their own lives. Look at Belle, launching her own business. And she'd always appreciated that Jeff had a real job, and earned real money, even though they didn't, technically, need it.

"What are you, Tim?" said Belle, thinking of how normal he looked compared to her canary-yellow husband.

"I'm just the date of the beautiful Mistress of the Dark," he said, giving Frost's shoulder a squeeze. She smiled weakly.

"Have you seen Sofia?" Frost asked her husband, looking around the room. Belle did, too, spotting the regular characters—Clara chatting with Gabby, in her *Autumn in New York*–Richard Gere–silver fox getup, and Gabby's wife, Margo, making a rare appearance, in a slip dress, her hair styled into a Winona Ryder pixie. There were Trina and Bud Cunningham, both in all white, designer ghouls. Then she saw her own husband, bright as a tennis ball, holding two drinks, one of which he handed to Belle, who accepted it gratefully. Jeff and Tim fist-bumped and then went off to find food, leaving the women alone.

They were interrupted by an ebullient Sofia, sashaying over. She was in an orange catsuit and had stuffed the already generous area around her hips with two balloon-like structures.

"I'm a gourd. Get it?" she said to the group, laughing. Sofia somehow pulled it off in a way that didn't make her look hideous.

"I'm also drunk," she said. "I got here by myself an hour ago, didn't see any of you, and so had to drink my way to the top floor." Belle had been surprised by the swiftness with which Sofia had integrated herself into their group, and by the readiness of their collective acceptance, including her own. But so many Atherton moms were too something or other: too uptight, too intense, too flakey, too weird, too clingy. Clara was too annoying. Ava was too bitchy. Gabby was too harsh. Trina was too boring. Sofia was none of these things. She completed their pod like the final piece of the puzzle.

"Frost! I love your spider bandage," said Sofia. "*Que linda.*"

"Speaking of, our private detective wants to talk to you about the scooter accident at some point this week, if that's okay?" said Frost. Sofia nodded.

They were joined by Gabby, sans Margo, who'd left for bed. Gabby was in an oversize gray overcoat, and she'd done her hair in a wavy, handsome way that really did resemble Richard Gere's. She was eating a bowl of perfect pasta pomodoro.

"What's the goss over here?" said Gabby. No one offered anything up. "Have you seen Armena Justice's outfit?" No one had yet.

"It's crazy," Gabby continued. "She's dressed as 'sixty-four,' the average temperature in New York in October. It's a funny idea—an odd idea—and she fully committed to becoming a sixty-four-year-old. She had the makeup artist who worked on *Benjamin Button* do it. You'll do a double take. It's like stepping thirty years into the future."

As if summoned, Armena Justice walked by, or what looked to be Armena Justice's mother—a tastefully dressed woman in her midsixties. She smiled at them, and Belle experienced a disorienting wave of déjà vu, like she'd witnessed everything that was happening before.

To get her bearings, Belle walked away from her friends and over to the pasta station, watching as Batali shoveled penne onto plates. A few moms she didn't recognize walked by, and Belle had the uncanny feeling they were glaring at her. She saw Dre Finlay and Caroline Press, whispering to each other, glancing at Belle, and then checking their phones. A different group of women, standing across the room, was laughing and pointing her way. What was happening?

Without getting food, Belle walked back to her friends, but they'd disbanded. Only Sofia was still standing there, her gourd hips protruding, a fruity sexpot. She was staring at her phone and looked startled when she glanced up to see Belle, like she'd seen a ghost.

"Come on, tell me what's going on," said Belle. "Are people talking about me for some reason?" Belle took a step toward Sofia, who, seemingly on instinct, backed away.

"What the hell, Sofia?" snapped Belle, harsher than she'd meant to. She was already feeling on edge about Hildy and unsettled by her encounter with Dr. Broker.

"You haven't seen it yet?" asked Sofia. Belle shook her head.

Sofia handed Belle her phone. It was open to Gmail and Belle saw she'd been reading an official email from Atherton, from the automated school address, with the subject line "Our Lice Journey." Belle's heart dropped as soon as she saw it—that was the subject of her email to the school nurse. She scrolled down to read, though she didn't have to; she'd written it herself.

Dear Nurse Weiss,

Belle Redness here, mom of Miles and Hildy, with some bad news to share. No, this time it's not strep (shocking, I know). It's . . . wait for it . . . I'll give you a clue: it rhymes with mice but it's creepy and crawly. That's right, it's LICE. Ugh ugh ugh. They've come for us. And we've ALL got it, including my husband and housekeeper. We just got the treatment from Licenders, thank God, because I could literally *feel* them on my head, making themselves comfy, like they were about to settle in for a season of *White Lotus*. I know it's standard policy to let you know. The kids will be back in school on Monday, lice free. Thanks for keeping this quiet! You know how all the Atherton bitches like to talk.

On that note, I'd advise you to do a thorough head check of the Finlay kids, the Klein clan, and the Corders—none of those dirty children appear to ever wash their hair; I don't know what their moms are thinking (probably . . . not much; they all suffer from the same empty-brain syndrome). Oh wait, also Becky Oranga's kid, "my Jesse." Just so she freaks out a little.

Cheers,

Belle Redness

Belle's breath came in sharp, painful bursts. She handed the phone back to Sofia, who put her hand on Belle's shoulder to steady her.

"I think . . . I think," said Belle. She couldn't get the words out. Everyone in the entire room seemed to be looking at her, shooting daggers out of their eyes.

"You are all right," said Sofia soothingly. Belle swore she could hear the words "lice" and "asshole" in the air, coming from all directions, everyone talking about her at once.

Ava and David, dressed as Louis Armstrong in a blue tux, holding a trumpet, took this moment to approach the women. They were holding hands, their expressions equal parts concerned and irritated.

"Hey, ladies," said Ava, stalling. Belle braced herself.

"Soooo, I suppose you know about the email we all just received from the school," said Ava, looking around the room, her eyes never settling on Belle. Coward.

"Well, everyone's talking about it, and some of the moms are, you know, mad about being named in it," said Ava. "It's truly not about the lice, but . . ." She paused.

"This is very rude! Belle has done nothing! *She* didn't send that email to the whole school," said Sofia, coming to Belle's defense, for which she was grateful.

But Belle knew where this was going, so she saved Ava—whom she was starting to hate with a visceral heat—the trouble.

"I'm leaving, don't worry," said Belle. If she could somehow preserve her relationship with Ava, for Pippins Cottage Home's sake, she'd do it. She needed to find Jeff and get the hell out of there. She could strategize with her friends later about how to recover. For now, she had to lie low.

Before anyone could say anything else, and without saying good-bye, Belle took off, sending Jeff a quick text—Where are you? I'm leaving now, there's an emergency, kids fine, meet me at home—and then running down to the second floor, scanning faces for Frost or Morgan or Jeff, the costumes so absurd it felt like she might be in a bad dream. She passed Art, or, rather, Ichabod Crane, wearing a green waistcoat and a hat that looked out of the 1800s. "Tell Morgan to call me," she said to him, not stopping. Partygoers were giving her the side-eye, the woman who'd committed the double sin of giving their children lice *and* shit-talking other Atherton moms. *That was a private email*, she wanted to shout at them.

The second floor was dark and smoky and crowded, and Belle could barely see in front of her. She felt along the wall, attempting to reach the stairs, focused only on getting to the entrance. She'd almost made it when she felt a strong hand on her wrist, once again pulling her somewhere she didn't want to go—the same room she'd been in with Clara.

Her eyes slowly adjusted to the blackness. She could see the skeletons above and the witches on the walls, but not who she was with.

"Hello?" said Belle softly. She felt very vulnerable and upset, and her too-small Jason Wu dress was beginning to suffocate her.

"Mrs. Redness," said a deep voice, which she instantly recognized to be Dr. Broker's. He took her hand again and led her to the corner of the space, hidden from view, even if the door were to open.

All of Belle's anxiety instantly melted into electricity. She didn't know why Dr. Broker had chosen to bring her here, but being in a dim room with him lit something up inside her.

"Um, Dr. Broker, I'm glad I ran into you," Belle stammered, trying to sound normal. "There are two things I'd like to discuss.

First, I heard something about nude photos that I don't think is true. Second, it seems that an email I sent only to Nurse Weiss was blasted to the entire school, and I need to know how that happened. A head has to roll, Dr. Broker. Not yours . . ." She was rambling now, unable to stop.

Before she could process what was happening, Dr. Broker had pushed her against the wall, pressing into her with what she could feel, even through his jeans, to be a large erection. He ran his hand over her Bulgari ruby necklace, and then his lips were briefly on hers, tasting of mint and rum. Nothing like this had ever happened to Belle Redness, a daddy's girl and rule follower. For a second, she felt like she might give in. He was so attractive, and his body was so . . . warm. But as Dr. Broker began to lift up Belle's Jason Wu dress, an image came into Belle's mind, the same memory she'd had earlier that evening, one of her younger self, sitting across from Jeff at a bar, laughing at something he'd said, their fingers entwined. She quickly ducked out of Dr. Broker's embrace.

"You know, I don't have lice anymore," she said awkwardly, wiping her mouth, wishing she hadn't let him kiss her in the first place. In the low light, she could see he was frowning.

Belle took the opportunity to dart out of the room, the wax witch looking on with a sneaky smile. Then she took an Uber home alone, reliving it all in her head.

A note from the host, Ava Leo

Hi, all,

Thank you so much for attending A Bouquet of Newly Sharpened Pencils! David and I were so thrilled you could make it—we had a wonderful time celebrating the start of the Atherton school year, and we hope you did, too. Below, a quick list of what was left in our apartment. Please claim them by early next week; after that, items without owners will be donated to the Atherton Parents Against Persons Experiencing Homelessness committee for neighborhood distribution. See everyone at drop-off on Monday!

All our best,

The Leo-Chungs

A pair of plastic antlers

Three vapes, wasabi flavor

One diamond drop earring

A black Celine trench (Ava is planning to keep this for herself, if
  no one claims it ☺ )

Six humanlike bones

A dime bag of weed (David will happily keep this one ☺ )

Three iPhones

One Google Pixel phone (loser)

A Chanel clutch with three condoms inside ( ☺ )

Various hair extensions—purple, orange, and gold

Did someone leave a hamster here?? Hazie seems to have
  adopted one, and we don't know how it got in the house.

Ava Leo was seriously exhausted. She didn't know why she'd volunteered to throw a theme party in the first place. On top of her job, on top of her travel schedule, on top of everything else. It had been David's idea, part of his constant need to show off. That's what Ava got for marrying a chef, she supposed. But it just hadn't been the right time. And they didn't have the money to do it. And now they had less. Way less.

David's restaurants were failing. The BaoFuku group, which consisted of five spots around the city, ranging from Michelin-starred fine dining to a hip fried chicken joint in Red Hook, was hanging on by a thread (a noodle?). It had been a long, stressful road, starting with the pandemic shutdowns. They'd rebounded nicely after that, but the restaurant industry was notoriously mercurial, and David had never been a great businessperson. They'd overspent and over-staffed and that, combined with the fact that David's signature style of experimental fusion was on the outs, meant they were on the verge of shutting down.

David was in denial, talking up his next great menu ideas, calling in all his celebrity friends for photo ops at the flagship. But the books didn't lie, and Ava wasn't quite sure what to do about it. It would be a huge fucking life disaster if it happened. And every day, they edged closer to the brink.

Ava also had her own job to worry about. Pinterest was great to her, sure. They'd hired her to be a face, and she worked her butt off doing it. But even tech companies were tightening their belts right now, and Ava was worried that at some point, a higher-up would look at her salary and do a double take, interrogating it in a way that no one seemed to have done when they'd hired her out of Hearst five years ago. ("You're paying *who* how much to do *what*?" Yadda, yadda.) Then what?

Maybe that's why she'd been so bitchy lately, Ava thought regretfully, walking through her trashed apartment the day after the party. The cleaning crews were waiting to get paid before they arrived, and Ava couldn't bring herself to do it. She'd have to tidy up herself; there was no way she was spending another $2,000 on this stupid event. When they'd looked at the final bill for everything this morning, over $75,000, it was like a punch to the gut. David had been so upset with himself that he'd left to go work the line at one of the restaurants, something he did when he wanted to calm down, his own form of meditation.

So that meant Ava had to deal with the mess, which felt like a metaphor for her entire life. David was always at a restaurant, working 24/7, leaving Ava to manage her own career, plus the girls' lives. What would happen if they went broke? They had some savings, but not enough to keep living the way they lived. First, Ava would have to take the girls out of Atherton. (She'd already called the school about potential financial aid and was waiting to hear back about it.) They'd have to sell the apartment, which would help, although they did have a huge mortgage on it. She wished she had any family money, but neither she nor David had inherited anything from their parents aside from tough love and enviable work ethics. All of Ava's friends seemed to come from endless trust funds. She supposed that was the only way to "make it" in New York anymore, starting with a huge leg up. Take Gabby, whose family owned like half of the buildings in Manhattan.

Ava had the thought to call Gabby right now. Gabby could at least make Ava laugh with an inappropriate joke or two. But Gabby was going through her own shit. No one knew this yet, but Gabby and Margo were about to file for divorce. Margo had made her final Atherton appearance last night at Ava's party; Gabby had begged her to, to keep face, as Gabby wanted to manage the messaging of their separation herself. Margo was leaving Gabby, but not for another woman. For a man. A man! Margo, as Pride as Pride could be, who'd proposed to Gabby at an Indigo Girls concert, had, out of nowhere, told Gabby that she'd been living a lie. That she was bisexual, and that she'd fallen in love with a guy. More specifically, she'd fallen in love with their veterinarian, Dr. Cuddles, and he and

Margo were going to start a life together, along with Gabby and Margo's two Westies, Gus and Van Sant.

When Gabby told Ava, she was weeping, inconsolable, confused, angry, scared for what it meant for her family and kids. Ava had attempted to make her feel better—"At least you're rich? I'm about to be living on the street with the homeless dude who attacked Belle, targeted by the 'Atherton committee for killing vagrants,' or whatever those bitches are calling it." But it hadn't worked. Gabby had kept crying while Ava sat there in silence, supporting her by just allowing her to let it out.

Grown-up life could be hard and disappointing, even if your dad owned the Empire State Building, Ava supposed. As Ava worked, sweeping, vacuuming, picking up pieces of jewelry that her wealthy friends had casually left behind, she thought about the little treat she'd give herself for living under such stress. Her daughters were spending the day with Ava's mom in Queens, and so after this Ava would go to the Sephora in Union Square. There, she'd peruse and test and smell and inspect until she found something she liked. Maybe a new blush? Maybe a perfume? She needed some new dry shampoo—perhaps one would catch her eye. Then she'd slip it in her Chanel purse and walk right out the doors, enjoying the rush of the illicit act. That would make her feel better. That would make her feel in control.

# PART II

## Winter

# WhatsApp Chat

*Atherton Lower School Moms*

*94 Participants*

**Dre Finlay**

Hi, Atherton mamas! Reminder that third grade moms' night out is this Thursday, February 5. We've locked down a venue—the upstairs bar at El Cantinero, on University—so get ready for plenty of guac and margaritas! Please remember to Venmo @DreF $100 if you're planning on coming. See you there, senoritas!

**Gemma Corder**

Will there be a gluten-free option for dinner?

**Dre Finlay**

I can check, Gemma! But it's bare-bones Mexican, so I wouldn't count on it . . .

**Sofia Perez**

Hola! First time in this chat, though I've been reading it all! I am looking for after-school soccer classes for Carlos. He played in Miami and wants to continue.

**Caroline Press**

Welcome to Atherton, Sofia! Ramy takes indoor soccer at Chelsea Piers. I'll send you the info. There are also options at Asphalt Green and the Y, but that's all the way uptown. Barf.

**Julie Klein**

Hi, all. I've started a separate WhatsApp group for the ice hockey team—Puck Moms—so let me know if you'd like to be included. Smelly equipment complaints welcome. ☺

**Jenna Worthy**

Sorry to be a downer, but here's a NY Times article link about the enormous risks for youth football and ice hockey players. It's something like one in every three players will get CTE in their lifetime, which increases the likelihood of dementia and suicide. ☹

**Julie Klein**

Thanks for that super-helpful info, Jenna. I assume you don't want to be added to the Puck Moms chat?

**Katrina Lowry**

Reminder: Please check your date for the safety patrol. Each parent is assigned one afternoon to walk the neighborhood from 3:30 p.m. to 5:00 p.m. Let's keep our kids safe!

**Cat Howell**

I heard the man who spit at Belle Redness is still on the loose! Does anyone have an in with the police commissioner? We can't have someone crazy like that near *Atherton*.

**Gabby Mahler**

Cat, this is New York, there are homeless people. Most of them are mentally ill, not *crazy*.

**Dre Finlay**

Don't forget to preorder your Atherton Valentine's Day cookies!

## Chapter 6

# A Night on the Town!

═══

Frost Trevor had just experienced one of those life-changing moments—the first time you meet the man you ultimately marry; the big job interview that goes your way; the double lines on the pregnancy test—that come about once a decade. She'd been walking on Houston Street, headed to Nolita for a quick dinner with Sofia, when she saw an unrecognized number pop up on her phone. She picked up (when you have children, you always pick up), fumbling with the device before putting it to her ear. Though she'd been out of the sling for months, she still felt a pang each time she bent her arm, reminding her of the accident.

Frost silently cursed herself for not buying earbuds because they were so ugly, remembering that her therapist had told her she needed to work on her practicality. She'd never been good at being practical.

"Hello, Frost? This is Ethel Zeigler. I own the Zeigler gallery on Twenty-Fourth Street. Nice to meet you." Frost held her breath. Why would Ethel Zeigler, one of the most famous art dealers in New York, be calling her?

"Hi, Ethel, I'm a big fan of yours. How can I help you?" Frost continued walking toward her destination—Peasant, on Elizabeth Street—as she spoke. The sharp February wind cut into Frost's exposed hands.

"Someone who shall remain nameless sent me pictures of your work. I'm interested," she said. Her voice was deep, with an old-school Brooklyn accent and a slight smoker's rasp.

"What? How? I'm not sure I understand," said Frost. She'd paused at the corner of Elizabeth and Houston, in front of a jeans store called Still Here. Inside, she could see a lithe young woman looking at herself in the mirror, inspecting her perky butt in the denim. Frost remembered when her butt used to look like that.

"I've seen your work. Your collaging. I like it. I want to see it in person. Do you have an agent I can call? I asked around, but no one seemed to know. I even thought about calling your mother, who I've known for years," said Ethel.

"Thank you for calling me directly," said Frost. She was having a hard time processing what Ethel was telling her. How could Ethel have possibly seen Frost's collages? They were stashed in her apartment on Twenty-Second Street. But that was a mystery to solve later. Now, she just had one thing to say.

"You can absolutely see my work. I'd be honored. A few are still in progress, but you'll get the idea. I don't have an agent; I don't even consider myself an artist," said Frost. "I never even thought about showing them. They were just . . . for me." She physically shut her mouth to stop herself from saying anything else idiotic.

"Well, maybe not, young lady," said Ethel with a laugh. "I only show what I can sell. I think you have a story here, and pieces that people will want to buy. Why don't you email me and we can set up a time for me to swing by."

"That sounds great. Thank you so much!" said Frost.

Ethel Zeigler was interested in her collages! Frost skipped along to Peasant, humming with happy energy, and saw Sofia already sitting at a table, sipping a tequila. Sofia was in an oversize black blazer, jeans, and suede boots, her thick hair blown out in flattering waves. She'd fully shed the bodycon dresses and logo'd bags for a subdued, quiet-luxury aesthetic. She looked very Atherton right now, and it suited her. Even her breasts seemed to have shrunk since September.

"*Mi amor*, how are you?" asked Sofia warmly. Over the past six months, Frost and Sofia had become a tight unit. Sofia was now always included in their mom drinks, was invited over for Sunday family playdates, and had become a permanent part of their drop-off clique. And she was proving herself to be an invaluable member of the Atherton Parents' Association, too. She'd joined the fundraising committee and volunteered to run the Christmas food drive, tasks that Frost, as a rule, staunchly avoided. New Yorkers liked to see other people *work*, no matter how much money they had, and Sofia's efforts had not gone unnoticed. It had been quite a speedy triumph, that's for sure. Frost knew of moms who'd been trying for years to be accepted into the downtown hierarchy. Some never got there at all.

"I'm good!" said Frost brightly, signaling the waiter to come over to get her a drink.

"Have you spoken to Belle? How's she doing?" said Sofia.

Belle had recently turned into a bit of a recluse. She'd never quite recovered from the lice email debacle, and had started avoiding school functions, for fear of seeing any of the moms she'd named in the now infamous note. She'd also been working overtime to ready The Dress for its big launch this month. Morgan, too, had been busy with Thyme & Time, which had recovered quickly from the robbery and was now going gangbusters, the most popular sound bath spa in all of Manhattan. At least Frost had Sofia to fill the friend void.

"I think she's pretty on edge," said Frost. "She's convinced someone leaked her email on purpose, though I have no clue who'd do that. How would they have gotten access to Nurse Weiss's account?"

Sofia shrugged, and Frost changed the subject.

"Have you figured out what you're wearing to Friendsgiving?" she said.

The next theme party was at Clara and Neil Cain's Financial District apartment, a five-bedroom duplex in a high-rise on Pearl Street, with wraparound skyline views. Clara had landed on Friendsgiving as a theme, though Thanksgiving was long past, celebrating "the bonds of Atherton's chosen community." All the moms were complaining about it on various chat threads—what the hell do you wear to a party about friendship?

"No costume ideas yet," said Sofia a little glumly. "It's kind of depressing to have to figure it out all on my own, without a partner."

The waiter appeared and Frost ordered a dirty martini. She wanted to cheer Sofia up. She was feeling good, maybe even great, and she wanted that feeling for Sofia, too.

"I got a very exciting phone call on the way here. An art dealer wants to look at my work."

"That's wonderful," said Sofia. "I'm sure you're an amazing artist—I can't wait to see your collages."

"I want to celebrate. How do you feel about going a little wild tonight?" said Frost.

Sofia's eyes sparkled, their golden rings catching in the restaurant's low lights.

"I'll text Maria that I'm going to be late," Sofia said with a smile. "Moms' night out! *Vamos!*"

"I'll text Morgan and Belle to see if they'd like to join," said Frost.

By 2:00 a.m., Frost and Sofia were dancing in a packed room at ZZ's, a private club owned by the Carbone guys that cost $50,000 to join and $10,000 a year after that. Neither woman was a member, but Frost was old friends with Mario Carbone's wife, so they had an easy in. A DJ was playing Madonna, and Frost was singing along to "Like a Prayer" at the top of her lungs, bumping up against Sofia, who'd shed her blazer long ago and was writhing in a damp white tank.

The place was packed with wealthy, let-loose revelers, and Frost and Sofia were both many drinks in. Frost, jumping up enthusiastically, hadn't felt this alive in years.

"Woohoo!" Sofia shouted throatily. A remix of Cher's "Believe" blasted over the speakers, and Sofia abruptly stopped dancing, a funny look on her face. For a moment, Frost thought Sofia might cry. Instead, Sofia turned to the attractive guy next to her and pulled him off the dance floor, motioning for Frost to join them. He, in turn, grabbed his friend, and the foursome stumbled into a banquette in the adjoining cocktail bar. There was a strong smell of cigar and cigarette smoke, and Frost inhaled greedily, transported to an earlier, happier time in her life.

Sofia grabbed Frost's hand under the table, smiling, seemingly back to her usual self, whatever passing cloud having lifted. The man Sofia had recruited, who looked to Frost like a young Paul Newman, was staring at Sofia in awe. The guy next to Frost, nearly as handsome in his own right, had already planted his hand firmly on Frost's upper thigh. She had Tim. She had Art. But this was something else. This was *exciting*.

"I'm Nick and this is Ryan," said Paul Newman, "and who are you two?"

"I'm Bluey and this is Bingo," said Sofia, without missing a beat. The guys, who appeared confused, obviously didn't get the mom joke. "What brings you to ZZ's?"

"We're out having fun," said Sofia. "Just two hot divorcées on the town." Sofia said it so naturally, Frost almost believed it herself. She felt the hand on her thigh snake up and didn't do anything to stop it. Sofia took Nick's head in her hands and kissed him, deeply, to Frost's surprise and amusement.

"You're beautiful," Ryan said directly into Frost's ear. She flooded with warmth.

"How old are you?" she whispered to him. His face was so smooth it reminded her of her sons'.

"Twenty-seven," he said, his fingers lightly massaging her leg. She didn't want him to stop. "How old are you?"

"Thirty-two," said Frost. The lie came easily. She felt thirty-two right then, if not younger.

"And you were married?" he said. "What happened?"

"My husband felt like a failure, and he took it out on me," she said. It felt freeing to finally say it aloud, if only to a stranger.

"That sucks," said Ryan. He gently kissed her neck and she let him. She looked over at Sofia and Nick and saw they were making out like teenagers, Sofia's hands running through his sandy hair.

"It certainly did suck," said Frost with a light laugh. "And so I fucked one of my best friends' husbands." Ryan also chuckled, thinking she was kidding.

Frost's bladder was about to burst.

"I have to go to the bathroom," she said. "But I want you to stay right here." Ryan nodded enthusiastically.

"Bluey, I'm going to pee," said Frost, poking Sofia, forcing her to come up for air.

"Okay! Come back soonest," she said. Frost then stumbled to the ladies' room, feeling like she was twenty again, out with a best friend, having fun, flirting with guys, her whole life ahead of her. Just because you're forty-two, does that mean you're dead? Frost still dreamed of so much.

The bathroom was down a winding, dim hallway, lined with individual stalls, all occupied. One cracked open, and Frost walked toward it, waiting for the occupant to leave so she could go in. A man came out, in jeans, a white T-shirt, and a black baseball hat, and it dawned on Frost that she'd seen him before. He strode down the hallway in the other direction, and she turned and followed. "Hey," she said, calling after him, walking faster, trying to catch up. "Wait, hey! You hit me with a scooter!" It was the guy who'd crashed into her, she was sure, she'd seen his face while she was lying on the ground. It was burned into her brain.

She ran back into club, the music pumping in the packed room, and looked everywhere for someone in a black hat. But there were too many people, and the scene was too chaotic. Had it really been the same guy? Was she just imagining things? When she got to the table, Sofia was still nuzzling with Nick, and Ryan was checking his phone. He looked up at her expectantly, but she shook her head. The night was over.

"Bingo and I must be going home now," she said, taking Sofia forcefully around the shoulders and dragging her away from her partner. "Hey, I thought *you* were Bingo," said Ryan, trying to get her to sit back down. "Noooo," Sofia groaned as they made their way out of the club and into the cold night. ZZ's was in Hudson Yards, all the way on the West Side, and the women had exited onto Eleventh Avenue. Though the neighborhood had been built up enormously in the past ten years, it was still desolate in the middle of the night, the surrounding buildings staring at them like goblins. Something didn't feel right.

"Hey, hey you two." Frost heard a male voice in the dark, but she couldn't see where it was coming from. Both women froze.

"I'm going to get you, pretty ladies," he threatened. Frost grabbed Sofia's hand and started to run, pulling her across the street, her heart pounding.

"I know allllll about you!" sang the man, putting on some kind of fake British accent, clearly trying to mask his real voice. It sounded like he was right next to them, though he was nowhere they could see. "I know who you're fucking! You slut!"

"Oh no, he didn't say that," said Sofia. "Are you calling *me* a *puta*? My friend a slut? Fuck you!" She shook loose from Frost and started running toward the voice, Frost watching her in shock. "Where are you? Where are you?" Sofia yelled out into the darkness. Frost had no choice but to follow her, sprinting down Eleventh Avenue all the way to Thirtieth Street, under the High Line, Sofia fueled by alcohol and an anger that Frost hadn't seen before.

"I see him!" called Sofia.

"Sofia! Wait!" Frost yelled after her, nearly out of breath, her high-heeled boots cutting into the sides of her feet. Sofia turned east on Thirtieth, and as Frost rounded the corner she saw who Sofia was chasing—the same man she'd seen coming out of the bathroom, in his black hat, gaining distance on them.

Frost put her hand against the building next to her, the concrete cold to the touch, pausing to catch her breath. She saw Sofia finally peter out as the man faded east, Sofia collapsing against the locked entrance leading to the High Line steps. Frost limped over to her.

Sofia was breathing heavily, trying to compose herself.

"What was that about?" said Frost.

"He called you a *puta*," said Sofia with a shrug. "Men shouldn't get to say that to us."

Just then Frost's driver, Jesus, zoomed around the corner in the Escalade, and the women hopped into the warm, safe car.

"I can't believe that just happened," said Frost, her body slowly coming down from the fight-or-flight adrenaline rush.

"Maybe it was just another crazy person. Like the guy at Atherton," said Sofia, resting her head back on the seat. "New York is scary. It's not like this in Miami," she said. "We have crime, lots of it, but this city is something else. Robberies. Bad men everywhere."

"The weirdest thing happened tonight," said Frost. "I could have sworn I saw the guy who hit me with the scooter coming out of the bathroom. And I think that's who you were chasing. That's impossible, right?"

Sofia sat up so quickly she nearly bonked her head on the back of the passenger seat.

"Really? I couldn't see him from behind. So many strange things are happening, no? I haven't told anyone this yet, but . . ." Sofia trailed off.

"Sofia, you can tell me anything, you know that, right?" Frost leaned in closer to her friend. Maybe she was finally going to tell Frost how she'd gotten into Atherton.

"I thought I knew the man with the gun at Morgan's party. I recognized his voice. But maybe I didn't."

Could this man be following them all? She'd have to alert the private detective. Frost knew a mom who'd been stalked by a random guy who'd seen her on Instagram. He kept popping up wherever she was, in restaurants, outside her tennis club. She'd finally been able to get a restraining order after he'd appeared at her kids' school. Was this something similar?

"Jesus, please put on Enya," said Frost now, closing her eyes and leaning her head back on the black leather seat. They were bathed in "Orinoco Flow."

"It's so nice that you like your driver," said Sofia. "Rodrick is such an ass."

"Why don't you just fire him?" Frost asked. Sofia shrugged and dropped it. Frost let the music wash over her. If she had a stalker, she'd deal with it tomorrow. She was excited about Ethel and the possibility that her art might be sold in a real-life gallery. That's what she'd focus on. But who had sent Ethel pictures of her work? Art had seen them, but why would he do that? Then there was Tim, who'd always been lightly dismissive of her creative drive. Her children? No way. And her mother didn't even know they existed; Frost was way too frightened of her reaction to even dream of it. It was too much to deal with at once, too many mysteries to solve.

"What are you thinking about?" asked Sofia. The music, plus the copious amount of vodka she'd ingested, was lulling Frost to sleep.

"I'm thinking about how pissed Tim is going to be when I stumble into bed," said Frost. It wasn't what she'd been considering at that moment, but it was true.

"It's not so bad being divorced," Sofia said now. They were crossing town on Fourteenth Street. The city was still fully awake, with groups of young people roaming the sidewalk, congregating outside of bars. Frost never loved New York more than after midnight. She'd spent so many years in the cover of Manhattan's darkness, cabbing from club to club, from a penthouse party to a VIP back room. She missed it more than anything, but that was life. Her boys got up at 6:00 a.m.

"Who do you talk to at night?" asked Frost, curious about this aspect of Sofia's life. She barely ever mentioned her ex, and Frost suspected there was more to the story than a friendly parting. That was the part of divorce that scared Frost the most: loneliness.

"I don't talk to anyone. It's perfection," said Sofia. "I put on the TV, pour a glass of wine, and enjoy the entire couch," she said.

"That sounds amazing, but I think I'd get sick of it," said Frost.

"Do you know anyone who's in a bad marriage?" asked Sofia, digging. "What about Morgan and Art?"

"They're fine, I think," said Frost carefully. Why had Sofia led with them?

"Something seems broken about it to me," said Sofia. Frost shrugged. "Or maybe it's just that Morgan is so . . . I don't know. Fake?"

"I don't think Morgan is fake," said Frost. "I've known her forever. She's always been the same. But I do think Belle is kind of sick of Jeff," she said, offering it up to avoid talking about Art. "But that seems pretty standard for our age." Neither Morgan nor Belle had answered Frost's text from earlier in the night, which had been a relief. She hadn't really wanted to see either.

They'd gone up to Twenty-Third Street and were crossing over Park Avenue, just a couple blocks from Frost's house. "Is it okay if Jesus drops me off first?" asked Frost. "I'm beat." Sofia nodded. Frost was starting to sober up; her head was now aching, and she was in desperate need of a large glass of ice water.

"How about you and Tim?" said Sofia gently, placing her hand on Frost's shoulder. Frost felt her eyes start to water. She tried to think about something else to stop the tears—Ethel's call, her artwork, her sons—but it was impossible. She'd had just the right amount of alcohol and was with just the right person (a new friend whom she trusted, who'd been through something similar). Frost then collapsed into sobs, burying her head in her own lap, the seat belt pushing into her chest uncomfortably.

"*No llores*," said Sofia, rubbing Frost's back soothingly. They'd pulled in front of Frost's house, which looked both alluring and foreboding at this hour, with its brick exterior and large, paned windows. Frost finally sat up, wiping the tears and snot that now covered her face.

"Tim and I are great!" she said, and both she and Sofia burst out laughing. "Except for that I'm pretty sure he hates me, and I have no idea what to do about it."

"I know the feeling," said Sofia. "I'll say it again—being divorced is fine. You are strong, you can do it if you must. The boys would be okay. But also, if you love Tim at all, give it a chance. I must tell you, from experience, the grass is not always greener. But love is important." Frost felt this deeply in her bones.

She hadn't had an evening like this in forever—drunken, dancing, crying. It felt invigorating. It felt fantastic. Frost gave Sofia a quick hug. "Thank you for paying for everything! Sorry I forgot my card again. Next time's on me," Sofia said as Frost jumped out of the car, raced up her steps, into her foyer, and all the way up to her bedroom, looking for Tim. She'd speak to him right now. This very instant. Tell him that if nothing changed, it would be over between them. She didn't know what she was going to do about Art, but that could come later.

She opened the bedroom door, expecting to find Tim asleep, but instead she saw him sitting up on the bed, his head in his hands. The bedside lamp was on, its soft glow illuminating the room.

"What are you doing awake? What's going on?" said Frost, instantly completely sober. "Is it one of the boys?" Her voice cracked on "boys."

Tim shook his head. He reached over to the nightstand for his glasses, placing them on his face and pushing them up his nose. It was a motion that, when they first were dating, Frost had found irresistibly sexy.

"Frost . . . I"—Tim paused, taking a deep breath—"I'm so sorry for how I've been acting recently. I've been under such stress about this project, which is going nowhere. I've been terrible to you. I love you, Frost. This family is everything to me. I'll make this right." He took her hand, and her heart seized. This is what she'd been wanting him to say for months, for nearly a year, but now it felt like it might be too late. Was it too late?

She sat down next to him on the bed. Tim leaned into her, touching the same place on Frost's neck that Ryan had been caressing just hours ago. Frost felt nauseated, the guilt and vodka rising into her mouth, nearly choking her.

"Oh, Tim," she said, stroking Tim's hair, still as thick as it was fifteen years ago, but now with gray creeping up the sides. He pulled her closer to him. She was, against her will, turned on.

"What were you doing out so late?" he said. She didn't answer. She didn't know what to say.

"Never mind, it doesn't matter. I'm going to stop being so controlling. If you want to be with me, you can. If you don't, I understand." And then he was crying, even harder than Frost had been crying in the car with Sofia.

He lay down on the bed, facing away from her, and she rubbed his back for what felt like hours, until he took her hand and slipped it over his penis, warm and hard. Then they had sex, Frost enjoying the comfort of her husband's shape and weight.

Afterward, Tim fell asleep, but Frost, feeling wired, couldn't. She wanted to tell him about the guy with the hat, to see if the private detective had turned anything up, but she let him rest instead.

By then, the sun was just coming up. Frost crept into the bathroom with her phone and shut and locked the door. She stared at herself in the mirror—her hair was knotted and frizzy, her makeup smudged under her eyes—then sat down on the toilet. She signed into her Gmail using the account she'd created for the purposes of communicating with Art.

I can't do this, she wrote. Something has changed. I'll explain later. But it's over between us. I'm so sorry.

She felt a flood of freedom; a huge weight off her shoulders. She sent a text to her live-in nanny, Flora, who was sleeping downstairs in her room on the basement level.

Can you get the boys to school today? I was out late and need to sleep. Thanks.

Frost quietly changed into her white Eberjey pajama set, throwing her clothes in a pile next to the bed. Tim was passed out on top of the covers, but Frost snuggled underneath next to him, collapsing into an intense, dreamless sleep.

She woke up hours later. Tim was gone, only his body's impression on the duvet remaining. She checked her phone to see that it was already 10:30 a.m. She pulled up her Gmail and saw Art had responded to her email. She opened it.

Okay, fine by me.

Okay? Fine by me? That was it? A year of sex and betrayal and sneaking around and all she got was: Okay? Men were such shits. She saw she had four unread text messages. One was from Flora, from 8:15 a.m.

> King and Alfred are at school. Drop-off was fine, though some moms were acting a little strange. Alfred sounds like he's getting a cough. I'm downstairs if you need me.

The other three messages were from Belle.
The first one read:

> Have you checked the Atherton WhatsApp?????

Confused, Frost opened the second:

> What were you doing out so late??

And then:

> Frost, call me. Whenever you get this.

Frost wasn't active in the Atherton WhatsApp group, which mostly consisted of moms discussing after-school activities and teachers' gifts with a heavy dose of passive-aggressive sniping. She navigated to the Atherton Lower School Moms channel. There were hundreds of unread messages, but Frost started at the top. Whatever Belle was referring to was recent.

**Dre Finlay**

Ladies, this isn't the correct forum to be discussing this! As administrator, I'm going to have to ask you all to please refrain from bringing it up again. What people do in their private lives is up to them. I won't have this channel devolve into Deuxmoi!

**Gabby Mahler**

You mean Deux Moms.

Frost scanned down the chain to a few hours earlier, where she saw someone had posted a link to a Page Six piece in the *NY Post*.

**Katrina Lowry**

Uhhh, has everyone seen this?

**Hattie McConBelle**

Wow, looks like I'm missing out by dutifully putting my kids to bed and having dinner with my husband . . .

**Dinah Grotton**

Eeeeekkkkk.

Frost clicked on the story in the *Post*, which had gone up at 7:00 a.m. It was tiny, no more than a photo with a large caption. The headline was UP WAY PAST BEDTIME, and underneath was a snapshot of Frost, her face partially obscured, dirty dancing with Ryan and Paul Newman on a banquette at ZZ's, just hours earlier. She could see Sofia's bare shoulder in the snapshot, but her face wasn't visible.

A feverish feeling came over Frost as she read on.

ZZ's, the exclusive members club from Major Food Group, is Manhattan's go-to spot for celebrities, influencers, and professional athletes. And as of last night, add one more category: New York's Hottest Mom. Pictured here is Frost Trevor, former It Girl and parent at downtown's most prestigious private school, Atherton Academy, seen dancing and reveling until all hours with a mom friend and some boy friends. Cool kids . . . meet the Cool Moms.

She read it over and over, in disbelief. She'd never been more humiliated in her life. Who would have sent this to the *Post*? Why would the *Post* even publish it?

She called Belle, the phone ringing twice before Belle picked up, sounding like she was in the middle of a workout.

"What the hell?" said Belle, in what Frost thought was an accusatory manner. "It's all anyone is talking about! Drop-off was insane."

"I don't really understand what the big deal is," said Frost, masking her panic. She'd had a few similar moments during her time in the spotlight, when negative items were written about her. She'd found then that the best way to move forward was to own it. But that was before she had a family. Before she had anyone other than herself to worry about.

"Sofia and I went out and had some fun, so sue us," said Frost.

"Yeah, it seems like you two have become *total* best friends," said Belle. "I was at Miles's hockey practice when I got your text, but if you'd told me beforehand, I could have arranged childcare. Everyone was gossiping this morning about you partying with young guys." Frost could hear Belle's hurt over the phone. On top of everything else, she had to deal with Belle's insecurity? Please.

"Aren't women allowed to let loose? Or does our ability to interact with the rest of the world disappear when we give birth?" said Frost, feeding Belle the lines she knew she'd parrot to the other moms.

"Well, you make good points," said Belle. "And who cares about those judgmental bitches," she said, now fully on Frost's side. "They all hate me already anyway. Next time I'm definitely coming!" Belle giggled, and Frost lay back down on the bed, exhausted.

I can't do this. Something has changed. I'll explain later. But it's over between us. I'm so sorry.

Ok, fine by me.

Art Chary was sipping a dry martini, sitting at a high top at the back of Le French Diner, a tiny restaurant on Orchard Street on the Lower East Side. He felt safe, with no fear that anyone from his Atherton life might somehow walk into this place at 5:00 p.m. on a weekday. He generally preferred going to hotels with his paramours, or, in the case of Frost, her apartment, but Tilly had insisted on meeting "out." He'd said fine, wanting to keep this new thing going, both to fight boredom and the melancholia that was lately cloaking him like one of his cashmere hoodies.

I can't do this. Something has changed. He reread Frost's message from the previous week, feeling the gin burn his throat as he finished his drink. He wondered what had changed. He'd never ask. Okay, fine by me, he'd replied. He'd known it was a bit of a heartless response, but what was he going to say? "No, please"? "I love you"? Impossible. A slightly sour feeling came over Art, and he tried to shake it off, knowing Tilly's arrival would help.

Did he love Frost? Yes. Did she love him? He didn't think so, though they'd never discussed such things. For her, it had been a great adventure, a way to regain the excitement of her fizzy youth, a distraction from her failing marriage. For Art, well, it had been more than that.

He thought back to the first time he'd met Frost, at an Atherton pre-K curriculum night. They were in the cozy classroom, with its little helper wheel and ABCs everywhere. Frost had been standing alone, inspecting a picture drawn by one of her boys, just a scribble, really, but admiring it in awe, as you would a painting at the Met. He'd noticed her expression first, the adoration for her child visible in the crinkle of her eye, and then he'd seen that hair, those wild auburn waves he'd wanted to bury his face in.

He'd introduced himself and she'd been polite, explaining that she and her husband, Tim, who'd been off that day at a film shoot, had twins, King and Alfred. He'd reciprocated with info about Gertrude. They'd chatted briefly about how they'd come to find Atherton, and how happy they all were to have landed at the best school in New York. A completely standard parental interaction, though the whole time he'd been thinking, Who is this gorgeous, charming person? Why aren't I married to *her*? Morgan had soon spotted them, striding over to interrupt, to befriend Frost by force, as Art had known she would.

"Hi there." It was Tilly, sitting down at the table, her face tilted toward him expectantly. Tilly was sweet, she was gorgeous, and she was amazing in bed, as Art had recently discovered, doing all the things women now seemed to think were standard but, in the old days, would have blown Art's mind.

"How are you?" he asked, thinking only of how much he'd rather be sitting across from Frost. As soon as Frost had broken

things off, Art had reached out to Tilly—he'd known she'd be interested. Tilly was lovely but she was a child.

"I'm good, I'm good," she said. "But I want to see you more."

"I know, but it's only been a week," said Art. "And as you know,
this is just . . . fun." He smiled at her with what he considered to be
his most persuasive, sexy smile.

Tilly frowned. Art was semi-worried she wasn't hearing what
he was saying. He'd had affairs before, many, but was always careful to choose women who had their own stuff going on: divorces,
bad marriages, no one looking to leave a life. That wouldn't have
worked for Art. He was tethered to Morgan forever, in health and
in sickness, since their first bloodstained meeting.

"I just don't want to feel used, Art," said Tilly, squeezing his
hand uncomfortably. He slipped his fingers out of hers.

"We're using each other!" he said lightly, trying to laugh it off.
What would Morgan do to Tilly if she ever found out? he wondered
uneasily. Perhaps that was the one upside to breaking things off
with Frost. He'd known he shouldn't have started anything with
her in the first place—taking advantage of her high at that party,
the exhilaration he'd felt touching her as he'd always fantasized of
doing. But the temptation had been too much. Art was ashamed
of his own weakness. He wasn't a bad man. Just a man who was
stuck.

"Would you like a martini?" he asked Tilly kindly. She shook her
head. "You know I don't drink, silly," she said. Art had forgotten;
these young people nowadays, sober, depressed, wanting to live forever but hating their lives. Poor Tilly. "But I'll have a mocktail if
they have one!"

Art went up to the bar, glancing out the large front window

as he did. He saw the flash of a woman in a hooded jacket as she spun around, hurrying to the other side of the street. Had she been looking inside the restaurant? Art knew he was probably just being paranoid. Being in public like this made him jumpy. Next time, he'd ask Tilly to come to the hotel room straightaway.

## Chapter 7

# A PA Meeting!

═══

Morgan Chary was winning. Everything was working out just as she'd hoped it would. The bookings for Thyme & Time were through the roof, and she'd been going in nearly every day, making sure the staff was happy, engaged with customers, and dressed to perfection. She felt great about the direction they were heading, though opening a spa had never been something she'd wanted to do. Her plan had been to launch Thyme & Time and then pass off the management to a partner, but now that it was humming along, Morgan thought she'd like to stay involved.

Physically, Morgan was also feeling good. She'd allowed Dr. Bossidy to tweak her Wegovy dose, pulling back so that Morgan didn't entirely forget to eat. Instead of nonexistent, her appetite was now a gentle tug, reminding her she needed fuel to keep going. She kept mini protein bars in her bags for such occasions, nibbling on them throughout the day. She loved how empty her body now felt, nothing to muddle her thoughts and desires and urges.

Morgan was on her way to meet Belle at the little Tribeca storefront Belle had rented for a Pippins Cottage Home pop-up, nestled between Thom Brown and Bubby's diner. Belle was hosting a press preview on Friday, and she'd asked Morgan for help setting up the event. The sky had opened into puffy white flurries as Morgan walked up to the entrance, the windows still covered in brown paper.

Morgan knocked on the door, the soft leather of her Hermès gloves making a muted rap. No one answered. She pulled her phone out and checked the time—11:30 a.m., right on time. Where was Belle? She knocked again, louder. Nothing. Then the door cracked open and she saw Belle's hand stick out, beckoning her to come in.

Morgan slipped inside, stepping over open cardboard boxes filled with The Dresses. She turned back to Belle and was surprised to see she looked like an absolute mess. Her eyes were red and swollen, her face stained with tears. Her hair, normally so perfect, was like a rat's nest, coiled and bunched up. Belle sat down in the middle of the floor, amid the boxes, leaving Morgan standing there awkwardly, still in her coat. Belle put her head in her hands. She didn't say anything for a few seconds.

"I don't think it's going to work," said Belle finally. "I think I'm going to fail." Her eyes filled with moisture, and Morgan could tell she was about to start crying. Morgan swayed, feeling unsteady on her feet, trying with all her might not to pass out.

"Don't be negative," said Morgan, holding on to the wall for support. "Pippins Cottage Home will be huge. You're the next Gwyneth Paltrow! You've been working toward this forever. Everything is perfect."

Belle scoffed. "I think I'm cursed," she said with a frown. Morgan, starting to sweat in the dry heat, took off her jacket and gently placed it on a nearby table. She sat down next to Belle, crossing her legs, her back Pilates-class straight, assuming her usual role.

"You're not cursed," said Morgan. She looked closely at Belle. They'd known each other for many years. "You've created a wonderful product that many women will love. I love it! It's going to work. I know you're nervous, but just power through. The worst that happens is that there's a slow start. But buzz will build, I'm sure. Plus, this space is gorgeous!" It felt so easy for Morgan to speak like this, to be positive and supportive, like stepping into a warm, comforting bath. "Now come on, let's get to it."

Morgan stood and started sorting through boxes, lifting The Dresses and shaking them out so their wrinkles smoothed. She spent the next hour helping Belle artfully arrange the furniture, creating an inviting display of Pippins Cottage Home clothing surrounded with other merch—expensive lip oils, moccasins made by an Indigenous tribe in upstate New York, some delicate beaded necklaces another Atherton friend made on the side. They didn't speak much beyond the work.

"By the way," said Belle, "Sofia had a great idea—she thought I should give out samples at the press preview and ask guests to wear them. What do you think about that?"

Morgan had already heard about this scheme from Frost. "What a fun exercise! Such an amazing idea from Sofia. That will be an awesome photo op," said Morgan. Belle just nodded, as if she hadn't heard her.

"Do you think it's weird how close Sofia and Frost are getting?" Belle said shyly, not looking directly at Morgan. Morgan could sense Belle was treading lightly, not wanting to sound jealous.

"A little," said Morgan. "I like Sofia, but . . ." Morgan trailed off.

"But what?" said Belle.

"It's nothing."

"Nothing what?" said Belle, fully focused now.

"Well . . ." said Morgan. "I don't know if I trust her, is all."

"Why?" said Belle, perhaps too eager to hear the answer.

"I heard something about her divorce, that it was messy. That she cheated and he didn't give her anything. That she was basically kicked out of Miami."

"Yikes," said Belle. "I wonder why she wouldn't tell us that. Maybe Frost knows. They're joined at the hip lately." She snorted with envy.

"I don't think Frost knows," said Morgan. "It's kind of like . . . what does Sofia want from us? She's become part of our group very, very quickly."

"Yeah, but it's because we like her, right? And she saved me from that homeless guy at the beginning of the year!"

"Maybe that was all part of her plan," said Morgan, laughing, letting the statement hang in the air.

Morgan had a PA meeting at Atherton at 1:00 p.m. and didn't want to be late. At 12:45, she stood to leave. Belle frowned at her.

"I know people are still talking about the lice email," Belle said. "You can't even imagine the death stares I get at drop-off. Atherton won't let us access their server, but I'm positive someone did it on purpose." Belle put her head in her hands again. "It's like I'm Atherton non grata." Morgan waved her hand dismissively, but it was true. Belle's status had been downgraded from a respected and popular mom to someone who was "accidentally" left off lunch invites and group texts.

"No, no, everyone's over it," Morgan said, lying. "They're all talking about Frost partying with those guys, and have forgotten about everything else." Frost was also the subject of much Atherton chatter, though she'd done her best PR jiujitsu to change the story from slut-shaming to "moms owning their own sexuality." Anyone who didn't get behind that framing came off as a prude, and no downtown mom wanted *that* label. As a joke, Frost had bought a $400 Lingua Franca sweatshirt embroidered with the phrase NEW YORK'S HOTTEST MOM. A few of the other moms were seen in the following days wearing the same one.

Morgan then went to leave, but Belle pulled on her sleeve, keeping her hand on Morgan's arm.

"Morgan," Belle said, her voice unsteady. Morgan leaned closer to her.

"I think another mom is out to get us. What if it's Ava? Maybe it's Dre! What about Becky Oranga? There's something kooky about her, right?" said Belle.

"Belle, stop spiraling," said Morgan sternly.

"Do you feel like something *weird* is happening to us?" Belle pushed on.

"What do you mean?"

"Think about it," said Belle. "The robbery at Thyme & Time. Frost getting the *New York Post* treatment. I mean, someone spit in my mouth! Frost got hit by a scooter! It just feels like a lot of bad stuff at once."

"I guess I see what you're saying," said Morgan. "But how could all that be connected? In my meditation practice, we've discussed this idea of negative event clusters. Sometimes stuff like this just piles up, and no one knows why. It could just be a cycle of the moon."

Belle pursed her lips dubiously. "It started on the first day of the school year. The day we met Sofia. Like you said!" Morgan didn't respond. "Anyway, thanks for the help," said Belle, deflated. "Enjoy the PA meeting. Does Dr. Broker go to those?"

"Sometimes," said Morgan. "Why?"

"Just curious," said Belle, brusquely opening the door for Morgan, who stepped outside alone, breathing in the fresh air. She was relieved to be out of that stuffy, stressful room. She saw she had two missed calls; one from Art, who'd also texted ("Honeydew, won't be home tonight until late, have more of those meetings. Sorry") and one from an unknown number, which had left a voicemail. Morgan put her phone back in her purse, feeling her needle pack as she did. She'd give herself her Wegovy dose at the school, as it was too late to go home before her meeting.

Her driver, John, got her to Atherton in no time, crossing over on Eighteenth Street to avoid the traffic in Union Square. Stopped at a light on Park Avenue, Morgan looked out the window to see Sofia walking toward the school—she'd joined the PA that fall at Morgan's urging. Sofia was in a camel coat, her cute black beanie covered in a light dusting of snow.

Morgan slowly unwrapped a mini protein bar as John idled in front of Atherton. She took two bites, swallowing with effort. Then she put her phone to her ear and listened to her voicemail.

"It's me," said the man on the other end. "When can I see you? I'm doing this all for you, and I expect to be rewarded. I *need* you," the voice begged. "Please?"

Morgan then typed a number into her phone and sent a text: "Soon."

She hopped out of the car and walked up the steps to the school entrance, the same steps that Sofia had toppled down those months ago.

Morgan nodded at the woman at the front desk, the longtime school secretary, Mary Margaret. "Hi, Mary! Just headed to the PA meeting. It's in the auditorium." Mary waved her on, and Morgan headed to the lower level, around a corner and down the marble stairs. The walls were covered in photographs of Atherton students, some dating back to the 1800s, in their suits and ties and little black hats. The school had a particular smell—cozy, like a grandma's old-timey kitchen. Morgan loved its historic grandeur, the way that people ooohhed and aahhhhed when she told them her children went there, the kindness and brilliance of the staff, especially the new headmaster.

As if she'd said his name aloud, up the stairs skipped Dr. Broker, dressed in his uniform of jeans and flannel. He smiled at Morgan, and she noticed his cheeks looked a little pink, as if he'd been working out on a treadmill.

"Hello, Mrs. Chary! Headed to the PA meeting?" He stopped a few steps down from her.

"Yes, thanks. Will I see you there?"

"Oh, no, not today. I have some pressing things to attend to. You know the drill."

Morgan felt hands on her shoulders, and turned to see Sofia on the step above, still in her coat, smelling like cold air, her long eyelashes nearly crystallized. Sofia stared at Dr. Broker in a way that made Morgan uncomfortable.

"Dr. Broker," said Sofia. "I got your messages about scheduling the Atherton Altruist ceremony, but I think it's not the right time yet. I really don't feel comfortable being the center of attention."

"That's too bad, Ms. Perez! We'd all love to honor you for what you did that day. Especially as a new mom to Atherton."

"I'll let you know when I change my mind," Sofia said faux sweetly.

"Please do, Ms. Perez. Enjoy the PA meeting, ladies!" At that, Dr. Broker headed back downstairs.

The pair walked through the hallway that led to the auditorium, entering to see the first few rows already filled with dutiful PA members, all moms plus one dad, Dreyfuss, whose husband, Rufus, ran development at MoMA. The room, which had recently been renovated and reopened to large fanfare, was shaped like a large oval, with a stage at the bottom center of the space and circles of plush red seats heading upward from there. The church of Atherton, Morgan always thought when she entered. Morgan spotted Gabby and Ava in the first row, heads bent down and together as if praying. Morgan and Sofia sat down next to them.

"Hello to my fellow suckers," said Gabby. She was in a fuzzy black sweater and looked a little tired. "Anyone know the topic du jour?"

"I think it's the annual benefit," said Ava. She was in her usual black top and miniskirt combo, her flat black boots coming up all the way to the tops of her thighs.

"Who's the lucky family this year?" said Gabby with a heavy dose of sarcasm.

"Why? What's the story with the benefit?" asked Sofia.

"The benefit is the most important event of the Atherton calendar," explained Ava. "And the PA has a family throw it, a kind of hybrid benefit-theme party. They found they raised more money when someone hosted in their own home; that the intimacy of it encouraged big, big donations. So it's just a lot of pressure on the person who volunteers, is all. But the upside is that the school pays for the entire party. Not that it matters to the parents here."

Dre Finlay, the president of the PA, stepped up to the podium and tapped the microphone. She was wearing jeans, a striped La Ligne sweater, and Le Monde Béryl flats, the outfit of about half the moms in the audience.

"Hi, ladies! Thanks for making the time. Today we've got an

important decision to make—which one of you will host the annual spring benefit. Whoever gets the honors has big shoes to fill. Caroline Press hosted last year, and we pulled in a record amount of money for Atherton. One million two hundred forty-five thousand dollars!" They all clapped. Caroline Press, sitting at the back of the auditorium, stood up and took a bow.

"You've had a year to think about it," said Dre. "So who's it going to be?" There was silence in the room. Ava jokingly grabbed Gabby's arm and tried to raise it against her will, and Gabby batted her away.

"Oh, come on. It's not so bad. We're all going to help. We basically just need a space." Dre looked around the pews for any takers, but no one said a word.

"Ladies," said Dre, her upbeat tone gone stern. "*Someone* has to step up. This is Atherton! My friend Whit told me Braeburn raised nearly two million last year. We can't be outdone by Lauren Parker and her uptown friends!"

There were some awkward sniffles. Morgan could see a line of perspiration beading on Dre's mustache area. Several women reached into their bags to check their phones, avoiding the increasingly tense scene.

Dre then broke into a huge smile. "Yes! I knew we could count on you," she nearly shouted into the microphone. Morgan looked around the room to see who'd volunteered but didn't spot any hands raised. She realized that the sucker was sitting right next to her. It was Sofia, her sharp red nails pointed toward the ceiling.

"Sofia Perez, for the win!" said Dre with relief, and the rest of the PA members cheered politely.

The meeting went on for another hour, with many topics covered (the school's mental health initiatives; the increased slots for neighborhood safety patrol; enforcing the rules for Atherton end-of-year gifts—there was a $100 per child cap on presents, but it had been roundly ignored). Morgan listened to the discussion distractedly, thinking of the voicemail she'd received earlier, and reciting her meditation mantra—"I'm a monster on the hill"—in her head.

"I heard that last year, one family gave Mr. Chin two tickets to the Eras Tour. In Berlin! With airfare!" said Ava to audible tsks-tsks. "Those cost thousands and thousands," she said.

Morgan took that moment to duck out, pushing through the heavy auditorium door into the hallway, then to the nearest bathroom. The Atherton facilities looked nothing like the ones she'd had in her public school growing up, with their rusty stall doors and scribbled graffiti on the walls. No, the bathrooms at Atherton were shiny and clean, with stainless steel faucets, Toto toilets, and toilet paper that felt like a cloud. The room was empty, and Morgan slipped into a stall and locked it. She pulled out her phone and sent a text—"15 minutes? This meeting is wrapping up." Then she took out her needle pack, quickly pulled down her pants, and gave herself the shot. Her thoughts went to Gertrude, who'd told her that sometimes she sat alone in the bathroom during lunch to cry. It made Morgan want to scream. Instead, she violently kicked the side of the stall as hard as she could, smashing her On running sneaker into the gleaming metal. Then she did it again. She felt better. Lighter. It would all be okay. She reminded herself that everything was going according to plan.

Morgan took a deep, calming breath ("I'm a monster on the hill") and opened the stall door, stepping out to see Sofia looking directly at her, hands on her hips. Morgan swallowed an expletive. She looked down at her purse to make sure she'd hidden her Wegovy, but it was sticking out, the top of the needle visible. She saw Sofia's eyes clock it before looking away. Morgan took her bag off her shoulder and shoved its contents down in one nonchalant movement.

"Sofia! You scared me," said Morgan with a little laugh. Sofia smiled.

"Why would I scare you? I had to pee, too," she said.

"But why are you standing here like that?" said Morgan.

"I was just thinking," said Sofia. "You must have been deep in thought, too. You didn't even flush!" Morgan felt heat rising up her face. "But I did hear you kick. Is everything okay?"

"I'm amazing," said Morgan lightly, brushing her off. "And I must have forgotten to flush. Silly me; there's just so much going on lately. It's exciting about the benefit," she continued, stepping around Sofia and heading to the sink.

"Yes, I think it will be a perfect first party for my new apartment," said Sofia. "I've even thought of a theme."

"Already? That was quick," said Morgan, washing her hands. The water was too hot, and her fingers were burning, but she kept going anyway.

"A surrealist ball," said Sofia. "With a New Year's Eve twist—though it's in May."

"That's clever," said Morgan, moving past her. "I'm going back to the meeting now. See you in there."

But Sofia blocked her from exiting, standing directly in front of the door.

"I really need this party to go perfectly," she said, putting her hand on Morgan's shoulder. "Will you do your best to help me? *Por favor?*"

"Of course," Morgan answered, shaking Sofia's hand off. The rings around Sofia's dark eyes were pulsating. "I'd do anything for a friend."

Morgan, who rarely made errors, silently cursed herself for underestimating this woman.

A Note from Mary Margaret, Secretary, Atherton

Greetings, Atherton mothers and fathers and caregivers,
We want to announce a change to front desk security, in the wake of a few concerning incidents in the surrounding area involving persons experiencing homelessness. If you plan on coming to the school for any reason—a PA meeting, to pick your child up for a doctor's appointment, if you're volunteering for the food bank—you must first register on our proprietary app, Atheroo, at least 24 hours in advance. There will be no exceptions granted. We all know that I know you, but please don't put me in the position of not allowing you into your own child's school. Thank you for your cooperation. We at Atherton appreciate your support, as always.

Take care,
Mary Margaret

Mary Margaret was two years to retirement, and it couldn't come soon enough. She'd worked at Atherton for thirty years, in various administrative positions, and had seen the school transform from a sweet, low-key haven for downtown families into the utter insanity of today, a mecca for super-wealthy, pushy parents holed up in $10 million apartments in the West Village and Tribeca.

Yes, the Atherton community still lived in New York City, but in an enclosed bubble of money, their children shepherded from place to place in black Escalades, experiencing nothing of Manhattan beyond the walls of their fancy private school, designer homes, and restaurants that were way too expensive for ten-year-olds to be eating in. Students coming in on Monday mornings talking about the omakase at Shuko and sitting in their dad's box at the Knicks game and flying private to London for a long weekend.

Why live in New York, anyway? Mary suspected it had to do with status, the desire to be hipper than their contemporaries in Greenwich and Chappaqua and even on the Upper East Side. So parents could *say* they lived there. In the old days, the children took the bus to school, they walked from their nearby apartments, some of them took the subway from Brooklyn. Alone! Not anymore. Mary had overheard a recent conversation between two fifth-grade boys, one expressing shock that the other had taken the 6 train to soccer practice in Central Park (with his nanny, of course).

"My mom would never let me take the subway," he'd said to his friend snidely. "That's why we have our driver."

In the last ten years, the moms had become more overprotective *and* more negligent, diverging traits that somehow overlapped in the Venn diagram of modern parenting. The kids had neither freedom—they were trapped in their rooms on their devices instead of sent out to explore the world—nor true attention from their mothers, who were all glued to their phones reading about the "right" way to parent instead of doing it. (Fathers had always been useless and continued to be.) It was certainly a toxic combination.

Mary had grown up in Garden City, Long Island, attending Catholic school. The nuns would slap you on the face if you misbehaved. Imagine a student getting hit now? Mary's childhood felt as far away as the Middle Ages. She still lived in the same town with her husband, who'd retired a few years ago from his job importing office furniture, in a small house they'd bought for $50,000 in 1979.

Mary was one of seven children and had four children of her

own, plus six grandchildren. She'd been around kids her whole life—babysitting for her siblings, raising her babies, helping care for her precious grandkids, and in her role at Atherton, which for years had been an absolute joy. She'd loved taking the LIRR to Penn Station every morning, then the N train down to Union Square, walking to the majestic school building from there, with its red brick and impressive white columns. She'd loved the smell as she entered for the day, the cookie aroma wafting from the kitchen, manned by Chef Nancy, a dear friend of Mary's.

Her job at the front desk meant she saw everything. She knew which child was depressed and which was a liar and which was going to crack if he didn't get into Harvard. She saw their fights, their fun, their breakdowns. She knew who was using vapes in the bathroom and who'd written a term paper with AI. She knew each mom clique and who was up and who was down. She knew that Gabby Mahler and her wife, Margo, were going through a divorce; Mary helped Sue Grossman, Atherton's psychologist, with her schedule. Mary knew that Ava Leo and David Chung were having money problems—they'd contacted the school about potential financial aid. She knew that Dre Finlay, the current PA president, was a total gossip. Mary had been in the bathroom when Dre and Julie Klein had come in after a recent PA meeting.

"Like, we get it Morgan, you're 'amazing' and no one else is quite as perfect as you. Ugh, it's so annoying how superior she is," said Dre. Julie clucked in agreement.

"I'm like a hundred percent sure she's on Ozempic," said Julie. "She's thinks she's fooling everyone, but she wasn't that thin last year."

"Look at Gertrude," said Dre, whispering now. "That's what Morgan's body *wants* to be. Mia told me that Gertrude is being even weirder than normal. Morgan seems to be so in the dark about that, or maybe it's just denial."

"Very sad," said Julie.

"But she's still the worst," said Dre. They both laughed before heading into separate stalls. Mary waited for them to finish and exit before coming out.

Mary knew that Morgan Chary, Frost Trevor, and Belle Redness, with that obscenely long hair, were, as they used to refer to it in Mary's day, the popular girls of Atherton. They were pretty and rich and social, and that status inspired jealousy among the other women. The golden trio had recently expanded to include the new woman, Sofia Perez, who was an absolute mystery to Mary. She'd never seen a new family get two nonentry spots, seemingly for no clear reason—she knew the donor list by heart and had never seen the name Perez on it. The admissions process was closely guarded, but even Heather Lipsky, who ran that department, had been taken by surprise by the Perez situation. Dr. Broker had pulled a headmaster trump card, and, Heather had confessed to Mary, basically gone rogue. It was all highly unusual.

Mary had adored the former headmaster, Dr. Summers, an inspiring educator: kind, patient, stern when it was needed, beloved by all. She missed him. He'd retired two years ago, and the school had gone downhill at a fast clip since. (To clarify, fundraising had soared, but Mary felt the school had lost its soul, and soul was more important than a state-of-the-art science lab or a professional sports-grade gym—to Mary, anyway).

Dr. Broker! Ha! He was a wolf in heartthrob's clothing, in Mary's opinion. The mothers were obsessed, and Mary watched them fall over each other to get Dr. Broker's attention, flirting with him as if they were giggly sorority girls and not forty-year-olds with husbands at home. And he encouraged it, flashing them that smile, attending those ridiculous theme parties they were all so fond of. But there was something off about that young man that Mary couldn't quite put her finger on.

In other news, poor Nurse Weiss was so distraught over the lice email leak. She prided herself on confidential communication with parents, and the breach was haunting her, to the point that she'd hired an outside consultant to look into it, without telling Dr. Broker.

Well, none of it was Mary's business now, was it? Mary waved goodbye to Morgan Chary, breezing out, leaving the building after yet another meeting about fundraising, or Atherton Gives Back, or whatever it was she was always coming to the school for, in and out of Dr. Broker's office. She was here more than any other mother, hands down. Her daughter, Gertrude, that strange little creature, was also always around. Mary had seen Gertrude bringing Dr. Broker coffee the other day, probably on the command of her mother.

Mary chuckled to herself thinking about Dre and Julie's little bathroom gossip session, how all these women were basically grown-up versions of their high school selves. For all their talk of self-reflection, for all the therapy they paid for, their meditation crap, they were still just mean girls, teasing each other on the playground.

Mary would get through her two more years at Atherton and then join her husband in retirement. That was a short amount of time in the scheme of life. She was old enough to know that.

## Chapter 8

# A Pop-up Party!

≡

Sofia Perez had successfully befriended the popular, wealthy women at Atherton, but she was starting to think that something was very, very wrong with them. A darkness hovering over the group like a cloud of gnats. After her mother had died, Sofia, distraught and grieving, had hired a psychic, an older Colombian woman who'd come recommended by one of the nannies. They'd sat together in Sofia's living room and the woman had held Sofia's hands, then shared that Sofia was being closely watched over by her mama. Her mother was worried for Sofia's well-being, the psychic said.

"But why? I'm fine, other than missing her," Sofia had protested. The psychic shook her head, squeezing Sofia's fingers tightly.

"You are not fine. You are about to enter a turbulent time. You will encounter evil. You will prevail, but it will be a long, hard fight."

Sofia had often thought of the psychic's words as she'd stumbled through her divorce, assuming "the people" the psychic had been referring to were JP and his family. But lately she'd been starting to think otherwise. Was the battle still ahead of her?

The entirety of February had been frigid, and Sofia, not used to New York winters, was perpetually chilled. She shivered as she entered the Pippins Cottage Home pop-up on Hudson Street. It was the preview evening for the line, and Belle had invited friends and fashion editors and the moms from Atherton who were still speaking to her. At the door, Sofia was handed The Dress in her size, then escorted by a young assistant to the luxe dressing room in the back.

The space was about half full when Sofia emerged in the ill-fitting garment. Guests were perusing the goods, most of them wearing The Dress, and Sofia laughed to herself looking at all these fashionable women modeling a version of what Sofia's grandmother used to wear to flop around the house.

Belle was standing in one corner of the room. She looked terrified.

"Sofia!" Belle came running up to her, embracing her with the force of a lonely child. Her hair was in a long ponytail, and she looked particularly young.

"Thank you for coming. I'm so nervous, I think I've sweat through my Dress two times already. We have all the right people here to start building excitement about the line. Your idea was genius! Have you seen Ava? I don't think she's here yet."

Sofia noticed that Belle's eye was twitching. Belle must have felt it at the same time, and she put her hand to her face, massaging it forcefully, causing a few of her eyelashes to rip off in the process.

"Everything looks great," said Sofia gently. "And I haven't seen Ava, no."

Frost and Morgan breezed in from the changing area, both wearing Dresses.

"Don't we all look fabulous!" said Frost with enthusiasm, doing a curtsy.

"Congrats! Now we are *both* newly opened business owners. Thyme & Time is booming, and I know Pippins Cottage Home will be the next big thing," said Morgan. Belle smiled tightly, and Sofia saw Frost roll her eyes.

Jeff approached them, twirling his Oura ring around his finger.

"It looks like everyone in this room has joined a sex cult," said Jeff, smirking. He was in his usual backward cap, beard, and sneakers combo.

"Jeff, shut *up*," said Belle, frowning. "That is *not* supportive."

"Babe, babe, I was kidding. You're just stressed," said Jeff. He patted her back and then, noticing an alert on his phone, stepped away from the group. Morgan changed the subject.

"Have you all heard that Sofia is going to host the annual benefit?"

"You're a hero, Sofia," said Frost.

"I do what I can," said Sofia. "The theme is a surrealist ball—start thinking of your wacky costumes now!" Sofia had volunteered to throw the benefit after she'd heard it was subsidized by the school. She'd figured it was a good way to solidify her standing on the PA and also get the word out about her own venture, which was beginning to take shape.

"Speaking of," said Frost, "I had an idea for this Friendsgiving party, inspired by you, Sofia. The women from *Sex and the City*." Sofia felt herself flush. To be included in their group costume, as a famous foursome, no less, meant Sofia had really made it.

"I love it," said Belle, entirely cheered up and always happy to be Frost's hype man.

"So who's who?" said Morgan. "Sofia, I know you're Samantha." Sofia smiled, though it felt like an insult. She scratched her arms. The Dress was starting to bother her.

"I can't wait," Sofia said gamely. "I'll just have to get a blond wig."

"I know the best wig place in NYC," said Morgan, her voice turning into what Sofia now recognized as Morgan's "Ask Morgan" tone. "It's where all the cool Hasidic ladies go."

It was settled that Belle would be Carrie, Morgan would be Charlotte, and redheaded Frost would be Miranda.

Belle went off to pitch her product to the editors in attendance, instructing the others to walk around the store and look *extremely* interested in everything. Sofia was bored. She was getting sick of this New York way of socializing—groups of women gathering to celebrate and "support" one another's ventures. It all felt fake and not the least bit fun. She went over to a display of gold necklaces, standing next to two attractive young women in matching pink lipstick, one blond, one brunette. Both were in The Dress. Sofia pretended to look at her phone while she eavesdropped.

"How many of these rich-lady-with-a-fashion-line previews do I have to attend in one lifetime?" said the blonde. The brunette shrugged.

"We have to cover it on the site because she's friends with a company board member or something—their kids go to the same school. But come on, if she thinks anyone will ever buy this sad, brown, scratchy thing, she's out of her mind."

"It *is* scratchy," said the blonde. "But I don't know. People bought the nap dress."

"Yeah, but that was during the pandemic, and everyone had lost their mind," said the brunette.

"What does her husband do again?" said the blonde. They both looked over at Jeff, still on his phone.

"I don't think anything exciting," said the brunette. "It's her dad with all the money. Imagine being that rich and then deciding, wow, what I really want to do is make some ugly dress. Wouldn't you just, like, do nothing?"

"I'd sleep in, have my nannies deal with my kids, and then go shopping all day," said the blonde. She scratched herself.

Belle swanned over, her Dress making an oddly stiff swishing sound.

"Girls! Thank you so much for coming," said Belle. "You both look gorgeous in The Dress." Sofia kept her back to them, shifting so she could still hear what they were saying.

"I appreciate your support for Pippins Cottage Home and can't wait to see how you'll cover it. Let me know if you have any questions about production or my inspiration. I've always wanted to be a designer, since I was a little girl, and The Dress is the result of playing with this idea of: 'What is the perfect piece for a capsule wardrobe?'" The two women hmmmed and ahhhed enthusiastically.

Sofia saw Frost across the room, chatting with another woman whom Sofia didn't recognize. The previous day, she'd secretly trailed Frost after drop-off, expecting her to go to her art studio on Twenty-Second Street, perhaps to meet Art. Instead, Frost headed straight to Friend of a Farmer, on Irving Place, waiting outside the restaurant until it opened at 9:00 a.m. Sofia had peeked around the corner to see Frost hugging a man who definitely wasn't Art. He was tall and leggy, with shaggy hair, and when he turned around Sofia saw that it was Tim, Frost's husband. Holding hands, they went into the restaurant together. Sofia, surprised, had rushed toward Union Square to escape notice.

Sofia now felt an arm slip through hers. It was Morgan's. She was wearing a turtleneck under The Dress.

"How are you?" said Morgan sweetly. Sofia didn't really feel like chatting.

"How are the kids doing? Adjusting to their new life okay?" Morgan tilted her head sympathetically. Sofia didn't know what Morgan was fishing for. Out of everyone she'd met, Morgan was the hardest to pin down. She didn't understand Morgan's motivations, and that upbeat-cheerful-*amazing* thing. Sometimes Sofia thought she got a glimpse of a monster inside of Morgan, a flash of bones, filled with the drugs she was taking to stay thin. Sofia had seen the needle the other day in the bathroom, after she'd heard Morgan kicking the stall. Who was Morgan so angry at?

"Yes, they both really love Atherton," said Sofia politely.

"You know, you never did tell us how you came to find the school," said Morgan, looking at Sofia intently. Morgan's face appeared to be pulled at the edges, like someone had stretched her skin over her cheeks. "It's rare that two siblings find spots in non-entry grades. You were so lucky!"

"I suppose so," Sofia said.

Just then, Ava Leo entered the pop-up, cutting their conversation short. After being accosted by an attendant and doing a double take when asked to wear The Dress, she reluctantly went in to change. She came back in The Dress, plus her own black blazer, rendering Belle's creation nearly invisible underneath. Ava walked up to Sofia and Morgan.

"I'm here!" said Ava jovially. "I have to run soon—I have a Gucci event in Midtown after this and then a Prada dinner after that, but I wanted to stop by." (Everyone in New York was always having "to run" as soon as they arrived somewhere.) "I got the sense that Belle might commit suicide if I didn't show. All good with you two?" Sofia and Morgan nodded.

Belle and Frost approached, Belle with a grin so big Sofia thought her face might crack in half. "Ava! I am *thrilled* you could make it!"

said Belle, as if greeting a long-lost relative instead of someone she saw nearly every day. Belle looked Ava up and down, her face freezing in disappointment when she realized that Ava had all but hidden her Dress under her blazer. Sofia ached for her.

"It all looks fab," said Ava. "So smart of you to ask guests to participate—we're like unpaid models!" She laughed, but Belle didn't. Ava fingered her Dress, as if touching a particularly pungent piece of cheese.

"Thanks for wearing it," said Belle. "It does feel like everything is coming together. The site goes live tomorrow, and I hope that this moment will solidify some orders."

At that, Ava took her phone out of her bag and starting snapping pictures. Belle's eyes lit up. Jeff walked over and put his arm around her.

"It's a triumph, babe," he said.

"Can you hold this for a second?" asked Ava, handing her phone to Sofia as she aggressively scratched one of her legs. At the same time, Sofia noticed that she, too, was feeling a little . . . itchy. She went from foot to foot, wiggling a little to try to relieve the feeling. She rubbed her leg. Then rubbed it again. She saw that Morgan was peeking underneath her shirt, and that Frost was inspecting her arms. Belle was facing away from them, watching the twenty or so women milling about. Everyone who'd agreed to put on The Dress seemed twitchy. Touching themselves as if swatting away a mosquito.

Sofia looked under her Dress to see that her skin was beginning to bloom in pink. Frost flicked Sofia, gesturing to herself silently, pulling The Dress up her arm enough for Sofia to see that she, too, was breaking out in an angry rash.

"Guys, I have to go," said Ava, continuing to scratch herself.

"I'm having some kind of allergy—sometimes I get a mild reaction to shellfish. Belle, there's no shrimp nearby, right?"

"Definitely not!" Belle said. "Ava, I'd so love it if you could wear The Dress for the rest of the night," continued Belle, her voice cracking in desperation. "I know you have some other events to go to, and it would be so wonderful if you were photographed out in Pippins Cottage Home!" There was a beat of silence as Ava decided how to respond. Sofia stared at the ground; the awkwardness was overwhelming.

"Aw, Belle, I'm sorry, but I have to say, I'm feeling a little uncomfortable in The Dress. I think the fabric doesn't agree with me. I have supersensitive skin . . ."

Belle audibly swallowed.

"Sure, I totally get it," Belle said, trying to recover. The women looked in diverging directions. Sofia wanted to disappear.

"But congrats again," said Ava. She then hurried to the dressing room, momentarily emerging in her regular clothes, waving good-bye to the jealous group.

"Please remember to post!" Belle shouted after her.

"Belle, I'm a little itchy also," said Frost, her fingers going up and down both arms. Morgan didn't say a word, but Sofia could tell she too was physically uneasy, her mouth twisting in a strange way.

Belle shook her head, confused.

Jeff, who'd been on his phone, looked up, registering his wife's concern.

"Why is everyone so quiet?" he said. Sofia felt like her legs were on fire.

"I think . . ." said Belle, nearly choking. "I think there might be something wrong with The Dress?" she said.

Frost held up her arm in the middle of the circle for them all to see. Scarlet bumps snaked up her skin. She grimaced.

The blonde and brunette from earlier walked over to Belle, who'd turned a ghostly white. Sofia began to fantasize about tearing The Dress off her hot, bothered body.

"Uh, Faith and I here are both having some weird skin thing? Like, it *really* itches," said the blonde. "What kind of fabric did you use? Is it mohair? It doesn't feel like mohair."

"It's pure cotton, a hundred percent pima, sourced from northern Italy," said Belle.

"Hmmm," said the brunette. "That's strange. How are we both reacting to cotton?" Belle raised her hands, as if to say "no idea."

"Did you two come in the same car? Maybe it was something from the Uber?" said Frost, trying to be helpful (and also trying not to scratch herself as she said it).

The blonde shook her head.

"Oh shit!" someone shrieked. They all turned to look. A willowy fashion editor type with a prominent beak nose was jumping up and down. She was in a Dress and black heels, her legs bare despite the cold outside.

"I need Benadryl!" she yelled, charging toward the door.

In an instant, everyone was making their way toward the dressing room, a herd of inflamed influencers, as Belle tried unsuccessfully to calm them all down.

"It's all fine! It can't be the fabric. The fabric is pristine," she was saying repeatedly, though no one was paying attention to her. Sofia knew that as part of the inner circle, she had to stay in her Dress until the end. But it was excruciating, like the biting sand flies that attacked her when she'd visited her relatives in Colombia.

"I'm calling my dermatologist right now," said someone. "I have her personal cell number."

"I feel like I'm burning up," moaned another, who Sofia recognized as a mom from Atherton.

"Belle, *what* did you make these out of?" said another.

Jeff was helping the door attendant find jackets and scarves. The guests, in such a rush to get out, left their Dresses in a discarded pile on the dressing room floor, a sad metaphor for the disastrous evening.

The friends stood there helplessly as Belle's dream was crushed by "textile contact dermatitis," as one wellness editor put it loudly, causing the rest of the room to google the condition.

After five frenzied minutes, only Sofia, Morgan, Frost, Belle, and Jeff remained, plus a couple of manic staffers (they'd been required to wear all black, to differentiate from the guests, and so had been spared). Jeff was rubbing Belle's back rhythmically, in the same way Sofia used to soothe her babies.

"I . . . I . . . I," Belle said. "I don't know what happened. Something must have gone wrong with the samples. I'm wearing an earlier version, and I don't feel anything." Jeff nodded sympathetically.

"Belle, I'm going to change now," said Frost. Belle sniffled her assent. Sofia and Morgan followed her into the dressing room, each heading into a separate stall. Sofia nearly ripped The Dress off, changing back into her jeans with relief.

They found Belle sobbing next to the jewelry display, Jeff stress-googling "contact dermatitis" and "cotton allergy" and "fabric malfunction."

"It's all ruined," cried Belle. "All my work. Everything. SOMEONE IS DOING THIS TO US. I know it." She stared at them imploringly, but no one volunteered any information.

"Someone is trying to fuck up our lives," Belle whispered.

"I'm not seeing a good explanation," said Jeff, still looking at his phone. Was he ever not looking at his phone? Sofia wondered. "There's no type of fabric that can cause a universal allergy. Unless the samples were tampered with, and someone put something on them that caused itching. But . . . *why* would anyone do that?"

Belle wiped her eyes. She gave them all a meaningful look.

"It doesn't make sense," continued Jeff, shaking his head in confusion. "Don't worry, sweetie. We'll get to the bottom of it. We'll get to the bottom of everything." He went back to his screen.

"Belle, I'm so sorry about all this," said Frost. Sofia could see that Frost's arms were still lightly red, the color mirroring the highlights in her hair.

"I'm also sorry that I have to go," she said. "I wish I could stay and help, but I told the boys I'd be home for bedtime. I've been spending a lot of time on my collages, and so I promised. But I know this will all work out. No one will even remember it tomorrow." Frost gave Belle a quick peck on the cheek, then waved goodbye to them all. "I'll start a chain about our Friendsgiving costumes!" she said.

"I also have to take off," followed Morgan. "I'll call you in the morning. You are a fighter. You're *resilient*. You're strong. You can survive anything. And we are here for you." Belle nodded solemnly.

Sofia glanced out the window to see a young homeless woman, possibly strung out, walking past the store. She pressed her face against the glass, squashing her nose, then locked eyes with Sofia, who couldn't bring herself to look away. Then she gave Sofia the middle finger and scurried off. No one else in the group saw. Sofia winced.

"My gorgeous friend, I also must leave," said Sofia. "Let me know if I can help in any way," Morgan had just exited, and Sofia rushed after her, making sure to stay far enough away so that Morgan didn't notice that Sofia was on her tail. Sofia followed as Morgan walked down Hudson Street and turned onto Leonard. One World Trade loomed ominously in the distance. Morgan kept going, walking so fast that Sofia had to jog to keep up with her.

Sofia thought about money as she followed. Everyone in New York was always thinking about money. How they'd get more of it. What they'd spend it on. Money equaled freedom from JP. Money meant Sofia would get to keep her kids. And she'd do anything for that.

Morgan eventually slowed, entering the park in front of the imposing white building of City Hall, Sofia staying a healthy distance behind. It was getting dark, and Sofia was cold in her Orolay coat, which she'd recently bought on Amazon (though it was hideous, it was affordable, and the moms all had one for some unknowable reason).

The park was relatively empty at this hour, and so Sofia was carefully striding from tree to tree, hiding behind trunks to avoid being seen. Morgan passed a statue of an old guy in a chair—HORACE GREELEY, the plaque read—and continued to the south side of the wooded area, finally stopping in front of a large fountain, its water off, a tall, cross-like structure rising in its center. The only other person in view was a woman sitting on a bench off to the side. She was piled in jackets, maybe five in total, and was scattering crumbs on the ground, attracting a sizable crowd of pigeons, the birds fighting each other for scraps.

Sofia wasn't exactly sure why she'd followed Morgan here. What did she suspect she'd be doing? But her gut had told her to go, so she had. Sofia shivered yet again, unable to shake the chill.

Maybe Morgan just wanted some alone time. Maybe she'd found out Art was cheating on her, and she was upset. Maybe she was worried about Gertrude. Sofia was starting to feel like a weirdo standing there, watching Morgan do . . . nothing. What was this stalking thing all about, anyway? Trailing her friends around the city like she was a private eye! *Estúpido.*

That's when she saw a man walking toward Morgan. His back was to Sofia, so she couldn't see his face. He was in a bomber jacket, and a black baseball cap was pulled down low on his head. As he approached the fountain, the bird-woman chucked a handful of bread onto the ground, and a swirl of pigeons swooped down, some of them flying close to the man's head. He ducked for cover, and as he did, turned toward Sofia, giving her a quick view of his profile. Sofia gasped. Then she ran away, fast, pulling her scarf tightly around her neck. The wind in New York was whipping.

# WhatsApp Chat

## Atherton Lower School Moms
### 94 Participants

**Dre Finlay**

Attention, Atherton mommies! I've got an important announcement for you all, so please read this all the way through.

The homeless man who has been loitering near Atherton, the one who terrorized us all on the first day of school, has finally been arrested, and it was all thanks to Atherton's safety patrol—namely, Gemma Corder and Julie Klein, who were on duty that day. Gemma and Julie saw the man in Stuyvesant Square Park, walking right through the reflecting pool, harassing nannies with strollers. They called the NYPD, who put this man in handcuffs and led him away. Atherton moms to the rescue! If you see Gemma and Julie at drop-off, please give them a huge thanks from our entire community for their bravery. We set up the safety patrol to protect our children, and we did just that.

**Jenna Worthy**

Wow, Gemma and Julie! We owe you one. The homeless problem in New York just keeps getting worse. Here's a story from the New York Post about the mayor's failure to control it.

**Caroline Press**

And don't even get me started about the migrant issue . . .

**Gabby Mahler**

Guys, we live in New York City . . . we have "right to shelter" laws here. These are people who are suffering!

**Caroline Press**

Like you're suffering in your Park Avenue castle. ☺

**Gabby Mahler**

I actually take offense to that, Caroline. We're all very privileged here. The least we can do is help those in need.

**Dre Finlay**

Everyone! Enough sniping! I just wanted to celebrate Gemma and Julie and the whole of Atherton's safety patrol.

**Katrina Lowry**

Gemma/Julie well done! Was it scary??

**Julie Klein**

It was a little daunting! We spotted him and called 911. I was thinking of our kids the whole time, and how this was all for them. That helped!

**Gemma Corder**

The police came quickly. He resisted a little, and that part was intense.

**Julie Klein**

Then they led him to their car. The whole time he was shouting: "She paid me! She paid me!"

**Dre Finlay**

You two are heroes. ☺

**Gabby Mahler**

Yes, bravely calling the cops on a man with mental illness.

**Dre Finlay**

Don't forget: today is the last day to sign up for the Atherton spring break camp in March! See you all at Friendsgiving. I, for one, am looking forward to celebrating the bonds of Atherton's chosen community.

# Chapter 9

## The Bugs Are Back!

Belle Redness was sitting in her kitchen, sipping herbal tea, staring out at One World Trade, taunting her with its message of resilience and strength. Fuck resilience. Belle's cat Duke jumped up onto the countertop, rubbing his nose onto Belle's, sensing she was upset. Belle gave him a kiss. Then she slowly lowered her face down, banging her head on the cold Calacatta marble. Duke, startled, leaped down to the floor. Then Belle hit her head again, harder. The pain felt good. It felt right. She did it once more, moaning a little. "Aaaarrrrgggghhh." Belle was losing her shit.

"Mom, what the heck are you doing?" said Hildy, who'd walked in without Belle realizing she was there. It was 11:00 a.m. on Tuesday and Hildy was home—she'd been diagnosed with strep throat the day before and had to follow Atherton's rule of twenty-four hours on antibiotics before returning. It felt like the Redness clan was suffering plague after plague after plague. Belle raised her head swiftly and sat up straight, hoping Hildy hadn't seen the extent of her feeling-bad-for-herself self-harm.

"Nothing!" said Belle, fake chipper. "Just resting for a moment.

I'm exhausted. How are you holding up?" Hildy was in plaid pajama pants and a blue hoodie, her twelve-year-old face half-hidden. She still hadn't gone through full puberty—she didn't have her period yet, though most of her friends already did. But her body was changing, and Belle knew how self-conscious that made her.

"Fine, my throat hurts, whatever," said Hildy, sitting down next to Belle. Belle noticed that Hildy had a smattering of pimples tucked away under her right eyebrow, and desperately wanted to lean over and pop them. She resisted. Hildy looked so much like Belle had at that age. Belle hadn't blossomed till she was in her late teens, when she'd suddenly gone from awkward to beauty queen, and she was praying that Hildy would take a similar path. Become gorgeous at the same time as Belle was losing her girlish luster. Oh, the irony. At least Hildy had time.

"You know, I'm still getting teased about your stupid lice email," said Hildy, shaking her head. "I wish people would just forget about it." An older kid had seen the email in his mom's inbox and had forwarded it to all his friends, and for months, boys had been itching their heads as Hildy walked by in the hallway. "I saw Donavan Klein laughing at me," she continued. Belle had always suspected that Hildy had a crush on Donavan and felt horrible if Belle had embarrassed her daughter in front of him.

"Sweetie, I'm so sorry," said Belle with a sigh. Belle had spoken to Dr. Broker at length about the email and had even offered to pay for a tech expert to come in to analyze Atherton's servers months after the incident, having given the school the proper time to run its own (inconclusive) investigation. But Dr. Broker refused, saying that it wasn't school policy.

Well, she'd done more than *speak* with Dr. Broker. Right after Christmas break, Belle had marched into Atherton on a mission.

She'd worn her favorite pink Oscar de la Renta fringe suit, which she saved for occasions when she wanted to feel powerful, and her hair loose down her back. "A real-life Rapunzel," he'd called her at Ava and David's party. Jeff had offered to come with her, but she'd told him that it was smarter for her to go alone, and that Dr. Broker would respond better to the pleas of a mother than the demands of a father. By then, the details of her, er, encounter with Dr. Broker had turned hazy in her mind; it had been so dark and so fast. Had it even really happened at all?

She'd gotten an appointment through Dr. Broker's secretary, Alice, but no one was at Alice's desk when Belle had arrived. Walking through the school in the middle of the day had given Belle the feeling of being in trouble as a kid, adding to her anxiety. Dr. Broker's office was on the fourth floor of the building, and she'd lightly knocked on the door, nerves causing her heart to pound wildly.

"Come in!" he'd summoned.

She'd entered to see Dr. Broker sitting on a black leather chair behind his antique herringbone desk in the large, sunny room. The space was filled with built-in bookcases, framed pictures of Atherton on the wall, plus Dr. Broker's various degrees. He'd motioned for her to sit down across from him, which Belle did, perching on the chair uncomfortably. Dr. Broker looked even more attractive than normal, his hair lightly tousled, his shirt hugging his chest.

"So, Mrs. Redness, let's talk about the email," he'd started off. Belle had swallowed. Was this just going to be a normal meeting?

"Yes, let's," Belle had said, stammering. "I've given the school time to figure it out, but clearly you haven't. My concern is that it wasn't a mistake, and that someone specifically hacked into Nurse Weiss's email and sent it around."

Dr. Broker had laughed softly, sending a spasm of desire through Belle.

"We pay not one, but two sixty-five-thousand-dollar tuitions to this school! I think we deserve some information," she'd said, trying to gather herself.

"Uh, Belle, can I call you Belle?"

Belle had waited a beat.

"Yes, Dr. Broker. Or should I say Paul?" When Belle got nervous in front of a man, her voice became soft and high-pitched.

"It's Dr. Broker to you, Belle."

He'd gotten up and walked around his desk to the office door, clicking a lock there that Belle hadn't noticed. Belle had raised an eyebrow. She'd bitten her front lip.

"People try to barge in when I'm in the middle of meetings, so I had Alice install this to keep everyone out." He'd said it as if it were the most logical thing in the world.

He'd come to where Belle was sitting, standing right in front of her. She'd looked up at him coyly. What was he up to? Then he'd taken one hand and placed it on the top of her head, stroking her hair, gently squeezing the back of her neck. After a moment, he'd bent down and started to place his other hand between her legs, but Belle had jumped up, putting a stop to it, repeating to herself: Jeff, Jeff, Jeff.

"Dr. Broker," she'd cooed, wanting to adopt a more adultlike tone but finding herself unable to. "This isn't right. I'm married and you're the headmaster. I really do want to talk about the email!" Red-faced, Dr. Broker had sat back down at his desk, and they'd had a five-minute, stunted chat about the fact that Belle and Jeff wouldn't be allowed to access the school servers. She'd thanked him for his time and swiftly unlocked the door and nearly toppled out, running the hallways to escape the school. As she'd left, Mary Margaret had gaped at her like her pants were on fire.

Belle came home with the story that Dr. Broker wasn't budging, and they'd just have to suck it up and accept that it was a technical glitch. Atherton was the best school in New York City. It was their key to the Ivies, which, most annoyingly, you couldn't buy your way into nowadays. Pulling the kids out wasn't an option.

"I wonder if someone is out to get our family, like in a TV show or something," said Hildy now. "Like, they want to extort you and Dad or something, and get all of Grandpa's money, and they're doing all this bad stuff first," she said. Belle patted her on the back. The only silver lining was that this whole thing seemed to have caused Hildy to soften somewhat to Belle. They'd spoken more in the last few weeks than they had in months. She'd been waiting for Hildy to bring up the story that Clara Cain had shared, the one about nude pictures, but she never had. Belle had assumed, with relief, that Ozzie Cain had been mistaken.

Belle's phone rattled on the counter—Frost's name appeared, but Belle didn't answer. Frost had been kind since the Pippins Cottage Home fiasco, helping Belle do damage control, using all her connections to try to keep it all out of the press. It hadn't worked. In the days after the preview, there had been a slew of spiteful mentions of the incident in industry outlets. *Puck* eventually caught on, running an item in Lauren Sherman's widely read fashion newsletter, the words of which were now committed to Belle's memory.

## AN ALLERGY TO FASHION

Fashionistas, get your Benadryl ready! All hell broke loose in Tribeca this week during the press preview of Belle Redness's new capsule line, Pippins Cottage Home. Editors and industry VIPs were invited to the event in a pop-up on Hudson Street and asked to don an item (the only item?) from the line—The Dress. ("It looked like a cross between a straitjacket and my aunt Teri's bathing suit coverup," sniped one attendee.) As the night wore on, guests started to feel a strange sensation, "like ants in your pants . . . or, rather, Dress," said one. The culprit? The Pippins Cottage Home fabric, which was causing editors and influencers to break out in ugly red rashes. Instead of posting on Instagram, the fashion crowd headed out the door and into the arms of their dermatologists. Downtown New York has never been so itchy.

The aptly named Redness, daughter of Joseph Connolly, former CEO of J.P. Morgan, had no comment when reached by telephone. Needless to say, Pippins Cottage Home won't be coming to a store near you anytime soon. "This line is finished," said a prominent fashion editor. "There's no way for it to recover." Another rich wife's vanity business bites the dust . . .

A rich wife's vanity business! Ugh. Belle had a BA in economics! Ugh. Ugh. She'd done her research, she'd sourced fabric with the utmost care, she'd employed talented designers to work on the line, she'd hired a marketing and PR firm to help with the rollout. And now it was all fucked, along with her reputation, by some mysterious, possibly nefarious error. She was so upset, so embarrassed, and so confused. The next day, she'd sent the samples back to the factory in Italy, and they'd inspected them thoroughly. Nothing! They'd found nothing. What could have happened? And why did it have to happen to her? That idea that she had a giant bull's-eye on her back had turned from a feeling into a belief.

"Mom, are you going to get that?" Hildy asked, looking at Belle's phone. Frost was calling again.

"No, I'll speak to her later," Belle said. She didn't want to talk to Frost. She didn't want to talk to anyone. She didn't need cheering up from her friends. She needed a time machine.

"Are you still upset about Pippins Cottage Home?" Hildy looked at her kindly. Hildy, her little baby Hildy. When Belle had gotten pregnant with Hildy, she and Jeff had been living in the East Village, on the third floor of a brownstone on East Fifth Street. The apartment was long and thin, and the kitchen was just a tiny nook off the living area (as an adventure, they'd decided not to take money from her father for a few years; after they had Hildy, that quickly changed). Belle had loved that shitty apartment, with its banging radiator and the windows that looked right out onto the trees. At night, she'd lie in bed, stroking her pregnant stomach and listening to people smoking outside bars, drunkenly chatting, their voices as clear as if they were in the bedroom with her.

"I'm still upset, yes," she said to Hildy. "I worked hard on that project, and it's not going to go the way I was hoping. Have you ever felt that way?"

Hildy cocked her head, thinking of an answer. "Remember last year, when we went to Aspen with the Charys and the Trevors?"

Belle nodded. The families had a tradition of skiing together in different locations each season—Aspen, Telluride, Big Sky, Alta—the kids dumped in ski school while the grown-ups enjoyed alone time. Belle didn't ski (though she loved expensive ski outfits), and so she spent her days napping, reading novels, getting spa treatments, and grabbing cocktails with the girls.

"When we got there, I decided that I'd dedicate the entire time to the downhill obstacle course. They had one for the ski school kids. I wanted to get really good, so I spent hours practicing that thing, going over the little jumps, around the cones. And by the last day, I was doing pretty well," said Hildy. Had Belle known that was happening? She recalled that she'd worn a brand-new Fendi ski suit during the trip, multicolored in pinks and purples and yellows. But she couldn't remember what her daughter had been up to.

"Then on the final run, I could *feel* I was going to break my record. And I was so proud of how fast I was going." Hildy paused.

"What happened?" said Belle.

"Gertrude messed me up," Hildy said.

"Gertrude?" Belle couldn't imagine what Hildy meant.

"Yeah, I think she actually, like, broke my ski on purpose," said Hildy. "I saw her near my equipment when I was walking back from the bathroom, and then during the race I crashed into a cone and slid the entire rest of the way down."

"I'm sorry, honey. That does sound disappointing. But how can you be sure Gertrude did that? Why would she?" said Belle.

"Uh, Mom, have you ever met Gertrude?" said Hildy. She'd turned serious, and Belle didn't know what she was getting at. Gertrude and Hildy had never been friends, as much as Belle and Morgan had pressured them to be. They just didn't click; Hildy was spicy and chatty, and Gertrude was, frankly, sad and kind of quiet. Morgan complained often that Gertrude was getting teased about her weight and that Atherton wasn't dealing with it properly.

"Of course I know Gertrude Chary," said Belle. "I've known her since she was five years old."

"Well, then you know she's an evil bitch," said Hildy.

"Hildy!" said Belle, surprised.

"Mom, it's true. She does bizarre things—steals stuff from desks, she copies people's work when no one's looking. But then she pretends to be innocent in front of the teachers," said Hildy.

"But maybe that's because she's being teased herself about being chubby—Morgan told me about 'Girthy Gertrude.' So maybe she's acting out in retaliation."

Hildy looked at Belle like she was crazy.

"What are you even talking about? Girthy Gertrude? Firstly, no one teases each other about weight at Atherton. What do you think this is, the year 2000? It's called the body positivity movement, Mom. Duh. And secondly, what seventh grader would come up with the name 'Girthy Gertrude'? Girthy? What does that even mean?" Hildy rolled her eyes so hard Belle was worried they might get stuck up in her brain.

The buzzer rang, interrupting them. Belle wasn't expecting anyone today. She'd been planning on holing up alone and continuing to monitor the internet for negative mentions of her event. Her best guess was that somehow the fabric had come in contact with an allergen during the shipping process, but how that could have happened, well, that's what Belle wanted to get to the bottom of.

"Maybe it was one of the moms from my lice email, trying to get back at me," Belle had posited to Jeff yesterday, both of them having coffee in the kitchen, Jeff slurping his unattractively. Did everyone get less and less attracted to their husbands as time went on? Or was that just Belle? Sometimes she'd look at him doing something normal, like bending over to tie his shoe, or flossing, or toweling off after a shower, and think to herself: *Ew*. And then a wave of guilt would come over her for feeling that way. It wasn't Jeff's fault that he was aging. She was, too, as much as she didn't like to think about it. And he still loved her just the same as he always had.

"I never should have had everyone wear something from the line."

"Babe, that was a good idea," Jeff had said.

He'd walked over and given her a long hug, and, in his familiar embrace, Belle's duplicity had hit her in the stomach like one of Miles's soccer balls. She'd let Dr. Broker kiss her. Sort of. Jeff could never, ever know.

"It was Sofia's idea, actually," Belle had said.

"Well, whatever, it was Sofia's good idea. All we know is that this definitely wasn't a random event," said Jeff. "We have to take it in context. Your leaked email plus this. There's a pattern here. I'm going to contact that private detective that Tim hired to look into Frost's accident—maybe he can do some digging for us, too. My thought is that both of you have been targeted."

"Targeted? That sounds sinister," said Belle.

Jeff had looked at her a little patronizingly, which had annoyed Belle. "When you're rich, people want things from you," he'd said. "We have money. People want money. It's as simple as that."

Now, getting up to see who was at the entrance, she thought about their conversation. She remembered Morgan's phrase— "negative event clusters." She wasn't generally a superstitious, karma-is-real kind of person, but it had occurred to her that by reveling in Thyme & Time's robbery she'd perhaps brought this on herself. Does the universe punish you for being a bad friend?

She saw Frost downstairs at the door, her red hair poking out of a white bucket hat, holding two shopping bags. Frost waved at the camera and Belle buzzed her in.

"It's freezing outside," Frost said as she stepped out of the elevator, which opened right into the apartment's bright blue foyer. "I tried calling you to tell you I was on my way, but you didn't pick up. I figured you were negging me because you wanted to feel sorry for yourself all alone." Frost took off her hat and shook out her hair. "But I wasn't about to let that happen."

Belle was happy to see Frost, as always. It had been that way since the first day they'd met, the kind of friend who you both love and are a little in love with.

"Look what I've brought over, you're going to die for it," said Frost. She handed her coat to Ivanna and walked past the colorful print from Rachel Perry's *Vogue* series, one of Belle's favorites, into Belle's library, the walls warm with purple felt. Belle was pleased with it every time she entered, a mark of a successful renovation. The Davids were worth every penny.

Frost opened the shopping bags and began laying out items of clothes—"Don't peek until I'm done!" she commanded. Hildy crept in behind them, having heard Frost's voice. She'd taken her hood down and looked brighter for it, more like the Hildy of old rather than the grumpy tween Belle was currently dealing with. Frost looked up and saw her there.

"Hildy, my darling! Give me a hug." Frost went over and swept her up tightly, causing Hildy to blush happily. Even Hildy couldn't resist Frost.

"I'm so sorry about your strep," Frost said, ruffling Hildy's hair, which was looking greasy from inactivity. Belle would make her wash it tonight. "What a crock of shit." Frost liked to curse around kids, and the children ate it up. It made them feel grown-up and in on the joke. Frost went back to arranging clothes on Belle's sofa.

"Okay, Belle, I'm ready for you!" said Frost. "First person to guess what these are from gets a cookie from Grandaisy." Frost held up a paper bag from the Tribeca bakery. Frost had laid out three fully composed outfits. One: a pink tank top, a tutu, and sky-high sandals. Two: the famous Dior newspaper dress. And three: an ethereal floral midi dress with pink stilettos.

"It's *Sex and the City*!" said Hildy, excited to have won the game. Frost ceremonially handed her the cookie.

"Yes, they're for our Friendsgiving costumes. Belle—I mean Carrie—take your pick," said Frost, gesturing to the clothing as if she were Vanna White.

"Where did you get these?" said Belle, gravitating toward the tutu, which she stroked gingerly.

"You know my friend Mike Bruno, who owns First Dibs? They have a whole pile of clothing that's associated with *Sex and the City*—either originals from the set or versions from around the same time. The tutu isn't the exact one from the show, but SJP did wear it in an ad campaign. Mike told me they're going to list it for close to two hundred fifty thousand dollars."

"What?!" Belle was shocked. She spent a lot on clothing, but not $250,000 a lot.

"So don't fuck it up." Frost laughed. "Here's a tip: drink white wine, not red."

Belle picked up the tutu and held it over her body. Frost started humming the *Sex and the City* theme song, and Hildy looked impressed, coming over to Belle and running her hand over the springy fabric. Belle felt cheered. Frost always made things better. Perhaps there was a way to salvage Pippins Cottage Home. This would all be cleared up, and they'd move on with their lives.

"I have options for all of us. Plus, we have to figure out the guys. Jeff will be thrilled to be Big, I'm sure," said Frost.

"Hahaha, Dad as Mr. Big," said Hildy, laughing. "That doesn't work! Shouldn't Art be Mr. Big? He's the fuckboi of the bunch," she said. "All my friends say he stares at their moms for a bit too long . . ."

Frost turned back to the couch, gathering up the rejects to return.

"Oh, Hildy, hush," said Belle. "That's our friend's husband, and it's not a nice thing to say about him."

"Whatever, Mom, it's true," said Hildy, shrugging.

The buzzer then rang.

"Ivanna, can you get that?" Belle called out. It was probably an Amazon delivery. Ivanna didn't respond. The buzzer went off again.

"Ivanna?" Belle shouted. Maybe she was in the bathroom. Belle walked out of the library to the foyer, peering into the video footage of the camera downstairs. She didn't see anyone standing there. Must have been a dropped-off package. But then she heard the elevator rumbling up to their floor. She toggled to the elevator camera and saw a man in a baseball cap, holding a small Amazon box. She couldn't remember what she'd ordered. The trade-off that Belle and Jeff made to live in their fabulous Tribeca loft building was that the security wasn't ideal. They had a state-of-the-art lock system, including a coded elevator, but no actual doorman. Belle wasn't sure how this guy could have gotten in.

Belle plastered a smile on her face, holding out her hands for a quick retrieval. As the doors opened, she registered that the man had replaced his cap with a ski mask, obscuring his face entirely. Panic flooded Belle's body. Was she about to be attacked? Where was Hildy? But the man didn't lunge or come into the apartment. Instead, he ripped the tape off the box and pulled out a bouquet of flowers, handing it to Belle as the doors closed back on him. Belle, suspecting the worst, looked closely at what she was holding.

The flowers were dead. Crumpled brown roses, lifeless pink tulips, shriveled white peonies. A rotten stench wafted up to her nose. She went over to the video monitor and watched as the stranger exited the building, his ski mask now traded back for his baseball hat.

Frost and Hildy arrived in the foyer.

"Mom, what is that?" said Hildy, sensing something was terribly wrong.

"Belle, who gave those to you?" said Frost.

Belle shook her head, confused. "A man in a ski mask," she said. "But I saw him on the security camera, wearing a baseball hat."

"What!" Frost exclaimed. Belle noticed that a small white note card was sticking out of the lower part of the bouquet.

"Here, I'll read it," said Frost, pulling it out. "It says, 'Dear Belle, Congrats on the successful launch of Pippins Cottage Home! We knew you could do it. Wishing you all the best, a friend.' A friend? How strange," said Frost. Ivanna had entered the room and Belle handed the flowers to her. "Just throw them out," she said softly, not wanting to upset Hildy. Ivanna headed into the kitchen, small pieces of leaves breaking off the bouquet and falling to the floor, leaving a trail of decay.

"Must have been a mistake at the florist," Belle said, trying to laugh it off for Hildy.

"I'm calling Dad," said Hildy, unconvinced.

"No, no, don't call him yet," said Belle. "You'll worry him. I'll speak to him later."

Just then, the elevator doors opened unexpectedly. Belle, on instinct, grabbed a miniature blue Jeff Koons balloon dog from the entry table, ready to bash the guy's head in. But instead of a ski-mask-wearing monster, into Belle's apartment stepped Sofia, her cashmere coat belted tightly, her hair freshly blown out. Her large grin turned to concern as she sensed the vibe in the room.

"Sofia!" Belle nearly barked. "I wasn't expecting you."

"I texted you to say I was nearby. I wanted to cheer you up, so I brought you this." She held out a tray filled with individual ramekins, each covered in tinfoil. "It's my special Colombian dessert, *postre de natas*. My mama would make them for me when I was feeling down." They all just stood there, no one accepting the offering. "Your building door was propped open, and I know your elevator code, remember?" Belle did—she'd given Sofia the code to her elevator a few weeks ago, when she'd had the girls over for wine and cheese.

A sharp squeal came from the kitchen. Sofia, startled, dropped her tray, sending ramekins flying every which way, South American pudding spraying onto the purple felt walls like streaks of white paint.

The women ran to find Ivanna standing at the kitchen island, the dead flowers strewn over the beautiful stone, dozens of large brown insects whirring around her head. "Aahhhhhaaaahhhh," yelled Ivanna, shooing the bugs away.

"Lanternflies!" gasped Belle. "NO!"

"They must have been in with the flowers," said Frost. Sofia picked up a roll of paper towels and started batting the flies down, one by one. Hildy grabbed a kitchen towel and helped, whipping it at the spotted creatures. Duke and Sky got in on the game, the two cats pawing at the lanternflies, pinning them with their fluffy paws. Belle watched them all in a daze while Frost comforted Ivanna.

After nearly five minutes of battle, the lanternflies were defeated. All that remained were their squashed carcasses, sullying the clean white imported tile, the cats playing hockey with the corpses.

Hildy disappeared with her phone, likely to call Jeff, and Belle sank down to the table.

Then she burst into tears.

An email to Frost Trevor and Tim Butler

Report from Greg Summerly, Private Detective

I wanted to send a wrap-up of my findings from the October 14 incident. Unfortunately, no huge reveals here, and for that I apologize.

On October 14, at 6:37 p.m., Frost Trevor was struck by a man on an e-scooter while crossing Hudson Street at Christopher Street. The man, in his twenties or thirties, wearing a baseball cap and an N95 mask, did not identify himself at the scene. He approached from the north, directly striking Ms. Trevor. He also fell off his scooter. Then he got up and continued south.

Ms. Trevor was with her friend Morgan Chary, who, after helping Ms. Trevor to her feet, then fainted herself. They were joined by their other friend, Sofia Perez, who they'd earlier had drinks with at the Odeon. Two witnesses initially helped Ms. Trevor after the accident, but I was unable to locate them for questioning. In the process of this investigation, I spoke to Ms. Chary and Ms. Perez, as well as two surrounding store owners, one of which, Good Guys cannabis shop, was able to provide me with security camera footage of the incident.

Unfortunately, the footage was very grainy, and though the accident was visible, any identifying features of the man were blurred. He appeared to strike Ms. Trevor directly, though it's unclear if it was deliberate. In my professional opinion, it was not. Neither Ms. Trevor nor Ms. Chary nor Ms. Perez could name any concrete identifying features of this man.

On February 1, Ms. Trevor, out at a nightclub, ZZ's, suspected she saw the same man in the bathroom area. She attempted to make contact with him but was unable to. She and Ms. Perez then left the club and were heckled by an unidentified man who yelled slurs at them. Ms. Perez ran after this man for two blocks but ended up losing him near the entrance to the High Line on Thirtieth Street. She was unable to get a close look at him.

ZZ's would not provide me security camera footage of that night, but it is my professional opinion that the incidents are not related. Ms. Trevor was admittedly drinking heavily that evening.

To summarize: In my professional opinion, Ms. Trevor was the victim of a common New York City crime: a hit-and-run by an inexperienced, reckless e-scooter driver. E-scooter accidents in New York City have increased 17 percent just this year, and many drivers use them dangerously.

I do not see the link between the incident with the e-scooter and the incident at ZZ's. The only commonality between the two is Ms. Perez.

Thank you for your business.

Best,
Greg Summerly

## Chapter 10

# Friendsgiving!

---

Frost Trevor felt okay, given that there may or may not be someone in Manhattan who was out to get her and her friends. Unlike Belle, Frost was holding on to the idea that it was all just a big coincidence. Or a misunderstanding. The private detective they hired had confirmed as much, sending them a succinct email basically saying: you're being paranoid. So Frost was trying to stay positive. Her marriage, which just months ago seemed to be on life support, had rebounded. She and Tim were talking, they were having sex, they were being open with one another in a way that they hadn't for years. (Well, open-ish; he could never know about Art.) She needed to focus on her husband and her sons. She'd been an asshole for too long. Frost was trying to be better.

The boys, however, were presenting a slight problem. Frost hadn't told this to anyone, particularly not Belle, but after school the other day, Frost had overheard Alfred and King, deep in Fortnite comas, talking about the "fake nudes." She'd sat them both down, basically dragging them by the ears, and forced the story out: a couple weeks after school started, King said he'd turned on his phone to find a text message from an unknown number. He'd opened it to see a slew of X-rated photos of Hildy Redness, whom he'd known since pre-K. He'd shown Alfred—but that was it!—and Alfred, with his eagle eye, had guessed that the pictures were doctored. "Hildy's boobs are not, uh, like that," said Alfred, turning crimson and looking anywhere but his mother.

King told Frost that a similar thing had happened at Dalton—some kid had used AI to make deepfake pictures of girls in his class and had gotten caught and suspended. He'd even heard that the kid might have to go to jail. With that in mind, King said he'd deleted the pictures and the text right away, but that "maybe" a few other boys had heard about it, including Ozzie Cain. Or maybe a few other boys had also received the text. He couldn't be sure. But both twins swore to God, no fingers crossed, that they didn't know who'd sent it.

"Does Hildy know?" Frost had asked, her heart sinking. As if Belle needed something else to worry about.

"I don't think so," said Alfred. "Bro, whoever did it is really perverted," he said. King nodded in agreement. "Maybe it was Gertrude Chary," said King offhandedly. "She's sus," he said, wrinkling up his nose. Frost didn't know what "sus" meant, but she wasn't concerned about Gertrude. Gertrude was sad, not evil.

"Hildy's not really our friend, but she's fine. She just does her own thing," said Alfred. At twelve, Frost's sons were men one moment and little boys the next. She'd tabled the chat and told the boys to let her know if they received anything else of the sort. "Don't breathe a word of this to anyone," she'd warned, and they knew her tone meant business. "And I'm not your 'bro.'" They both laughed. Frost's hope was that somehow it would never surface—she wasn't going to tell Belle, and maybe it would all just blow over.

And honestly, she was too busy to deal with yet another Belle meltdown. Because Frost Trevor's dream was about to come true: she was about to become a *real* artist. She'd shown Ethel her work after that initial phone call, hosting her at Frost's apartment on Twenty-Second Street. Ethel had arrived dressed in vintage Yohji Yamamoto—an oversize black tent dress—and pink eyeglasses, her long gray hair in a slick braid. Frost, who never got intimated, had been intimidated, showing Ethel her collages shyly, carefully watching Ethel's face, wrinkled in an attractive, artistic way, for reactions.

"Young lady," said Ethel finally, pulling her glasses off to reveal large, blinking blue eyes.

"I like these. They are . . . thought-provoking, striking, and I think people will want them for their homes. I'm going to sell them, if you don't mind," she'd said. "Though I know you don't need the money." She'd cracked a wry half smile. Well, Ethel was right about that, but Frost didn't care. To be validated for something that wasn't her father or mother, her looks, or her husband was thrilling. She'd had a dawning, disturbing thought that she'd never been so happy in her entire life. Maybe when her sons had been born, one right after another, that final push to get King out of her body, the hormones and fear and love and panic assaulting her all at once. This was close.

In a nod to the exhibit's theme, they'd chosen to repurpose the old Bungalow 8 on Twenty-Seventh Street, now abandoned and tenant-less. "This place is a shell of its former self, just like the women in your work," Ethel had said as they'd toured the dilapidated club. (Perhaps Ethel didn't remember that Frost had incorporated herself into a few of the pieces. Or maybe she did.) Frost had brought Sofia along for the visit, and it amused Frost to watch Sofia gingerly stepping over the exposed wires in her stiletto boots. "I love it," Sofia kept saying, about nothing in particular.

Frost had been spending lots of time alone with Sofia over the past few months, the four friends operating more as two separate duos. There wasn't a schism or anything like that—no one was fighting, no feelings had been outwardly hurt. That Frost knew of, at least. But Frost was having a hard time stomaching Belle's depressive pall and baseball hat–conspiracy theories, and Morgan's hardcore Morganing: obsessing about Thyme & Time, barely eating or drinking anything, being chipper but no fun at all.

There was something intoxicating about making a new best friend in your forties; it reminded Frost of falling in love. She craved Sofia's presence the way she used to crave a new boyfriend's touch. She wanted Sofia to *like* her, and so when they were together, Frost became the best version of herself: witty, stylish, go-with-the-flow. The person she used to be when she was younger and unattached, not the woman she was currently, navigating a troubled marriage and nearing a possible midlife crisis.

Frost looked over at Tim now, in the back of their chauffeured SUV. They were headed to Friendsgiving, at the Cains' apartment on Pearl Street. Tim and Frost were in the middle row, and Sofia was in the back, in a blond wig and a Samantha Jones–inspired belted trench coat (and nothing else). Tim, for his part, was dressed as Steve to Frost's Miranda, and it made Frost laugh to look at him, in his sleeveless Puma B-ball shirt, small, wire-framed glasses, cargo shorts, and low-top Converse All Stars. Tim had embraced the challenge, even buying his outfit himself after doing internet research on the character. Frost grabbed his hand in hers and he turned to her and smiled.

"Looking hot, Hobbes," he joked, pinching the sleeve of Frost's gray blazer, part of the skirt suit she'd chosen to wear as Miranda, the one from the famous "he's just not that into you" episode. She was planning on saying that line to people all night.

As much as Frost loved a party, she was anxious going into the evening. Even the pulsing pop music (Cher's "Believe," at Sofia's request) wasn't quite enough to clear the murky, what-else-could-go-wrong feeling hovering over Atherton like an impending storm. Belle was convinced that there was a sicko out there who'd found them together in an Instagram photo and was trying to ruin their lives, one by one, like in a David Fincher film or something. Tim wasn't so sure—"Don't bad things happen to bad people?" he'd joked to Frost the other day.

"Belle and Morgan aren't *bad*," Frost had said defensively. "And what about me?" Little did Tim know. They were sitting in their living room on a pink Bellini sofa, having a drink before dinner, discussing how the search to find the man who'd scootered into Frost had reached a dead end. To push it forward, Frost would have had to make an official police report, and based on the detective's meager findings, she'd decided against it.

Spending alone time together was something Frost and Tim had been trying to do regularly, on the suggestion of their couples' therapist. She'd set her vodka down on her Mario Lopez Torres wicker grasshopper side table, its antennae pointing right at her. Why had she purchased that piece, again? At the time, she supposed, she'd thought it was cute. Now it just looked creepy.

"Oh, come on," said Tim. He was sipping a scotch, one of the expensive ones he'd bought at auction.

"You know how I feel about Belle and Morgan," Tim continued. Tim thought Belle was a rich, whiny daddy's girl, and that Morgan was a fake-happy pain in the butt. "Anyway, it seems you have a new best friend. And I like this one!"

Frost wondered if her friends would be annoyed that she and Sofia were arriving at the party together. Probably, though neither would ever admit it.

The car pulled up to the Cains' building, a shiny glass tower facing the waterfront. Tim helped both women down from the car, and when Frost saw how strikingly glamorous Sofia looked in her coat and wig, she instantly regretted her more humorous choice of unflattering workwear. To complete her look, Frost had a stylist pin her red hair under to resemble Miranda's shaggy short cut.

"Ugh, I don't look like Miranda, I just look like a dowdy lesbian," Frost whispered to Sofia as they were waiting for the elevators to take them up.

"I'm a lesbian, and I heard that!" It was Gabby Mahler followed by Ava Leo. "Hello, Frost, hello Frost's shadow, Sofia," said Ava with a smirk. Sofia scowled at her. Gabby had curled her short blond hair and was wearing a cropped white T-shirt, a purple button-down tied around her waist. Ava had mushroomed her bob—as if she'd stuck her finger in a socket—and was in a graphic T-shirt and a black suit vest.

"I think I know who you two are . . ." said Frost.

"Party on, dudes!" Ava and Gabby interrupted in unison, collapsing into a giggling fit. They were both carrying electric guitars.

"Who are you?" Sofia asked.

"All we are is dust in the wind, dude," said Ava solemnly.

"Bogus!" said Gabby. They couldn't stop laughing.

"I don't understand this costume," said Sofia. Ava rolled her eyes at her—it was the second time in so many minutes that Ava had been rude to Sofia. Ava wasn't particularly nice to anyone, but there was a pointed dismissiveness to her interactions with Sofia, which Frost assumed was classic female jealousy. How boring.

"We're Bill and Ted! From the movie!" said Gabby, snickering still. Sofia shrugged.

"Guess it didn't make it down to Miami," Sofia said with a sweet smile. "Or maybe you guys are way older than me."

"Burn," said Gabby, elbowing Ava.

David Chung then entered the lobby, dressed as Abraham Lincoln in a top hat and long beard, a bit player from *Bill & Ted's Excellent Adventure*.

"Welcome to Friendsgiving, guys," said David. "Or should I say Samantha and, um, Miranda, and what's your name again, Tim? Sam?"

"Steve," said Tim, in his best high-pitched Steve voice.

"This hat is making my scalp itch," said David with a grimace.

"Where's Margo?" said Frost to Gabby, who waved the question away.

"Too tired to make it, plus all three kids have strep," she said.

The small elevator arrived, and Sofia, Tim, and Frost got in without the other three. "Be excellent to each other!" Ava yelled at them as the doors closed.

"Morgan and Belle are here; let's find them," said Frost as the doors opened into the party. She took Sofia's hand, leading her through the cluster. Frost waved bye to Tim and saw him drift over to Art, who was standing close to the entrance. Frost's stomach seized; she hadn't seen Art since they'd stopped speaking, and she was annoyed that his presence made her feel nervous. He'd come dressed as Trey MacDougal, Charlotte's first husband—Morgan had explained to Frost that he'd been too vain to wear a bald cap as Harry Goldenblatt—and so he was in a red plaid kilt. He caught Frost's eye and then looked away.

Frost and Sofia pressed into the ruckus in search of the completion of their foursome. Frost wanted to get as far away from Art as possible. Plus, the costumes only really worked when they were all together. The enormous duplex apartment had floor-to-ceiling windows throughout. You could see Brooklyn from one side and New Jersey from the other, the Statue of Liberty holding her torch in the distance. Frost cringed, thinking about the number of women who'd been sexually harassed so that Clara Cain, defense attorney to sex pests, could afford this place.

Frost quickly saw that the Cains had leaned into the *Friends* in Friendsgiving, and had turned the apartment into a nearly identical re-creation of Central Perk. There was worn, velvety furniture, wooden tables, and a perfectly set up coffee bar at one side of the living room that made it feel as if you were stepping into the famous TV show. The waiters, actors who resembled the cast of *Friends*, were passing around espresso martinis. Frost and Sofia both took one from a David Schwimmer look-alike. "Thanks, Ross," Sofia trilled. "This show *did* make it to Miami," she said happily to Frost, who was still trying to spot the rest of their crew.

Before she could, Clara approached. She had on a wavy, long blond wig and was in some sort of gaudy lace evening gown.

"Ladies! Welcome!" she said brightly, giving them each a wet kiss on the cheek. "I love me some *Sex and the City*! Did you know that Dre Finlay, Genevieve Thomas, Caroline Press, and Jessica Hillton came as the fab four, as well?" Clara gestured over to a nearby group, and Frost saw that their costume idea wasn't so novel after all. There was a Carrie in a tutu, a Samantha in a red halter gown, a pregnant Charlotte in a black-and-white polka-dot dress (Jessica was seven months along). Plus, it looked like Caroline Press, in a slinky black dress with a sheer panel on top, had opted for sexy Miranda over frumpy Miranda. Frost was beyond annoyed.

"Thanks for having us, Clara," said Sofia. "Such a great event."

"I can't wait for yours!" said Clara. "A surrealist ball! It's brilliant."

"What are you dressed as?" asked Frost politely. She really just wanted to find Belle and Morgan, but Clara was the host, and so they'd have to dutifully put in their time.

"Ah, well, I was just *so* busy at work on top of all this party planning," said Clara (Sofia made a face at Frost), "and so the costume came together very last minute. I'm Kate Winslet, and Neil over there"—she pointed to her husband, in a classic tuxedo, his stomach straining against the buttoned jacket, taking a napkin out of his pocket and blowing his nose with it, loudly—"he's Leonardo DiCaprio," said Clara. Frost let out a barking laugh, but then pivoted to a cough to cover her tracks. Clara, pretending not to notice, went on.

"Kate and Leo are such good friends. They met while filming *Titanic* and have remained close since then," said Clara.

"Oh . . . do you *know* them?" asked Sofia, confused.

"No, I don't know them," said Clara, shaking her head. "Though I'm surprised that Leo hasn't called me yet, based on his history of dating, um, young women," said Clara.

"Perhaps one day soon," said Frost dryly. Clara smiled at the thought.

"It's a great costume idea. And a great party," said Frost, trying to end the chat. She couldn't see Belle or Morgan anywhere.

"Did you hear they arrested the homeless guy who'd been hanging around the school?" asked Clara. Frost and Sofia nodded.

"The rumor is that someone was giving him money to stay in the area," said Clara. "That's what Julie Klein told me. She was there. Why would anyone do that?"

"Have you seen Morgan or Belle?" asked Frost now. She was done talking to Clara.

"I think they're upstairs," said Clara. "And, well, how are the boys?" She said it as if she knew something that Frost didn't want her to.

"They're fine, why do you ask?" said Frost, worried about what she was hinting at.

"Ozzie told me that they'd been involved in the Hildy-nude-photo thing," said Clara, who was clutching a large espresso martini. She was a little slurry, and Frost realized she must be drunk. Fuck.

"They're all good," said Frost swiftly. "Here's to Atherton's 'chosen community!'" Frost raised her glass to Clara and grabbed Sofia's arm, pulling away.

"And congrats on your art show, Frost," Clara yelled after them. "I can't wait!"

As they speed-walked to the stairs, Sofia squeezed Frost's wrist, getting Frost to slow down, even though Frost knew what was coming and didn't want to discuss it.

"Frost, what nude photos?" Sofia was wide-eyed.

"It was all just a mix-up," Frost said hurriedly. "Someone sent some fake nude pictures to Alfred, and he opened the attachment without knowing what it was."

"Of Hildy?" said Sofia.

Just then, they saw Morgan and Belle heading down the stairs toward them, Morgan floating along in a strapless white lace wedding dress, a shawl wrapped around her neck, and Belle in her tutu, twirling theatrically, her impressive hair set into Carrie ringlets, carrying a nearly full espresso martini.

"We're all together!" said Belle. The sound system was blasting "I'll Be There for You" on repeat, and it was getting difficult to hear, between that and the ambient chatter.

"We've been looking for you, but we got detained by Clara," said Frost.

"Oh God," said Belle, subtly pointing at the other *Sex and the City* pod. "They stole our idea!" Dre Finlay saw them staring and did a passive-aggressive bow in her tutu.

"Belle, I haven't seen your Mr. Big," said Frost, looking around for Jeff.

"He's probably hanging with Trey and Steve." She laughed at the absurdity of it all. "Sofia, you look hot," Belle continued. Frost was proud of Belle for making it out to the party—the moms were still whispering about what had happened with Pippins Cottage Home, everyone expressing sympathy to Belle's face while snickering behind her back and calling it karma for being a bitch. Belle and Jeff had hired the private investigator Greg Summerly to look into the lanternflies incident, but he hadn't gotten anywhere yet. It was all pretty much a disaster.

"I'm so happy we have a Samantha in our group. Finally!" said Belle. "I love being in a foursome. I'm glad you joined our little pod."

Clara then sauntered up to the group, accompanied by Ava and Gabby, looking like hooked fish.

"We were just, uh, chatting with Clara here, and wanted everyone to join in," said Gabby, winking at them when Clara wasn't looking. Ava, her hair springing in every direction, gave "help us" eyes.

Clara was sloshing her espresso martini, sending it raining over the edges of her glass.

"I love you all, did you know that?" Clara said. Frost, wanting to run interference for fear of what Clara might say, jumped in.

"I think we should check out upstairs," said Frost. The other women nodded, happy to be saved.

"I know you all don't like me as much as I like you," said Clara, mournfully, trapping them there. "It's so nice you have each other. I feel like I'm always working, and never get to do any of the fun mom stuff, the pickups, the class picnics, the PA meetings." Out of nowhere, Clara started to cry. No one knew what to do. Morgan eventually went over to Clara and patted her back stiffly.

"And to think," said Clara in between sniffles, "Frost and Belle can still be best friends, even though Frost's sons were sending around naked pictures of Belle's daughter!" Fuck, fuck, fuck. Frost peeked at Belle to see if she'd heard what Clara had said. Oh, she'd heard. Her cheek color mirrored the pink of her leotard.

"*What* did you say, Clara? Frost's boys had pictures of *Hildy*?" Belle's voice was high, too high, that girly lilt in overdrive.

"I thought you knew?" said Clara, realizing what she'd done. Or maybe it had been on purpose. "The pictures were fake, so at least there's that. Ozzie told me the whole story."

Belle turned to Frost, her nostrils flaring with anger. Carrie Bradshaw on fire.

"FROST!" Belle was nearly screaming over the music at this point. "Why didn't you tell me?" Frost looked down at the ground. She didn't have a great defense and didn't want to get into it here. She and Belle could have coffee tomorrow to discuss. It was all a misunderstanding. But Belle didn't relent.

"Listen, you . . . you . . . you," Belle said loudly. People in their immediate vicinity started to look over, keenly aware that something was *happening*. Belle Redness was having a tantrum. How juicy was that?

"Belle, please, let's talk about this later," said Frost quietly. In the eight years she'd known her, Frost had never seen Belle lose her temper in public. A few feet away, Frost saw a group of women dressed as the Spice Girls pointing at them and guffawing.

"I'm sure we can figure out what happened, like grown-ups and friends," said Sofia, trying to make peace.

Belle then did something that Frost would never have expected her to do, not in a million years. She lunged at Frost as if they were playground enemies, the jerky movement causing Belle to dribble some of her espresso martini down the front of her tank top. Belle then registered, with horror, what she'd done. "Tell your First Dibs friend I just cost him two hundred fifty thousand dollars!" she shouted. In a rage, Belle flung the rest of the martini directly at Frost's face, a complete liquid shock, the alcohol dripping down Frost's cheeks into the neck of her gray suit.

"*Dios mio*," said Sofia with a start. Frost tried to wipe the drink off with her hands. Her eyes, watering with tears, felt like they were burning.

Frost heard someone say loudly, "Holy shit, Belle Redness just threw a drink at Frost Trevor." And then the scuffling of high heels and loafers toward their area, everyone trying to get a good look at her, wanting to be the one who could retell the story with accuracy and fun details. ("Frost's suit was soaked!" "I thought Belle was going to murder her!" "Aren't those women best friends? I guess not . . ." "Belle Redness, lice queen, ruining another Atherton party!")

Belle, who had the look of someone who'd shocked herself, stomped away, running up the stairs alone. Clara, that troublemaker, took off for the front of the apartment. Gabby and Ava scurried to the bar.

"Listen, we all make mistakes. I'm sure you two will be great in no time. You're amazing friends!" said Morgan limply. "Belle has just been having a rough time of it lately." Frost knew that was true, but she also knew she'd messed up. She'd been messing up so much lately. "Maybe because that son of hers is such a little beast," said Morgan under her breath, almost to herself. Belle's son? A beast? Miles Redness was a sweetheart. Frost caught Sofia's eye; she must have heard her, too.

Then came a loud banging sound, which turned out to be Clara, hitting her espresso glass with a spoon on the other side of the room. The music finally, mercifully, turned off. With difficulty, Clara stepped up on a milk crate, which had been set down next to the bar. The lights dimmed and a small spotlight was pointed toward Clara. In the glare, it turned out the Kate Winslet dress was nearly see-through, giving her guests a clear view of Clara's high-waisted Spanx.

"Everyone please quiet down!" Clara ordered. No one did. "Everyone! Please!" A waiter handed her a microphone.

"A toast," she screeched into the mic, causing the entire party to cover their ears in pain.

"Atherton parents, welcome to Friendsgiving," said Clara proudly. Occasionally, Frost regretted inventing this bloody theme party tradition. It hadn't been her aim when she'd hosted that Valentine's Day party those years ago; she'd just been bored and thought it'd be fun. Fun used to be Frost's thing, though perhaps not so much anymore, she thought ruefully, the espresso martini still wet on her collar.

"I love that you all took the theme so seriously and came dressed to the nines for the occasion. I see the cast of *Seinfeld* over there, and I know there are a few Taylor Swift squads floating around. And I love the *Sex and the City* crews, plus I saw a Magic Johnson and a Larry Bird, and also the Spice Girls!" A few lone "yeahs!" emerged from the crowd as their costumes were mentioned.

"It's so lovely that we've formed such close bonds as parents of children at the same wonderful school. I think I even saw Dr. Broker walking around! Dr. Broker, can you say hello?" People eagerly looked for their headmaster, but he didn't seem to be in the room. Clara gave it a few seconds and then shrugged unhappily. "My hope for this party, and really the whole purpose of the theme, is that we expand *beyond* our own friend groups and meet some new people. I know from my personal experience as a working mother"—Frost heard a couple low groans at that—"that it's difficult to foster new Atherton relationships, particularly between men and women. So right now, let's solve that."

"Where is she going with this?" Sofia said softly into Frost's ear. Frost was happy that at least one of her friends wasn't pissed at her. She wondered where Belle had gone.

"I have here a box filled with every male attendee's name on a piece of paper," said Clara, gesturing to a large wooden cube on a table next to her, decorated with the word TIPS. "I need all the women to line up, grab a name, and then find that person and have a meaningful conversation with him. That's an order!" she finished. No one moved. "I'm not kidding, folks," Clara continued, sounding embarrassed. "Do I have to speak like I'm in court here? Please line up. Now." Frost heard grumbles before the moms started making their way to the box. Frost grabbed a slip of paper: Bud Cunningham. Ugh. Frost didn't want to have a conversation with Bud Cunningham. She wanted to go home and dry off.

She looked around for her friends; she needed to find Belle. She needed to explain the whole story. Clara still had the mic and was instructing the partygoers that the bar wouldn't reopen until they'd paired off and chatted for at least six minutes.

Frost searched halfheartedly for Bud. She passed Tim, who made a face at her, mouthing, "What happened??" She gave him a peace sign, their signal for "we'll discuss it later." She then spotted

Trina Cunningham, wearing pink overalls and a pink cap. Her hair was plaited into two braids. Trina ambled over to Frost, her braids swinging. "Trina, I pulled Bud," said Frost. "Do you know where he is?" Trina shrugged. "No idea. Last I saw him he was upstairs, drinking with the guys. He's wearing red overalls, a rainbow shirt, and a red hat. He's My Buddy and I'm Kid Sister—the dolls that were supposed to be your best friends?" Frost nodded. These theme parties gave people license to be fucking weird. "What happened with you and Belle?" Trina asked, a gleam of good gossip in her eye.

Frost took off for the second floor instead of answering, in search of a grown man in a doll's outfit. She saw that couples were pairing off and wondered if this party game, in some instances, might lead to more than friendship. She thought back to the Zoo-ly Fourth party, walking down to the beach with Art, the ketamine coursing through her body. How different she felt tonight, only one martini in, and a husband whom she felt recommitted to. Where the hell was Bud Cunningham, anyway? She scanned the top floor for someone in overalls. There was a Kramer speaking to Posh Spice. There was a guy dressed as Snoopy talking to a member of Taylor Swift's squad, Karlie Kloss. Oh, wait, no, that was the real Karlie Kloss. Frost forgot that she and Josh Kushner had a kid in kindergarten. She waved at Karlie, who waved back. They knew each other from around town. But still no Bud.

The area was set up to look like the *Friends* apartment, and the drinks station was within a suburban-size kitchen, which the Cains had painted blue for the party. Frost felt a tug, and she looked up to see Art standing in front of her, so close that she could smell his musky scent. She glanced around for Morgan but saw no one from their close circle of friends in their vicinity.

"Frost, I'm . . . I'm. Frost, I miss you," said Art softly, leaning into her. Frost felt her usual tug to him. "I'm sorry about the way we ended. I didn't want to be short with you. I need to tell you something," he continued. "It's about Morgan . . ." At that moment, Frost saw Morgan coming up the stairs, her wedding dress costume taking up an impressive amount of space. She instantly spotted Frost with her husband and made a beeline toward them, not leaving Frost with time to say anything to Art other than "You should work on your marriage. I'm working on mine." Then Frost spun away. She saw a green door, which she figured led to a powder room, and opened it haltingly, not wanting to walk in on anyone who'd inadvertently forgotten to lock. The lights were off, and so she patted her hand across the wall until she felt a click. The room was illuminated, and Frost saw that she'd walked into Ozzie's bedroom. Whoops. Frost went to turn the light back off, but as she did, she saw some movement near the closet door, which was slightly ajar. She then saw the flash of a tutu.

"Belle?" Frost called, confused. "Is that you? Are you in the closet?" Belle peeked her head out.

"Frost! Yes, it's me," she said. She stepped out of the closet and smoothed her Carrie curls guiltily.

"Are you alone?" Frost asked, though she knew the answer to that question already. Belle shook her head, then put her finger to her lips. Frost had a bad feeling.

Just then Sofia entered, likely looking for Frost.

"What's happening in here? I just had to get away from Hugo Corder, his breath was so stinky," she said, waving her hand in front of her nose. "Ah, did I interrupt? Are you two making up?" she said to them.

The closet door squeaked open, and Belle ran back to it and shut it tightly.

"Is someone in there?" said Sofia, an eyebrow raised. Belle shook her head.

"Well, then, I'm glad I have you both here, because I need to tell you something," said Sofia. Frost wasn't sure what she was talking about, but she was more concerned about who was hiding in the closet. Whoever it was, it certainly wasn't Jeff Redness.

Sofia went on.

"I've decided what I want to do with my life . . ." she said. Her blond wig was askew, her shiny brown hair visible from the front, too beautiful to be contained.

Then into the bedroom walked Morgan, looking from one woman to another, her face inscrutable.

"Am I missing an important powwow?" she said.

At the sound of her voice, the closet door popped open again, and Dr. Broker appeared before them. His hair was mussed, and Frost could see that his small nod to the theme was a stack of beaded friendship bracelets on his wrist.

"Mrs. Trevor, Ms. Perez, Mrs. Chary, I hope you're having a nice party," he said genially, as if greeting them in the halls of Atherton. Belle looked at the floor, then at the door, anywhere but at Dr. Broker or her friends. As Belle squirmed, Frost could have sworn she saw Morgan and Dr. Broker lock eyes, but only for a brief second.

Dr. Broker cleared his throat strangely and, without another word, moved past them out of the room.

"It's not what it looked like," said Belle softly. "I know this is going to sound crazy, but he's been hitting on me! And, I don't know, I guess I like the attention, but nothing has happened, I swear. I wouldn't cheat on Jeff, though sometimes I fantasize about it." Frost believed Belle.

"I guess . . ." said Frost, knowing now wasn't the time to deploy the Miranda line but unable to resist, "you're just not that into *him*." No one laughed. Frost felt like they were all going slightly insane.

"Ay, ay, ay," said Sofia with a whistle. "Don't worry, Belle. This will stay between us. I'm very good at keeping secrets." Sofia then gave Morgan a long, hard glare, confusing Frost even more.

The *Friends* theme song came on again, blasting its insipid melody into Ozzie Cain's room. The four women stood there, staring at each other suspiciously, their expensive costumes deflated and stained.

A Note from the Host, Clara Cain

Dear cherished Atherton community,

Neil and I wanted to send a quick note to say a warm thank-you for coming to our Friendsgiving theme party last night. We hope you enjoyed your time at Central Perk! We know there was some groaning about the "friendship exercise," and we want to apologize to anyone who found it to be at all awkward. That certainly wasn't our intention! We so value the bonds that our amazing school creates and fosters, and we hope last night gave everyone the opportunity to expand their circles and talk to someone new and interesting. Remember: we'll be there for you when the rain starts to pour. Wink, wink. See you all soon.

All our best,
The Cains

Not one person had replied to Clara Cain's thank-you email yet. Did everyone hate her? She knew she was an unpopular mom, just like she'd been an unpopular kid. Were some people destined to go through life that way? Clara had been the smartest girl in her grade, in her whole town, really, a small suburb outside of Cleveland called Bay Village. She'd gone from there to Harvard and then to Harvard Law, brainy, hardworking, always the first to raise her hand in class.

She'd met Neil when they were both associates at Cravath. He was still there, a litigation partner, and Clara had gone out on her own, smartly seeing the hole in the market for a female lawyer to represent the Harvey Weinstein types. A woman by their side helped make the man palatable, though she knew that what she did turned the other Atherton mothers off. But she was a *lawyer*. She wasn't endorsing her clients' behavior. Didn't people get that?

Clara was a beast at work. She felt no moral ambiguity. Everyone had the right to an attorney, and she'd defend her clients to the best of her ability. She didn't care if they'd sexually harassed someone; that wasn't her problem. She felt no insecurity in front a judge or jury, and always had confidence that what she was saying was the right thing at the right time. It was the opposite of how she felt around the moms at school, like she was constantly putting her foot in her mouth, saying the dumb thing, the embarrassing thing. Talking too much about how she was constantly working. Revealing things when she shouldn't and withholding information at the wrong time. It painfully transported her back to her childhood, when she was teased for being a know-it-all, a kiss ass, a try-hard loser. "Clara the cunt," the popular girls used to chant as Clara crept through the halls of high school.

Well, she may be a cunt, but she knew a lot of shit about a lot of bad men, shit that could hurt people if it ever came out. She'd been confidentially approached by more than a handful of Atherton dads seeking legal advice. Bud Cunningham called her some years ago to discuss how his name was part of the Ashley Madison leak. Did he have legal recourse? (No, he didn't, but he was lucky enough to avoid getting caught; Trina had been so blissed-out on psychedelics that she completely missed that news cycle.) Dre Finlay's husband, Peter, had needed Clara's help after a young woman at work claimed he'd been sending her unwanted dick pics. (They'd reached a settlement without Dre finding out.) And now there was Art Chary, who'd recently given her a retainer. It turned out he was a cheater; Morgan didn't know. Or Art said she didn't know. But from Clara's experience, the wives often just looked the other way, not wanting to rock the boat of their privileged lives.

Art had been fucking Tilly, the sound bath specialist from Thyme & Time (in which Welly was the main investor), and he'd heard rumblings from inside the company that people knew about it. Welly depended on Art's reputation as a do-gooder CEO, and he couldn't have that kind of situation on his hands—his shareholders would crucify him. Clara didn't judge, though the employer-employee power dynamic of it all did give her creeps. Her job made her grateful to be married to Neil, a lovable doofus who thought Clara was the best.

Art claimed that his dalliances were out of desperation. That Morgan was a sociopath, and that he was "scared" of her. When Clara asked him why they hadn't gotten a divorce, Art had said that he thought she might murder him if he asked, so instead had resorted to sex outside the marriage. He even said he'd fallen in love with another mom! Clara didn't believe him for a second. She knew Morgan was sweet and helpful and cheerful. She was nicer to Clara than almost any of the other moms.

Clara was sitting with Neil in their living room, which the party planners had reassembled perfectly this morning, hauling out all evidence of Central Perk. Neil was reading the *Times* and sniffling; he had a near constant postnasal drip. Ozzie was out at soccer. Clara cringed, remembering how she'd burst into tears last night in front of the queen bees, the result of her sucking down too many martinis on an empty stomach. And she'd also spilled the beans about King and Alfred and those deepfake nude photos of Hildy. Clara was the holder of so much confidential information at work; you could torture her, and she wouldn't reveal any seamy details about her clients. But when it came to mom-gossip, she just couldn't keep it inside. Those two things were likely related, but Clara didn't have time to go to therapy, unlike all the stay-at-home moms. (What did they talk to their therapists about? Clara often wondered. Their feelings of inadequacy at SoulCycle? Their filler-regret?)

Clara's phone buzzed. It was a message from Art. Shoot. She'd just wanted to have a relaxing Saturday morning. But work called.

Clara opened up the text and Neil blew his nose loudly. "Sorry, honey, it's just these goddamn allergies," he said. She smiled at him and then got up to go to her office. She needed to call Art Chary back.

# PART III

## Spring

# Chapter 11

# A Happy Headmaster!

Dr. Broker, call him Paul, used to love his job as headmaster at Atherton Academy. Leading up to this appointment, he'd held various positions at prestigious private schools (he'd graduated from Harvard with a master's in early education and also held doctoral degrees in English and comparative literature from Columbia University). His career was in his blood. Paul's father, Martin, now deceased, was the longtime head of school at Deerfield Academy in Massachusetts. His mother, Nancy, currently in an assisted living home, had been an American history teacher at Deerfield. Paul, an only child whose parents had him when they were well into their forties, had grown up on the famous prep school's campus, soaking in the idea that molding the country's best young minds was a mission comparable to religion.

And so landing the top job at Atherton, one of New York City's finest schools, was like ascending closer to God. The redbrick building with white columns, tall and strong, the long history of the Quaker tradition emanating from the impressive classrooms, the teachers with their Ivy League credentials—it all brought Paul a nearly orgasmic

amount of pleasure. And, yes, Atherton leaned Progressive (no let-
ter grades, no uniforms, a play-based curriculum until third grade),
compared to other Manhattan schools like Collegiate and Trinity. But
Paul appreciated that aspect of its character. It was one way he felt
he could differentiate his career from his father's—"the hippie-dippie
one," as Paul remembered his father referring to Atherton, years ago.
Anyway, Paul's young age, forty-one, would have precluded him from
the headmaster roles at most uptown schools. There was always time
for that. If he made his mark at Atherton, with its highly influential
community, the world would be his oyster.

For the past year, he'd been doing just that. Improving parent-
teacher communication, leading a record-breaking fundraising round
in order to complete the new school theater, forging partnerships
with downtown Manhattan cultural institutions such as the Whitney
and the revamped Ellis Island museum. He'd recruited star teachers
and specialists, and also implemented an updated Atherton code of
conduct for today's fraught political environment, with guidelines
about gender tolerance and neo-antisemitism and, most popularly
(among parents), a phone ban until eighth grade.

In short, he'd been killing it, and had been proud of the progress he'd achieved in so little time in his role. Both the students and
parents respected him, and he was exceptionally popular among the
mothers, no doubt because of his good looks and charm. Paul had
never denied the basic advantages his face and body gave him. Did
donors appreciate that he looked like a midbudget rom-com actor
instead of a dowdy principal? They did. Did he purposefully flirt
with the richest mothers to squeeze even more money out of them?
Sure. But that was part of his job, and he'd never crossed a line with
any of them. Until recently, that is. And now he'd crossed line after
line after line.

Paul lived close to school, in an Atherton-owned prewar two-bedroom near Gramercy Park. It was big and sunny and had been renovated right before he'd moved in, a demand he'd made before signing his contract of $800,000 a year, the going rate for head-masters at top private academies in the city. He was lounging on his couch, a formal number from Restoration Hardware—his taste ran traditional, leather chairs and Moroccan rugs, from years of living amid eighteenth-century architecture at Deerfield. He was reading the latest issue of the *New Yorker*, giving his brain a break from the academic journals and Atherton parent "communication."

Paul had known of the rabidity of New York City parents by rep-utation and had experienced similar, if lesser, amounts of intensity at his previous administration jobs. But nothing could have pre-pared him for the pure onslaught of craziness he'd encountered at Atherton: the pestering, the competitiveness, the attention-seeking, the attempts at bribery! Parents emailed him directly, morning till midnight, sometimes, he suspected, drunk or high, asking all sorts of inappropriate questions and making ludicrous demands.

Leo handed a paper in late, and Mr. Chin docked his grade. This is preposterous. We were away, sailing in Greece with Barry Diller. How was Leo supposed to hand it in on time?

We think Charles isn't being challenged enough in his kindergarten class. Can he take math with the fourth graders?

Alexia is having an issue with Jemina, something about not liking Jemina's breathing patterns, so I'm asking that they be separated in science.

We'd really love for Marc to be in Mrs. Rolf's class next
year, we've heard such great things. We've also heard
you're a baseball fan. Jason has box seats to the Yankees
that he'd happily give you, even a playoff game! We really
can't wait for Marc to have Mrs. Rolf. ☺

These people, Paul supposed, had never heard the word "no."
At least at Groton and Phillips Academy, there had been an iota of
respect for the educators' opinions, a semblance of "teacher knows
best" that Paul hadn't found—at all—at Atherton. He'd thought
that, maybe, because Atherton was downtown, and the families
didn't all hail from financial fortunes, that the vibe would be a little more . . . low-key. He'd thought wrong. Creative money, tech
money, generational wealth. It was just money all the same. And
some New Yorkers had too much of it, while others, Paul knew,
didn't have any at all.

His phone rang, startling Paul from his *New Yorker*, his doorman
calling up.

"You have a guest, Dr. Broker. A woman."

"Yes, send her up, John. Thanks."

Paul was surprised, but not unhappily. He straightened the pillows on the couch and cleared the coffee table of his snacks. He
went into his kitchen, which was eat-in, with a small breakfast nook
and high-end appliances, including a Viking stove, which he'd never
turned on. There he opened a bottle of expensive cabernet that the
Finlays, who owned a vineyard in Napa, had given him a case of as a
Christmas present. There was a knock, and he went into his entry-
way, feeling himself harden into an erection as he did.

He opened the door to see Morgan Chary, sheathed tightly in
exercise clothing. She pushed in past him, grabbing his hand, pull-

ing him onto the couch, its width nearly that of a full-size bed, so that they were facing each other, prostrate, like two mummies in a tomb.

Morgan reached into Paul's sweatpants, firmly massaging his hard penis with one hand, the other carefully putting pressure on his balls, squeezing rhythmically, as if to some unheard musical beat. They locked eyes.

"Do it now," said Morgan commandingly. Just her words made Paul want to finish, but he resisted. Then he reached over to Morgan's delicate neck, warm and soft. He could feel her tendons underneath, her pulse beating fast. He wrapped his fingers around, locking them at the base of her hair. And then he started to squeeze. Softly at first, just a bit of pressure.

"More," she said. And he squeezed harder, then harder still, to the point that he could feel her windpipe starting to cave, dangerously.

He finally felt her pinch the top of his thigh, their signal that it was over for now. He let go, and as he did, semen gushed into his sweatpants, seeping out, dripping onto the RH cushion, which he'd make sure to send off to the dry cleaner. Paul was nothing if not tidy.

Morgan sat up and patted the space next to her, a signal for him to join, as if he were a child. There was a red ring around her neck where his hands had been, but other than that no indication that Morgan had been very close to dying a few moments before. Maybe that was an exaggeration. She'd been close to passing out, not dying. Paul comforted himself with this thought. He scooched in next to Morgan, nuzzling his face in her tender skin, which smelled of a perfume that reminded him of his mother. She rubbed his head, massaging his scalp. He whimpered in pleasure.

Paul had met Morgan right when he'd started at Atherton. They'd spoken at a welcome-back cocktail reception on one of the first days of school, held in the old auditorium, which had been converted into a grand banquet hall for such occasions. The parents were eager to get his attention; the new, impossibly handsome headmaster of Atherton Academy! He'd succeeded the famous Dr. T. Summers, who'd been at the school for two decades, and who'd led the search that had resulted in Paul's winning of the job. (Terry Summers had been good friends with Paul's father—academia was just as susceptible to nepotism as any industry, and Paul, as in many aspects of his life, leaned in to the advantages he was lucky enough to be born with.)

Paul had been standing in a corner of the room, receiving family after family, as if he were getting married, his head starting to hurt from the constant speaking, smiling, and the mental energy of trying to remember everyone's names. Morgan and her husband, Art, had sidled up to him, a tall, good-looking Indian man and a wife who, on first glance, looked like so many of the others: thin, polished, with blond highlighted hair and expensive jewelry. But there was something odd about this woman that Paul hadn't been able to place. She kept staring at Paul in a way that was both off-putting and alluring, like she *knew* things about him. But how could she?

"I'm Art Chary and this is my wife, Morgan," the man had said. He had a deep, smooth voice, a shiny smile, great eye contact. Art Chary, Paul knew, was a cofounder of Welly. Paul had committed the richest and most powerful of the Atherton parents to memory, and the Charys were high on the list.

"I'm going to go grab a drink, but I know Morgan would love to chat. She's very active on the PA, and I'm sure will have many questions for you! Morgan knows everything and everyone." He'd given Paul a firm handshake and walked off, leaving Paul with Morgan, who'd stepped very close to Paul in her husband's absence.

"I feel like I know you," she'd said in a voice so low that Paul could hardly hear her. He'd shaken his head, trying to act normally, but had felt a chill run up his spine.

"Either way," she'd continued, her voice morphing into that of any overbearing mother, and Paul had met a million of them, "our daughter, Gertrude, is a shy one. She's in Mrs. Victoria's class, and I think there are some children who might be acting cruel to her." Paul had nodded with care, his signature move, and she'd gone on in that way.

Their interactions over the next few months had been more of the same. There was PA business to discuss, and also Morgan's regular emails regarding Gertrude. Paul had spoken to Gertrude's teachers about the situation, but nothing had ever come of it—Mrs. Victoria strenuously denied that anything was happening to Gertrude on her watch, and Paul had no choice but to believe her.

Then one day, last spring, everything between them changed. It hadn't been Paul's fault. Well, it wasn't like she'd forced him to do anything. But still . . . Paul hadn't been looking to have an affair with a mother. Paul, with his impressive job and kind eyes and perfect hair, didn't need to resort to that for sex. Besides, Morgan wasn't even Paul's type. Paul liked zaftig brunettes, with curves and meat on their bones and large eyes and soft hair, women more like Sofia Perez. Morgan was as taut as a guitar string.

He'd been sitting in his fourth-floor office at school, in between meetings, and heard a light knock on the door. Alice had been out at an appointment—she was in her late sixties, close to retirement, and was recovering from knee replacement surgery. Two times a week, she left for an hour in the middle of the day to go to physical therapy. Anyone familiar with his schedule would have known that.

"Come in," he'd said, thinking it was likely one of the teachers with a quick question. Instead, Morgan Chary had entered, shutting the door behind her. She'd smiled at him and then, before he'd had the chance to say anything, come around to his side of the desk. She was wearing black leggings and a cropped sweatshirt, which was riding up to expose her flat, pale, nearly concave stomach.

"Uh, Mrs. Chary, what can I do for you?" Paul had said. She'd kneeled next to his chair, her chin perched on its arm, as if expecting him to plop a dog treat into her mouth. Had she lost her mind? Then she'd taken his hands in hers and placed them around her neck. Paul, who'd been on the verge of calling the police to report a crazy mother, had immediately gotten hard. Morgan had looked down at his pants with amusement. "There you are, Mr. Squeezy," she'd said teasingly.

Like everyone else at this school, Paul had a secret. His was an uncontrollable penchant for erotic asphyxiation. In simpler terms, he liked to choke women during sex. It was something he'd discovered about himself gradually. In his twenties, he had a girlfriend who'd been into rough foreplay. She liked when he'd held her arms down, pulled her hair, bit her hard. He'd found himself extremely turned on by these acts, thinking about them constantly. He'd started to fantasize about doing . . . more. But when he'd touched her neck while they were in the throes, she'd balked. "What is *wrong* with you?" she'd said, sitting up in bed, naked and scared. He'd been so ashamed that he'd buried the impulse for years, satisfying himself with standard lovemaking in real life and strangulation porn online. He'd created a digital alter ego—Mr. Squeezy—to discuss the ins and outs of erotic choking on Reddit, plus as his log-on to OnlyFans, where he paid to watch women get choked by other men.

He didn't know what it said about him that this murderous act was his ultimate turn-on. He'd grown up in a pleasant, calm, intellectual household. Nothing to give hints that the good-looking, bright son might suffer from some sort of deviant kink. Over the past couple of years, he'd read the trend stories about choking during sex with interest. Women's magazines were now saying it was "normal" and that "everyone was doing it." Everyone *who*? Paul had often wondered. None of the women he fucked, that was for sure.

And somehow, Morgan had found out. He'd never figured out how. Morgan was *into* it. "Mr. Squeezy."

They'd started seeing each other regularly, mostly at Paul's apartment, and occasionally, thrillingly, in Paul's office when Alice was out. He'd installed a lock on the inside of his door, claiming his need for privacy, that he didn't want teachers and parents bursting in when he was trying to focus. Morgan would arrive when she wanted to, holding all the power in the relationship. It was always the same. They'd lie parallel to each other, on the couch, on the bed, on the floor of his office, and Morgan would initiate foreplay. When she was ready, he'd put his hands around her neck and squeeze, squeeze, squeeze, until she pinched his thigh. Then he'd orgasm.

Afterward, if the mood struck her, which wasn't that often, Morgan would hand him a small, egg-shaped vibrator that she kept in her bag. It was a happy pink, the color of Easter candy and babies' bows, and he'd turn it on and push it on her firmly, under her leggings and over her underwear, until she was warm, shaking, biting her lips, and done. Then she'd leave, sending Paul into a panic that she'd decide to never come back. The thought that she could take everything away made him itchy with anxiety.

Was he even attracted to Morgan? Not in the traditional sense, no. But he was obsessed with her, that was for sure. She'd given him something that no one else ever had, the license to be open about his darkest desires.

So, when she'd started occasionally for asking for things—Gertrude to be with a specific teacher the following year, his support on whatever PA initiative she was pushing—he'd obliged. It was never anything that was outrageous, particularly compared to the requests he got from other parents.

One day, toward the end of the school year, they were lying on the floor of his office after the act. Paul was on his back, looking up at the ceiling, completely relaxed. Morgan was next to him, massaging his hand with her own. He'd never met anyone like her. He was bewitched. He wondered if Art appreciated her as much as he did. They'd never discussed him.

"I have something else I need from you," she'd purred.

"Anything." He wondered if he could choke her one more time before she left. He had ten minutes until Alice returned and Morgan could sneak out before anyone noticed.

"There's a mom I know who needs to get her children into Atherton. Messy divorce. She lives in Miami but is moving to New York. It's a boy and a girl, nonentry grades, but they're a lovely family and, well, you know I wouldn't ask if I didn't need it."

Paul continued to stare up instead of looking at her. He didn't answer for a moment. That would be breaking all the rules. He didn't even know if it was possible. His head of admissions at Atherton took her job very seriously, and spots in nonentry grades were extremely limited and generally went to enormous donors.

"I don't know, Morgan . . ." said Paul slowly. He wanted to help her, he really did. But this was a big one. People would start asking questions.

"Do we have a few minutes? Do you want to have another round?" she'd asked sweetly, changing the topic. Paul silently vowed to do everything he could to get this woman from Miami's children into Atherton. He couldn't let Morgan down.

And he hadn't. He'd contacted Sofia Perez out of the blue, telling her a friend had suggested he get in touch, that the best place for a family like hers was Atherton. He could get her two spots, he said, not letting her interrupt or ask questions. He knew she'd accept. They were the hottest school in Manhattan.

Then, soon after, Morgan had asked him to seduce Belle Redness. She didn't tell him why. Morgan never told him anything. It was killing Paul that he'd been unable to get Belle to relent. He knew she wanted him, but she refused to give in. It was unexpectedly admirable, he supposed. Maybe she just really loved her husband, who Paul had always thought was a bit of a twerp. Atherton was full of surprises.

Morgan was still rubbing his head. He stifled a cough; he'd been fighting something off these past few months, feeling tired and weak, though perhaps it was just stress. He stood up.

"Would you like a glass of wine? I opened a bottle from the Finlays' vineyard."

She shook her head. She didn't drink, but he always offered her something anyway. She was a woman of few appetites. He'd have a glass alone after she left.

"I'll make you a special tea," she said to him. Morgan always carried expensive tea bags with her, and she'd often make him a calming cup after they'd finished. She went into his kitchen, and a few minutes later the kettle whistled.

"Listen, I know that everything is getting . . . complicated," said Morgan as she came back to the living room, handing him an Atherton mug. Paul pursed his lips, blowing on the hot liquid before taking a sip. He'd thought many times over the past few months about untangling himself from Morgan. If they were somehow discovered, it would mean the end of his career. What if someone saw her walking out of his building? What if Alice came back early from an appointment? What a field day the *New York Post* would have the story—DR. BROKER IS A CHOKER: HEAD OF TONY ATHERTON ACADEMY CAUGHT GETTING KINKY WITH CLASS MOM. Paul couldn't let that happen. He had to get out of this. But he didn't want to. He couldn't.

"I know you're doing your best with Belle, and I think we have enough, for now. You can also drop trying to get Sofia to do the Altruist ceremony. It's almost over," said Morgan, pulling her turtleneck sweater back on, concealing the imprints of Paul's fingers. "I promise."

# iMessage Text

### Belle Redness, Frost Trevor

**Frost Trevor**

I wanted to say hi and sorry. I should have told you sooner about the pictures, but I honestly thought that it was better if you didn't know. I regret you finding out from Clara Cain, of all people. I deserved the drink in the face! It was pretty refreshing. ☺

   PS we never have to speak about you-know-who again. I believed what you said about him. Anyway, can we please make up? You have to come to my opening tonight. I need you there!

**Belle Redness**

You should have told me. That is my DAUGHTER. And I had to tell her about it, because I didn't want her hearing from anyone but me. She's already getting teased about lice, and now she hears this? It's not great.

**Frost Trevor**

Poor Hildy, I'm so sorry. Is she okay?

**Belle Redness**

She'll be fine. She knows they were fake, so it's not like it was *her*. But she doesn't know who would do that. I'm convinced it was the same person who sent me the flowers! Though there was one person Hildy mentioned . . .

**Frost Trevor**

Who? Ozzie Cain, that little shit?

**Belle Redness**

Weirdly, she said Gertrude.

**Frost Trevor**

Gertrude??? Hmmmm. Now that you mention it, the boys recently said that
Gertrude was an oddball.

**Belle Redness**

Anyway, Hildy seems intent on ignoring the situation, so I'm going to let her
do that. PS what do you think Sofia was going to tell us when you-know-
who came out of the closet? I wonder sometimes what Sofia is hiding.
Maybe she's the one who's been ruining our lives?

**Frost Trevor**

Sofia? Why would Sofia want to ruin our lives? She's our friend.

**Belle Redness**

I don't know, ask Morgan, she's so suspicious of Sofia. She told me something about her divorce, that she needs money or something . . . Has she
ever told you?

**Frost Trevor**

No, and I haven't asked. But she has a nice apartment . . . And the kids go
to Atherton. I can just ask her. We're close.

**Belle Redness**

Don't ask her! Then she'll know we were talking about it. Maybe we should
"Ask Morgan!" She always knows everything.

**Frost Trevor**

Fine, moving over to that chain.

# iMessage

*Belle Redness, Frost Trevor, Morgan Chary*

**Frost Trevor**

Morgan, Belle and I have a question.

**Morgan Chary**

Hiii!!! Have you two made up??? That's amazing! Frost, I can't wait for your opening tonight!

**Belle Redness**

Yes, we made up. We have a question about Sofia. What did you hear about the divorce? You said something to me but I'm blanking.

**Morgan Chary**

Weeeellll . . . You know I don't like to spread rumors!

**Belle Redness**

Oh, come on. Yes, you do.

**Morgan Chary**

She was cheating on her husband. He caught her, and then gave her basically nothing in the divorce. Like, destitute nothing. I heard he's paying for the apartment and school, but that Sofia has very little for herself. I also heard that there might be a custody play in the future, and that Sofia is desperate to make some money of her own to avoid losing her kids.

**Frost Trevor**

WHAT!?! Why would she lie to me? How do you know that?

**Morgan Chary**

A little birdie told me.

**Belle Redness**

So if she needs money . . . Do you think that's why she's friends with us?
Jeff has this theory that whoever is doing this weird shit to us is going
to come back with a request, like, "If you don't pay up, more and more
trauma's about to go down." It's like the ten plagues of Atherton, and she's
the angry God. Oh, shit, you know . . . she never does pay for anything. Have
you ever noticed that?

**Frost Trevor**

No, I don't believe Sofia would do that. She's a good person.

**Morgan Chary**

There's another thing I've been holding off on telling you both . . .

**Belle Redness**

**Morgan Chary**

When Frost was hit by the scooter, I got a quick glimpse of the guy who did
it, but I didn't recognize him. The other day, I was at Atherton when Sofia
dropped her kids off. When her driver came out to open the door to the car,
I could have sworn it was the same man. I'm like 99% sure.

**Frost Trevor**

Wait, you're saying that the guy who mowed me down with an e-scooter
is . . . Sofia's driver? No way. No way! *That's* the guy with the baseball hat?
The one I thought I saw at ZZ's?

**Morgan Chary**

Look him up on Facebook. Rodrick Beneto.


**Belle Redness**

THAT'S THE GUY THAT DELIVERED FLOWERS TO ME I'M LOOKING AT HIS FACEBOOK PAGE NOW. I'm calling you guys on a group FaceTime.


The three women's faces appeared as tiny tiles on their phones. Frost was in her apartment on Twenty-Second Street, surrounded by her collages. Belle was in her kitchen, a mug of coffee set down in front of her. And Morgan was walking through Central Park, wearing sunglasses to block out the glare, a tennis racket sticking up into the frame.

"Fuck. Fuck. Fuck," said Frost. "It's him. Should we call the police? I need to speak to Sofia. What if he's violent? He's driving around her children! Morgan, why didn't you tell us this sooner?"

"I wasn't sure!" said Morgan. "But then I saw him at drop-off, and it all came together. I'm nearly positive he's also the one who robbed us at Thyme & Time."

"But wait," interrupted Frost. "I still don't get it. Sofia was going to blackmail us or something? So she had her driver harass us? That makes no sense."

"It was her idea to have everyone wear The Dresses . . ." said Belle, her doe eyes wide. "And why didn't she appear in the picture in the *Post* with you, Frost? Maybe she's a criminal mastermind! Frost, she's your best friend." Belle said this with some bitterness, which the other women picked up on.

"You guys are my best friends," said Frost, a bit too quickly.

"I don't think we should get the police involved yet," said

Morgan. "Let's keep talking about it. But right now, I have to get to my tennis lesson."

They nodded at her sage counsel and then hung up.

An email to Belle and Jeff Redness

Report from Greg Summerly, Private Detective
Hi folks,
Here's my final wrap-up for your records. I'm sorry I couldn't find out more. Please don't hesitate to contact me with questions.

On March 5, at 1:45 p.m., an unidentified man of indeterminate race rang up to Belle and Jeff Redness's penthouse apartment. Belle buzzed him up, thinking it was an Amazon delivery. During the elevator ride, the man switched his baseball hat out for a ski mask, handing Belle a package as the doors opened, and then traveling back down. Belle never saw the man's face. We have no evidence, as of this moment, that the man was Rodrick Beneto.

The package contained a bouquet of dead flowers, concealing nearly twenty live lanternflies, plus a note congratulating Belle on the launch of her new business, signed "a friend." No one involved in the incident recognized the handwriting. An analysis from a handwriting expert concluded that it was the work of an adult female.

According to the building's security video, the man accessed the lobby via the correct security code, which only residents of the building are supposed to know (admittedly, many residents, including the Rednesses, share the access code with friends for convenience's sake). Unfortunately, the man's face was never visible on camera. There was no surrounding security video available.

At the time of the incident, Belle was with her friend Frost Trevor, her daughter, Hildy Redness, and the family housekeeper, Ivanna Boyko. After the perpetrator exited the building, Sofia Perez, a family friend, entered the lobby—she said the door was propped open, and video footage confirms this. She wasn't buzzed up, but rather input the correct elevator code to reach Belle's apartment, surprising the women when she arrived.

To summarize: In my professional opinion, this was a prank orchestrated by someone with a vendetta against Belle Redness. Earlier this year, an email that Belle privately sent to Atherton's nurse was leaked school-wide, and in it Belle named a few women in a negative context, including Dre Finlay, Julie Klein, Gemma Corder, and Becky Oranga. It's possible that one or a group of these mothers were behind the incident as revenge. None of them consented to an interview.

It is my professional opinion that neither Frost Trevor nor Ivanna Boyko had anything to do with the incident.

Belle and Jeff Redness also have expressed concern that there is a connection here to Frost Trevor's scooter accident and/or to an incident in which samples of Belle Redness's dress line caused skin rashes, among other, recent, inexplicable occurrences.

After review, the only commonality between any of these events is Sofia Perez.

Thank you for your business.

Best,
Greg Summerly

Greg Summerly, private detective, was not Greg Summerly, private detective. There was a real Greg Summerly, private detective. He lived somewhere in Florida and had a small, picture-less online presence, enough so that if you googled the name, you'd think that these two men were one and the same. But they weren't.

This Greg Summerly was in fact Jed Goggins, an out-of-work actor, who'd been approached by an anonymous employer on Task-Rabbit, where he'd listed himself as an aspiring thespian/handyman for hire. An inquiry had come in for some kitchen cabinet installation. He'd replied that he was available and had gotten this response: "Are you up for more? Maybe something risky that taps into your acting skills? I pay well, let me know."

Jed was up for whatever. He'd moved to New York right before the pandemic, with a BFA in acting from the University of Minnesota, hoping to make it Off Broadway, or Off-Off, or maybe even get a walk-on role on *Law & Order*. But when he'd arrived, he'd realized that his chances of any of this were basically zero. Less than zero. He had a couple auditions before the world shut down in 2020, and had been scraping by on odd jobs since, as a handyman, as a "man with a van," as a dog walker on the Upper East Side. Anything to pay his rent, which was $700 a month (he shared an apartment in Astoria with two other guys his age). He'd given up on acting but didn't have an alternate plan. He was stuck, broke, and finally about to move back to Minnesota, into his parents' house, to work with his dad, a local contractor, which he felt was a fate close to dying a painful, sad death.

The TaskRabbit emailer had offered him $30,000, in cash, to impersonate a private detective. It involved meeting with a few wealthy people, listening to their complaints, and then going his merry way. That was literally it. For $30,000! For that amount, he'd be able to stay in New York for another year, at least. Maybe he'd be able to get into Actors' Equity. Maybe, with that runway, something might finally open up.

So he'd ridden up in private elevators, to enormous, fully decorated places that someone like Jed thought only existed in magazines. People actually lived like this! Jed couldn't believe it until he saw it with own eyes. Even the cats looked rich. The families had maids, or "housekeepers," as they called them, and patterned wallpaper in their bathrooms, and art that probably cost more than Jed's parents' house.

And they wanted Jed's, er, Greg's help. They were desperate for it. Strange shit was happening to them—accidents, email breaches, other stuff that Jed didn't even really understand—and they were counting on this Greg Summerly person to figure it all out. Sometimes, Jed felt guilty about it, but then he'd set himself straight: he wasn't a bad guy, he just needed cash, and these people had loads of it. This was just some kind of game to them, like a grown-up, twisted version of Life, and Jed was happy to play his part for a price. He was an actor, after all.

So Jed had asked questions, furrowed his brow when needed, wrote details in a notebook, pretending, pretending. The role of his life! Sometimes their kids would walk in, demanding this or that, speaking to their parents as peers, which blew Jed's mind. He'd laugh to himself comparing these "moms" to his mom, who'd worked as a manager at Home Depot while also making sure there was dinner on the table and the homework was done and that Jed and his brother got to hockey practice on time at 5:30 a.m.

Jed had no clue who his employer was; they communicated via TaskRabbit only. For all Jed knew, he or she was one of the people he'd spoken with, using him as a cover. There was one woman, the one who looked like a Latin movie star, who seemed different from the rest. Speaking to her was the only time he'd felt an iota of regret. She resembled them, but she wasn't of them. It made Jed feel bad, tricking someone like that. But this wasn't a long-term gig. He'd go back to dog walking soon. Picking up shit on the sidewalk as these assholes passed him by without a second glance.

## Chapter 12

# An Exhibit Opening!

===

Sofia Perez was not a criminal mastermind. She was just a mother who'd been forced to move from her home, from her state, with all the uncertainly that comes with a messy divorce. She was trying to forge a life for herself, a life in which she didn't have to depend on her vindictive ex, JP, or worry about him trying to take her children away. And, so, yes, she'd become close to the women at Atherton for a reason other than companionship (though she did enjoy that part, particularly with Frost). But no, it wasn't so that she could *steal* their money, or somehow blackmail them into giving it to her (though she did have information which could help with that, too). She needed the mean moms on her side because she needed customers.

Because . . . Sofia Perez was about to become a travel agent! After a quick online course, she'd joined a company called Omni Travel group as a luxury travel adviser, specializing in Florida and the Caribbean. It wasn't a salaried job—she'd earn commission. For that reason, she'd done everything in her power to break into the Atherton world. She knew rich women well enough to know that once one of the moms hired her, the rest would follow, not wanting to be left out, or to be seen as doing the wrong thing. She could book trips for all of them. It was a perfect plan.

Sofia should have been feeling optimistic. But instead, she was fully freaked out. Because Sofia had seen something she knew she shouldn't have: Morgan Chary meeting with Sofia's driver, Rodrick, in City Hall Park, the night of Belle's pop-up party. The same guy who drove Sofia's children to school in the morning, the one whom JP paid to keep an eye on the family. Were Morgan and JP in cahoots somehow? What did Morgan want from Rodrick? He'd always been a bit of a jerk, but Sofia had chalked that up to his loyalty to JP.

Since then, Sofia had been following Morgan around every chance she got, trying to figure out how everything—or nothing—was related. She'd trailed Morgan to Whole Foods on Houston, to restaurants in Tribeca, to Thyme & Time and Atherton and back again.

At first, nothing had struck Sofia as suspicious (beyond the number of Tracy Anderson classes Morgan took). But then, yesterday, at around 4:30 p.m, Morgan had left her town house on Grove Street and walked east. She'd made her way across Washington Square Park as Sofia hung about a block behind, stopping every now and then to make sure Morgan couldn't catch sight of her. Sofia had thought Morgan might be heading toward Atherton, for yet another PA something-or-other. Instead, she'd turned on Third Avenue and kept walking uptown until she'd reached Twenty-First Street, turning left and then stopping in front of a pretty prewar doorman building. Morgan disappeared inside and Sofia hadn't waited for her to come out. She'd texted herself the address and then hurried away, grateful she hadn't been caught.

Later that night, after the kids were asleep, she'd googled the building, turning up the usual StreetEasy listings (a $4.5 million three-bedroom; a $2 million one-bedroom bargain). Lower down she'd found an article about the building on Curbed, a New York City real estate website. The story was focused on the sale of one specific apartment, but buried in the text Sofia found an illuminating aside—"The building is also home to artists and musicians, as well as an apartment owned by the prestigious Atherton Academy, which is used as the residence (and quite a perk!) for its headmaster."

An Atherton apartment! So Morgan had been visiting Dr. Broker. Rodrick, Dr. Broker . . . Morgan was up to something fishy, and Sofia was determined to figure out what.

"You will encounter evil." The psychic's words followed Sofia as she arrived at Frost's art exhibit opening. It was on the far West Side, on Twenty-Seventh Street and Tenth Avenue, the location of the old Bungalow 8. Sofia had taken the C train up from Tribeca, as she couldn't afford an Uber and there was no way in hell she was asking Rodrick, of all people, to take her anywhere.

Sofia entered the low, squat brown building. It looked nearly derelict, but Sofia knew that was all part of the show. IT GIRLS, BY FROST TREVOR read a small sign welcoming Sofia in. She opened the heavy door, keen to get out of the drizzle, to see the old club converted into a chic exhibition space. Frost's collages hung in zigzags along the exposed brick walls, the faces illuminated by track lighting, giving each an otherworldly appearance. Sofia had arrived early for moral support, and there was already a smattering of attendees inside, sipping champagne and admiring the collection.

Sofia spied Frost in the center of the small group, in a stunning teal silk jumpsuit, her red hair spraying out in wild waves. Her eyes were lined in black; her lipstick like blood. Sofia had never seen her look as beautiful as she did at that moment.

Sofia grabbed a champagne from a nearby tray and walked through the exhibit, stopping in front of each collage and studying her friend's work. Young women, most of whom Sofia didn't recognize, posing in old, blown-up photographs that Frost had decorated with seemingly random objects. A dirty shoe glued on. Some paint streaks here and there. Pictures from a fashion magazine sewn into the scenes. Sofia didn't understand any of it, but she murmured appreciatively anyway.

A couple whom Sofia didn't recognize walked past, the man with an oversize monocle hanging from a chain attached to his suit, the woman makeup-less other than sparkly bright blue lipstick.

"This feels very now," said the woman to the man. "We're past MeToo, beyond the gender wars, in the second Trump administration, flying by the fifth—sixth?—wave of feminism. She's commenting here on all of it." The man nodded solemnly.

"The portraits draw me in, but then the objects repel me. It's that push and pull that she's captured brilliantly." He spoke in a loud whisper that Sofia understood was meant to be heard. The duo floated past, and Sofia spied Frost momentarily alone, looking overwhelmed. Sofia hurried over to her, heels clacking on the stone floor, embracing Frost in a warm hug. Frost smelled like Blush by Marc Jacobs, her signature scent.

"This is so wonderful, Frost, really," said Sofia. "You are so talented! I can't believe it. A true artist." Frost beamed before pulling away abruptly.

"I have to speak to you about something." Frost's voice was urgent. "It's important. Morgan and Belle think you've been up to something. That *you're* behind what's been happening at Atherton. You can't tell them I told you."

"Me? I haven't done anything at all!" said Sofia, flabbergasted.

"Sofia, I . . . I saw you," said Frost, eyes downcast. Sofia's heart fluttered but she tried to keep her composure.

"Saw me doing what?" she said.

"I saw you following Morgan. The other day. Near Morgan's house. I was in that neighborhood running errands, and I saw Morgan walking alone on the other side of the street. I tried to call hello, but she couldn't hear me. A few seconds later, I saw you walking behind her, all incognito in black. I know you never wear black! What were you doing? Did you have anything to do with the lanternflies? With the *Post* article? Sofia, you have to tell me the truth. Belle and Morgan—"

Before Frost could continue, Gabby and Ava arrived in front of them, connected at the hip as usual, Gabby in a smart pinstripe suit and Ava in a black minidress. Frick and Frack, as Sofia thought of them.

"Frost, so, so, fab," said Ava, taking out her phone and doing a quick spin around of video. "Here's the amazing artist herself!" she said, pointing her camera at Frost, who smiled and did a little bow. Ava put the phone back into her teeny tiny bag, which reminded Sofia of one of Lucia's doll accessories. "I'll post that tonight," she said. "People are going to go mad for this. Former It Girl and her It Girl art show, I love it soooo much. Are the boys here to celebrate with you?"

"No, they're at a lacrosse tournament upstate, which is a shame," said Frost. "But hopefully this won't be my last opening!"

"Dude, I have to hand it to you," said Gabby. "No offense, but I always thought you were, like, beautiful and cool and that's it. But it turns out you have talent, too. I especially love the Chloë Sevigny portrait. What a babe." Frost's face went from flushed to cherry.

"Thanks so much, guys!" said Frost, nearly bursting with excitement. She looked around the room and gave Tim, standing alone near the drinks station, a quick wave. He waved back, and then did a nerdy thumbs-up. When they'd first met, Sofia had sensed a pall over Frost that had since lifted. She didn't know what had happened with Art, but it seemed Frost was moving on with her life in a healthy way.

Frost then got swept away into the crowd, shaking hands and receiving congratulations. Sofia saw several Atherton moms in a group off to the side, plus some society types whom she recognized to be Frost's former friends-about-town. Ethel Zeigler was at the other end of the space, showing off Frost's work to potential collectors.

Belle then walked into the exhibit in a floral dress, her hair clipped back into a long braid. She was followed by Morgan, in a trench coat, its collar popped. Sofia followed Morgan's and Belle's laser-beam gazes as they both focused on the same person at the same time: Dr. Broker, who'd somehow slipped in without Sofia noticing. Sofia remembered what it felt like to see Michael and wondered if either Belle or Morgan ached for Dr. Broker the way Sofia had for Michael.

Sofia had to gather her thoughts in light of what Frost had just told her. She walked to the bathroom, into a hallway of stalls separated by wooden slats, each more run-down than the next. She picked the cleanest option and went inside, locking the door. She sat down on the closed toilet with a sigh. Morgan and Belle thought *Sofia* was out to get them? She most certainly was not. These women were the crazy ones! Lying to each other, competitive beyond belief, screwing each other's husbands, their kids torturing one another. Sofia had never experienced anything like it. It made her miss the mom-drama of Miami, where the fighting revolved around whose son was better at soccer and whose husband bought them more diamonds.

The bathroom barriers were thin, and there was a rustling in the stall next to her. Yuck. She really should try to find Frost—she needed to explain why she'd been trailing Morgan. She got up to leave but heard voices. She paused to listen.

"Morgan," a man hissed. "There's no one else in here. Open up. Now."

Sofia pressed close to the splintered wood, noticing a small gap between the slats. She pushed into it and was able to see into the stall. There was Morgan. She unlocked the door and Dr. Broker entered. He went to Morgan without saying anything, pulling down the collar of her coat to reveal her skin, which was covered in light bruises. Dr. Broker then quickly kissed the hollow of Morgan's throat before placing his hands around Morgan's neck, pushing his fingers in and squeezing. Sofia had to put her hand over her mouth to prevent herself from shrieking. "Harder," Morgan croaked. "Harder." Dr. Broker moaned lightly. He continued to choke Morgan for what felt like an eternity. Sofia couldn't believe what she was seeing. Morgan finally pinched Dr. Broker's leg, clearly some kind of sign for him to stop, as he let go of her immediately.

Morgan then bent over, catching her breath, while Dr. Broker grabbed a wad of toilet paper to clean himself off. Then he looked in the mirror, fixing his hair. Sofia took that moment to step out of her stall, racing to the end of the hallway, tucking herself into a corner, unseen by anyone exiting the bathroom area.

Dr. Broker strolled by, licking his lips. Soon after, Morgan followed, glancing left and right, pulling her coat back up higher on her neck. Sofia took the opportunity to saunter over, purposely bumping into Morgan from behind.

"*Hola*," said Sofia casually. Morgan turned around to see who it was, annoyed.

"Hi, hi, you look amazing," said Morgan, semicordially.

"Did you see that Dr. Broker is here? He's such a lovely man. So gentle and caring," Sofia said, emphasizing the word "gentle." Morgan narrowed her eyes. If Morgan was out to possibly screw over Sofia, Sofia wouldn't take it lying down. She might not be wealthy anymore, but she was scrappier than any of these soft, privileged women. And she had ammo.

"No, I haven't yet," said Morgan. Sofia blinked a few times, gearing up for her next move.

"I forgot to mention, I saw you after Belle's press event," said Sofia. Morgan sucked in her cheeks but didn't say anything.

"You were meeting with some guy near City Hall. I was going to come say hi, but you seemed to be having a very intense conversation."

At that, the lights in the venue went out, sheathing them in complete darkness, confused murmurs rising from the partygoers. Sofia felt her way to a wall, leaning against it for stability, wondering what on earth was about to go down.

"It's okay, probably just an outage," someone half yelled over the noise. Someone else had opened the door, letting in the damp, spring-y air, but basically no light. Sofia could see a few people streaming out of the exhibit, but she felt bad ditching Frost like that; she must be in a total panic. Sofia felt the whoosh of someone running past, their sneakers padding on the floor. Then a strange, chemical smell hit her nose. She stood very still, trying to get her eyes to adjust. A few tense minutes passed, in which Sofia could only hear concerned murmuring, someone sneezing, a phone ringing, someone fumbling in a bag, trying to pick it up. Then the lights went back on. She could hear grunts of relief before noticing flyers stuck to the walls, on and among the artwork, not unlike those papers plastered to the pedestrian signal poles around the city. But instead of political statements and missing dogs, this one was an image of a naked woman kneeling on a bed, touching herself, her red hair wild, her eyes half closed in ecstasy. Frost. It was Frost. The word CHEATER was emblazoned over the picture in black blocky letters.

Frost was in the middle of the room, spinning in a circle as she surveyed the damage. Tim was close to a wall, inspecting the pictures of his wife. Sofia saw Dr. Broker and Morgan slouching out of the exhibit, one after another. Then out of the melee arose a violent howl, not unlike something out of a horror film. It was so loud, so impossibly high-pitched, that Sofia momentarily covered her ears with her hands.

"My hair!" the person yelled. "My haaaairrrrrr!"

There was Belle, standing in the corner, holding something in both of her hands like it was a sacrifice to the gods. On first glance, Sofia thought it might be a snake—might as well be, the world was basically ending. But as she walked toward Belle, thinking only of how she could help her friend, she realized that it wasn't a reptile at all. It was a braid. It was Belle's braid. And someone had cut it off. "You!" roared Belle accusingly, staring at Sofia, who'd frozen in place.

Terrified, Sofia turned around and fled into the rainy New York City night, the downpour drenching her as she walked down Tenth Avenue toward home. She thought of Michael, and of Carlos and Lucia, and of how she got into this mess in the first place. The picture of Frost, naked, posing for a man who was clearly not her husband, stuck in Sofia's mind. Belle, violated, holding her precious hair in her own two hands. For the first time since moving to

New York, Sofia was deeply, miserably homesick. She pulled out her phone and texted Frost.

Mi amor, I am so sorry about your beautiful artwork and about everything. I have so much news to share with you, if you'd like to know the truth. Tu amiga, Sofia. Sofia saw the three dots wiggling, so she knew Frost had read her message. But then she didn't respond.

Sofia, newly licensed luxury travel adviser, kept walking, too drained and soaked to find anyone to follow.

# WhatsApp Chat
## Atherton Lower School Moms
### 94 Participants

**Dre Finlay**

Good morning, good morning! As we near the end of the school year, I'd like to send out a few reminders about Atherton's schedule. First, the annual play, "Friends Forever"—which has gender-neutral casting and costumes—will take place on Thursday, May 6, at 5:00 p.m. Remember: Filming is *not* allowed. The school will send the produced video after the fact. That's real, folks: If you try to take a video, you'll be escorted out by Mac from the security team. Can't wait for the show! It's always so cute. And second, please RSVP to the Surrealist Ball benefit if you haven't! The caterers need final numbers.

**Jennifer Smyth**

What's a gender-neutral costume?

**Gabby Mahler**

You know, like Ken, beneath his underwear. ☺

**Armena Justice**

It just means anything in a primary color, pants and shirts, no dresses or suits and ties.

**Jennifer Smyth**

Honestly, that's so sad. Little Jordy has the most adorable tie that we were planning to send him in.

**Armena Justice**

I'm sure the tie is just precious, but costumes are gender-neutral so as not to offend any child who feels between genders.

**Jennifer Smyth**

Not to get all culture wars on you, Armena, but that's insane.

**Armena Justice**

Take it up with Dr. Broker! It's not my rule!

**Kim Berns**

Hi, ladies! I'm somehow still on this chat, all these months later. Can someone *please* take me off? Please! I'm begging you!

**Morgan Chary**

Reminder to place your order for Atherton beach bags and towels for the summer before May 15! Email me for more info.

**Jessica Hillton**

Also, a note from the PA: Don't forget to give to the Annual Atherton Fund before the end of the year. We have 78% participation from the lower school so far and are hoping to reach 100% before the last day of school, June 6.

**Valerie Greg**

Wait, I'm confused. What's the Atherton Fund? Is that different from Atherton Gives Back?

**Jessica Hillton**

Valerie, Atherton Gives Back directly benefits local charities, such as neighborhood food banks and homeless shelters. The Atherton Fund donations go to the school and its facilities, things like our new gyms and the eighth-grade trip to Paris.

Valerie Greg

I'm still confused. So what does our . . . tuition pay for?

Jessica Hillton

Everything else.

Valerie Greg

And we're supposed to give on top of that? And send our kids to sleepaway camp for $20,000 a pop? And Randall's Island Fucking Tennis Academy for $15,000? And goddamn Russian Math for $10,000 a semester? And also buy an Atherton beach bag?? No. Just no. NO.

Dre Finlay

Valerie, I'll offline with you. ☺

## Chapter 13

## A Coffee Catch-Up!

═══

The week after Frost's disastrous art show, Belle, Morgan, and Frost sat in Frost's colorful living room, on that funny pink couch of hers, sipping tea. Sofia had been so fully integrated into their daily lives that it felt strange to be without her. Like they were plotting something, which maybe they were.

Frost kicked it all off.

"So, guys . . ." She trailed off, adjusting her thoughts. Morgan picked up a cracker from a cheese board that Frost had set out and then put it back down again without taking a bite.

"I've had a very stressful, upsetting few days." Frost was on the verge of tears, her lips pursed and her eyelids red. "You, too, Belle, I know." Belle mournfully ran her hand through her new bob, which she'd had fixed up at by Jennifer Matos at Rita Hazan (Ask Morgan!). She felt naked without her hair, and still couldn't believe what had happened. After the lights had gone out, Belle had felt someone tug her braid. She'd tried to whirl around, confused, but the person who did it was quick: snip, snip, snip, and her hair—her *identity*—was gone, fallen to the dirty floor. Negative event cluster? No way. This was war.

"Tim is, um, well, we're just taking a little time apart," Frost said, her voice straining on "apart."

"We were doing so well before, but as you can imagine, the, er, picture of me was too much for him."

"Frost, I'm so sorry," said Morgan. "If you want to share anything with us about who the picture was taken by, we are all ears. No one is here to judge you."

Frost shook her head.

"There are no leads yet about who might have postered the walls and butchered Belle's lovely hair," Frost continued, her eyes starting to water. Ethel said Frost would recover, and that the collages could still eventually sell, but Ethel was putting her efforts on pause until the hoopla died down. It broke Frost's heart. "The security cameras weren't functioning properly," Frost said. "The property manager thinks they were tampered with."

"I saw him," said Morgan. She was in a high-necked green sweater, the color bringing out her blue eyes.

"Who?" said Belle, leaning in. Belle was in a lacy long-sleeved dress, not of her own design. She'd shut down the Pippins Cottage Home website the other day. Her hair had been the last straw. She was defeated.

"Rodrick. Sofia's driver. I saw him putting up the posters. I was waiting to tell you both until this meeting. It's Sofia. It's been Sofia all along. Maybe when Rodrick was working on the posters, *Sofia* cut off Belle's hair. Did either of you see her afterward?" Both women shook their heads.

Frost wasn't sure what to believe. She wanted to think that Sofia was incapable of hurting them in this way, but everything was pointing toward her being the one. Sofia hadn't explained why she'd been following Morgan, and while Frost wasn't about to share that little tidbit with the group, it cast so much doubt in Frost's mind.

Frost was still in shock about what had happened at her opening, all those months of toiling, of creating, only to be met with that humiliating end. Art's picture of her for all to see. She'd thought about reaching back out to Sofia, answering her cryptic text, but she'd just wanted to have a clear head. She needed some distance.

"This is the perfect opportunity to discuss our plan going forward," said Morgan.

"What would we *do*?" said Belle. Over this past year, Belle, particularly, had suffered. Behind her back, "pulling a Belle" had become the current Atherton shorthand for failing. Your kid blew it at a tennis match? He "pulled a Belle." You were the slowest in your spinning class that day? You "pulled a Belle." Other parents were delighting in the fact that "perfect" moms like Belle and Frost had been met with such blows. So much for "the bonds of Atherton's chosen community." The various WhatsApp channels were lighting up with schadenfreude. Moms snickering to each other about Belle's unwanted haircut. About Frost's sexy (adulterous!) pose. No Lingua Franca sweatshirt was going to get her out of that one.

"So it was Sofia behind those horrible bugs?" said Frost, in her own world, not really following.

"Lanternflies," Belle clarified, frowning. "Greg Summerly, the detective, mentioned that Sofia was the common denominator among, well, everything!"

"And the Hildy deepfakes? Sofia sent them to my son? And had someone hit me with a scooter? And rob us at Morgan's spa? No way," said Frost, an eyebrow raised. "I don't believe it."

"Yes!" said Belle. "Or, I don't know, maybe the scooter was just New York being New York. Those things are crazy dangerous."

"Sofia is a mother. She wouldn't do that to Hildy," said Frost. She was having a hard time wrapping her mind around these accusations. If Belle and Morgan were so sure, let them retaliate. Frost just wanted to mourn in peace and try to fix her marriage. Maybe she deserved this. She'd cheated, after all. She was guilty of that. Tim had been furious, livid, betrayed. He'd demanded a name and she'd refused. He said unless she told him who she'd slept with, he'd leave. And now he was gone. Staying in the Chelsea Hotel to get his thoughts in order, as he'd put it. And Frost was all alone and totally miserable.

The incident had sparked numerous newspaper articles, from the *Times* (FORMER IT GIRL'S EXHIBIT VANDALIZED) to the *Post* (FROST TREVOR'S ART SHOW DEFACED BY MIGRANT. SEE THE NUDIE PICTURES INSIDE!). The already on-edge Atherton crowd was flipping out. Frost had received a few texts from moms saying they were considering moving to Connecticut or Westchester. The city was "dangerous." Criminals were "everywhere." "No one is safe!"

Just then, Alfred and King came bounding in, bringing with them a buzzy twelve-year-old-boy energy.

"Mom, Mom, can we play Fortnite now, please? Flora's saying we can't," said King. He was tall and reedy, like Tim.

"Could you please say hi to my friends?" said Frost, smiling at them.

"Hi, Belle, hi, Morgan," said Alfred sweetly. He looked just like Frost, with a shock of red hair and sparkly brown eyes.

"No Fortnite. Sorry, guys. You know the rules. Now go down to the basement and play chess or practice piano. You have football uptown at three." The twins stuck out their tongues in protest but obediently left the room, lightly pushing each other and laughing on their way. Frost and Tim had told them that Tim was going on an extended set visit and would be back in a couple of weeks. The boys didn't know that their parents' marriage was in trouble, and Frost wanted to keep it that way.

"What if Sofia *drugged* you?" said Belle to Morgan. "And that's why you fainted after the accident?"

Morgan took a deep, thoughtful breath before answering.

"Oh my god. That's horrifying," she said. "But it could be."

Belle and Morgan went back and forth this way, riling each other up, more and more convinced that Sofia, their kind new friend, was a villain.

Frost wasn't having it, but she played along. She was too tired to fight, and some of what they were saying was convincing. Why was Sofia's driver following them around? Had he somehow found Art's picture of Frost? Leaked photos of Frost to the *Post*? None of it added up.

"We have to get her back," said Morgan, with a finality that Frost and Belle recognized, the same voice she used when she declared any goal—"We have to raise one hundred thousand dollars for the new auditorium"; "I have to run the marathon in under four hours."

"We want her gone, right?" continued Morgan. Belle nodded, though she looked a little unsure.

"But how would we do that?" said Belle.

"We're going to ruin her party," said Morgan. "Give her a taste of her own medicine. She'll be humiliated enough to slink back to Miami." Frost was suddenly scared for all of them. "I think," said Morgan, a gleam in her eye, "she might be crazy."

They disbanded with a plan, a plan that Frost thought was silly and juvenile and horrible all at the same time.

"If you guys want to do this, I won't stop you," said Frost as she held open her door for them to leave. "But I'm not going to actively participate."

"Oh, come on, Frost. It'll be fun," said Belle. Was Belle totally confident that Sofia had bad intentions? No. But Belle was also sick of being the butt of the joke at Atherton. She'd had enough of this year, enough of being thought of in the same breath as Clara Cain, a loser, an asshole; lice-y, bitchy Belle Redness. She hated her new hair. It was someone else's turn to go down.

"Remember, just avoid Sofia. It'll be easy—everyone's leaving for Memorial Day weekend, and she's probably going back to Miami," said Morgan. The elevator opened for them to leave, and Tim walked out of it. He looked a wreck, tired and weepy, and mumbled hello to Belle and Morgan, the doors closing on their embarrassed faces.

Frost glanced at her husband, whose mouth was twisted in pain.

"I'm sorry," she said, wrapping her arms around him. "I'm such a jerk."

"You are the worst," he said. He returned her hug, and she knew it was going to be fine. For now.

"Bad, bad people. I'm telling you," said Tim as he dug his thumbs into her tender neck. "Your friends are *bad*. I think they're rubbing off on you. Sofia is a good egg." Frost sank into the embrace of her husband. She didn't know who to trust.

## Chapter 14

## A Surrealist Ball!

━━

Morgan Chary always accomplished what she set out to do. At the start of each year, she'd write down her goals in her green leather Smythson Happiness journal. And so last January, after a satisfying meditation session ("I'm a monster on the hill; I'm a monster on the hill"), Morgan had taken one of her favorite pens, a ballpoint Montblanc, and handwritten the following list in her perfect cursive. She'd been sitting on her bed alone. Art had been out at a work thing. Or so he'd said.

1. Improve marathon time from 3:55 to under 3:45.
2. Find the best blueberry muffin recipe.
3. Take Gertrude on a mother-daughter trip, anywhere in the world she wants to go.
4. Finally learn how to play mah-jongg.
5. Carve out time for monthly date nights.
6. Ruin Frost Trevor's life.
7. Ruin Belle Redness's life.
8. Aim to read a book a week.

Yes, Morgan was going to ruin her best friends' lives. If that sounded a little dramatic, well, Morgan was an intense (and intensely cheerful!) person. When she was younger, she would play little vendetta games—a frenemy from gymnastics had mysteriously broken her leg on a faulty beam; a college acquaintance who'd made out with Morgan's boyfriend had been roofied, ending up asleep, naked, in the middle of the quad; a nutritionist competitor had lost her entire business after allegations of emotional abuse emerged on a Reddit thread.

Morgan was extremely good with details, and with covering them up, and she loved the internal satisfaction of quietly defeating her enemies, no one the wiser. From a young age, Morgan had understood that she *liked* hurting people, that she was different from her friends. She would lie for fun—creating elaborate stories for no reason, telling teachers things that were wildly untrue, crafting narratives to get what she wanted: better grades, money from her friends, attention from men, among other things. She loved to steal, even small amounts, sneaking into her friends' parents' wallets and taking a dollar or two when no one was looking.

She didn't understand "feeling bad" about something. Her friends always "felt bad." What did that mean? Her parents had been in denial, Morgan was sure, because they must have seen it in her. The family didn't get pets because her dad was "allergic." But really it was because they'd had a cat, Ollie, and her mom had caught Morgan systematically pulling off its whiskers, one by one. No more cats after that. Ollie was quietly euthanized.

After a while, Morgan had developed into, well, Morgan. She'd adopted that "amazing," "so cool," "love it" exterior as a shield. She took up gymnastics as a way to channel her rage. How could anyone suspect someone so nice of being so cruel?

No one knew this about her besides Art, and even he didn't know the full picture. (That romantic comedy scene of how they'd met? Morgan had orchestrated it, crashing into the bar on purpose, cutting her head to secure Art's attention. He had no idea.) Over the years, Art had witnessed little things here and there, bad, bizarre, darkly coincidental things happening to women whom Morgan disliked.

Art, insatiable, stupid Art, didn't think Morgan was aware of the extent to which he cheated on her, but Morgan knew everything. She knew about Julie Klein. She knew about Margo Mahler. She knew about the sound bath bimbo, Tilly. But Art was Gertrude's father, and Gertrude was Morgan's everything. She'd never do anything to hurt Gertrude. So Art was safe.

But Frost? Last spring, Morgan had put her nose to Art's discarded clothes only to smell the unmistakable stench of Blush by Marc Jacobs. It was Frost's favorite perfume; she stocked up on it on eBay, as it had been discontinued for years. How could Frost look Morgan in the eye? Frost wasn't like Morgan; she had a conscience, she had morals, she "felt bad." How could Frost spend time with Morgan and laugh and act as if she weren't turning around and fucking Morgan's husband? Frost with her red hair like guts and her dreams of being an artist and her useless husband, Tim, and her twins with their shaggy Gen Z hair. Morgan would kill her.

At the same time, Gertrude had started coming home, day after day, sobbing about how mean Miles Redness was to her. Pinching Gertrude's side when she wasn't looking. Whispering "fatty Chary" and "Girthy Gertrude" when she walked by. So Belle was put on the list, too. But really, Belle was more about Morgan's recent mood to destroy. She'd been all pent up since Gertrude was born, trying her best to keep it in for her daughter's sake, denying herself opportunities because she worried it would somehow—though she didn't know how—come back to haunt Gertrude. It was as apt a metaphor for motherhood as anything, swallowing Morgan's own self for this new person and this new life role.

But, for Morgan, it was never going to last. Twelve years was long enough. Twelve years of "Hiiiiii!" and "You look so great!" and "Can I bring anything?" and "Thank you for a wonderful evening!" and "Love it!!' and "Looking forward!" Twelve years of channeling her rage into exercise, into starvation, into thank-you notes and PA memos and unbearable family ski trips. Twelve fucking years of "Ask Morgan!"

Tonight was the night it all would come together. Sofia's Surrealist Ball. It felt as if Morgan was about to attend her own prom, that's how excited she was to make everyone around her suffer. She'd thought long and hard about her costume—a custom-made fabric clam covering her whole head, plus a slinky white Versace dress. She'd put Art in a similar getup, as a life-size oyster, in a glimmering silver suit, plus an enormous replica pearl, the size of a tennis ball, sitting on his shiny hair.

Because Morgan was on the PA, she'd arrived early at Sofia's apartment to help set up. Sofia lived in the same building as Hailey and Justin Bieber, in a slick four-bedroom loft with twelve-foot ceilings and eight-foot-high casement windows. To see the place, you'd think Sofia was rich, rich, rich; apartments in the building *started* at $7 million. But Morgan knew better. The benefit was an Atherton affair, paid for by the school, and so Morgan had been sure Sofia would volunteer to host. Having Sofia join the PA was all part of the plan.

Everyone was already in costume when Morgan walked in—surrealist moms gone wild. Dre Finlay was dressed as a unicorn, one large horn cemented to her forehead. She was speaking with Gemma Corder, who'd come as a living clock, in a nude bodysuit with numbers painted on, and giant clock hands that were, somehow, ticking around and around.

Morgan saw Sofia across the room, directing the party planner here and there, pointing out areas that still needed themed decor. She was in what looked to be a Schiaparelli tear dress, though it must have been a reproduction, as the originals were museum-quality pieces. It was white with pink fabric "tears," plus the matching hooded veil, covered in the same pattern.

Like now, Morgan had first spied Sofia from afar. A few years ago, in Miami at one of Art's work dinners, Morgan had spotted a stunningly voluptuous woman at the bar, waiting for her party to arrive. The woman was drinking a large martini and had ordered snacks—olives, cheese, cured meats—which she was enthusiastically sucking down, licking her fingers after each bite. Morgan had been captivated by the woman's erotic flesh, her flushed cheeks, the way her mouth chomped, chomped, chomped. It was so . . . animalistic. So different from the control that Morgan exerted over her own body.

One of Morgan's dining companions had gotten up to say hello to this woman and had shared her name afterward: Sofia Perez. And so Morgan did what Morgan always did: She found out everything about this Sofia Perez, about her family, her life, her marriage. And when the time came, Morgan had used that knowledge to get Sofia to New York, to import the perfect scapegoat for all that she wanted to accomplish. She'd ordered up a South Beach bimbo, a mom who'd cheated on her husband with her trainer (eye roll), who wanted money so badly and nakedly that it would be easy to convince Belle and Frost that she was after theirs. A kind of stock character whom Morgan could use and dispose of. But Morgan had made a mistake. A big one. Because Sofia wasn't like that at all.

Morgan went over to a group of PA moms and asked if there was anything she could help with. She needed to pretend to be busy until she made her next move. Tonight was a night without helpers (other than Belle, who was useless), and so Morgan needed to zone in. She was on the defense, which wasn't a place she was used to.

Morgan and Sofia hadn't spoken since the night of Frost's art show. They'd been on the same WhatsApp chains, sure, moms asking about summer schedules, end-of-term logistics, sending memes about the craziness of being a parent in May. But they hadn't communicated directly since Sofia had told Morgan she'd seen her at City Hall Park, with a "guy."

That man had been Rodrick, Sofia's driver; the man with the baseball hat, the man whom Morgan had been paying to torment Belle and Frost, to threaten them and photograph them and do them bodily harm. Morgan wasn't sure if Sofia had seen his face, but from the way she'd said it, Morgan was concerned that she had. And then what? Morgan hadn't planned for that possibility, and thinking about it was giving her hives. But she also felt confident that tonight's events would prove definitive, and then she wouldn't have to worry about Sofia ever again.

There had been others involved in her schemes; Rodrick wasn't nearly the only one. There was the homeless man, now cozily ensconced with all the other crazies at a mental health facility on Morgan's dime. There was Greg Summerly, the "private detective." There was Art, unwitting Art, who'd taken nude pictures of Frost in their little love nest on Twenty-Second Street. He'd deleted them from his phone but not before sending them to his own email, to which Morgan had the password.

She'd studied the pictures alone one night in bed, the curve of Frost's breasts, Frost's hand caressing herself. In the background, Morgan had seen Frost's collages, and so she'd sent them anonymously to Ethel Zeigler, knowing Ethel would be interested in that sellable storyline of a former It Girl and her It Girl artwork. Setting Frost up to tear her down.

Sometimes Morgan did the dirty work herself, like rubbing itching powder into the samples of Belle's Dresses when she was helping her set up for the event. And cutting Belle's hair had been a highlight. Morgan had even used her own scissors, those sharp ones she'd bought after reading about them on Wirecutter. In some ways, she'd been lucky: the fake nudes of Hildy? She didn't know who was behind those, but it hadn't been Morgan. Just a middle-school prank, probably, possibly Ozzie Cain acting out.

Then there was Dr. Broker, the most helpful of them all. Paul. So easily manipulated by his frankly pedestrian kink. So willing to do whatever she'd asked, including alerting Morgan to Belle's lice email, and then blasting it out to the entire school for her. Morgan had to admit, she'd enjoyed their time together. But it wasn't like she "felt bad" about what was about to happen to him. He'd soon be out of Atherton, and with him the risk of Morgan getting exposed. It had been in the works for a long, long time.

Morgan went up to Sofia to say hello.

"Hiiii, this place looks amazing!" said Morgan. Sofia, who'd been bending down to arrange a vase filled with gigantic ceramic bananas, stood up, surprised.

"*Gracias*, Morgan," she said. "And thanks for coming with the PA girls to help. You have a nice break?"

"Oh, yes, we went to our Hamptons house," said Morgan. "I can't wait for summer to officially start. How about you?"

"Ah, I just stayed in the city," said Sofia. "The kids went down to Miami to see their dad. I was supposed to go but decided to have some alone time here instead. I missed them, but it was nice to have some days to myself." Morgan nodded understandingly. Both women were saying nothing, acting the parts they were supposed to act.

"How's Thyme & Time going? I walked by the other day! It looked busy!" said Sofia. Polite, polite, polite. Isn't that how moms always were with each other?

"Great!" said Morgan, matching her tone. "We're actually thinking about opening up a second location, if you can believe it."

"So I guess the robbery was just a tiny problem to overcome," said Sofia. "A liiiiittle blip. Too bad Belle hasn't been so lucky with her business." Belle had made the choice to shut down Pippins Cottage Home for good; the taint of all that negative press had been too big to overcome. The combo of Morgan's business succeeding while Belle's failed had been particularly traumatic for Belle.

"I almost forgot: I had a nice, long conversation with a friend of mine from Florida, Andrea, who I hadn't spoken with in a while," said Sofia now, her face brightening. "I told her my kids were at Atherton, and she mentioned she knew someone there, a woman named Morgan Chary! Isn't that funny? She even said that she was the one who'd told you about me, years ago, and also that you two had a gossip session a few weeks before I left town. She really couldn't remember the details." Sofia lowered her voice. "I think she might have a drinking problem, if you know what I mean."

Morgan felt her heart quicken. Was she going to faint? Shit. Fucking Andrea, that stupid lush, had such a big mouth.

"That's so funny," said Morgan. "I certainly know Andrea. Her husband does some business with Welly, so we occasionally get seated together during work dinners. She's lovely. But I don't remember speaking about you!"

"Huh," said Sofia. "I have to run around and get everything set. People will be here in no time! I love your clam head, by the way. So fun. Like a big vagina." Sofia smiled at Morgan, a large, fake smile, and swished off, leaving her thrown.

But Morgan had no time to dwell on it, because she had things to do, and a timeline to stick to. And Morgan was always on time.


Belle Redness wasn't sure about any of this. She wasn't sure about this scheme that Morgan had concocted. She wasn't sure that Sofia deserved it. And she definitely wasn't sure about her costume—a red, Anita Zmurko-Sieradzka dress, with a large bump near the shoulder, like a fabric tumor, and no armholes at all, trapping all of her limbs inside the garment. She'd had to hobble out of the car; Fred had dropped them off on Hudson, but the building's entrance, it turned out, was actually on Desbrosses, and so Belle had to hop like a kangaroo across the sidewalk. Surely not the strangest scene in New York at that very moment, but perhaps in the top ten.

This costume had been a mistake. Even Jeff, who rarely gave her any sartorial feedback, had lightly advised her to change.

"Babe, you won't be able to move. It's a party. How will you hold a drink?" he'd said to her as they were leaving. "I do love your new hair, even if it's not what you wanted," he added kindly, giving her a quick hug. Jeff had been supremely nice to Belle recently, and she did appreciate it.

He was in a much more reasonable outfit than she, a black leather suit, plus a penguin head that he was holding (when he'd put it on, he'd felt claustrophobic, so she'd compromised and said he could just carry it all night, and maybe wear it for a couple of pictures).

Belle felt like hopping back to the car and going home. She didn't want to face the other moms, sighing with sympathy about everything that had happened to her. Belle was starting to hate Atherton, now that she was no longer on top. Being an outcast was no fun, and if Belle had learned anything this year, it was that she probably should have been better to everyone when she'd had the power. Belle was not a deeply introspective person, but even she could see that she'd been a bitch. Hildy had been right.

Belle and Jeff took the elevator up, just the two of them, not speaking to each other as they traveled to the party. Belle was thinking about Dr. Broker, whether he'd be there, what she'd say to him. She hadn't spoken to him one-on-one since the night of Friendsgiving, the night her friends had caught them in the closet. Belle, so angry at Frost, about The Dress, about everything, had run into him on the second floor of Clara's apartment, after she'd doused Frost with that drink. Dr. Broker had been sipping an espresso martini, those adorable friendship bracelets on his wrist. She'd been in such a state, so stressed and embarrassed and not feeling like herself. He'd grabbed her wrist and dragged her to Ozzie Cain's room, into that closet, which smelled of a twelve-year-old's dirty socks, plus Axe body spray. He'd tried to kiss her, but she'd ducked, wanting to but not wanting to, which is when Frost had come in and saved her.

Thank God for Jeff, she thought, looking over at him now in the elevator, holding that stupid penguin head, a decapitated bird out of a depressing *Planet Earth* documentary. She wished she felt comfortable broaching the topic of marriage counseling with him, but she couldn't bring herself to. It was lodged inside her throat like a chewy piece of Balthazar steak.

The family had been down in St. Barths over break, staying at the Cheval Blanc, their favorite, and it had been so nice to get away from the city, away from the chaos, the failure, and the creepy stalker (Sofia?). Belle had nearly felt like Belle again, lounging in an Eres bikini, sipping Aperol spritzes. Hildy had been in a better mood, too.

"I've moved on," Hildy had said to Belle at one point. "The nude pictures aren't of me, everyone knows that. And Alfred and King did apologize." They'd been lying in a cabana on the beach, Belle flipping through old *Vogues* and Hildy on her Kindle, reading one of those dragon books she loved. Miles was splashing around in the ocean, and Jeff was off at a yoga class.

"I'm glad, honey," Belle had said.

After a pause, Hildy had spoken again. "Mom, I'm sorry about Pippins Cottage Home, but maybe it was a sign you weren't meant to be a fashion designer." Belle had been surprised. That possibility hadn't even occurred to her. But she'd sat with it. Was Hildy was right about . . . everything?

"Jeff, I love you," Belle said now. She hadn't even meant to say it aloud. She was seized with worry that her non-affair would somehow come out. Her friends had seen them together! Jeff and his penguin head looked over at her, confused. "I forgot to tell you—that new detective emailed me that he found something interesting. He's going to call to discuss tomorrow," Jeff said. The elevator doors opened into the party.

Sofia and the Atherton PA had outdone themselves, turning Sofia's loft into an upside-down wonderland, filled with objects that were either way too big (wineglasses the size of water jugs) or too small (miniature chairs, which guests were using as purse-holders). The main area was flanked in what looked to be large picture frames, nearly the height of the ceiling, and there were life-size taxidermic animals; a seven-foot-tall bear holding a whiskey, a hawk, dangling from the ceiling, its skinny bird neck covered in Mardi Gras beads. The cumulative effect of the place was disorienting, like you'd un-wittingly taken shrooms. Belle and Jeff walked away from each other, Belle on a mission to find Morgan, to make sure everything was going the way it was supposed to go.

But first she saw Frost, standing alone near the bar, in a fishnet dress, a freaky-looking raven hat on her head. She looked stunning, as always.

"Uh-oh," said Frost, smiling at Belle like it was the old days. "We're near a bar—do I need to duck? Are you going to pour an-other martini on me? Never mind, I see you don't have any arms to throw a drink with."

Belle snorted. "That was a onetime thing, you know that," she said, relieved to inject some levity into the situation. "Speaking of, can you help me sip a vodka? I don't have any hands."

Frost flagged the bartender, who was wearing a gladiator costume, his chiseled abs exposed by an armor crop top, and then held the full cup of alcohol gingerly to Belle's lips. She slurped it like a baby. "Hits the spot," said Belle, feeling the familiar closeness with her friend returning.

"I really do love your new hair, even if you didn't technically choose to go short. It's so cool," said Frost.

Ava and Gabby waltzed over, each wearing a large orange ball around her body, stretching from neck to their knees, with tentacle-like structures protruding out. The getups were covered in black polka dots. They seemed delighted with themselves, twirling to show off, crashing into everything as they did, a happier couple than most of the spouses in attendance.

"Do you know what we are?" asked Ava, the line of her bangs even sharper than normal, as if someone had taken a ruler to them. Belle and Frost shook their heads no.

"We are a Yayoi Kusama painting come to life!" said Gabby. "She's a famous ninety-five-year-old Japanese artist. And she *made* these costumes for us. Can you believe it?" Knowing how much money Gabby spent on the theme parties, Belle could.

"I love this red thing," continued Gabby, caressing Belle's dress. "It's like you're a sexy sausage." Ava laughed. Belle wanted them to scram.

That's when Belle saw Dr. Broker passing by, in jeans and a white T-shirt that said DALÍ.

"Hey, Dr. Broker, come here!" called Gabby, pulling him over by the arm. He looked uncomfortable to be there, not making eye contact with the women, sipping his drink instead of chatting. He was usually so smooth. Belle wondered if she was making him antsy. She felt like an idiot in her armless dress.

"Dr. Broker, my good man," said Gabby. "First question: How are we doing with the Atherton Fund?"

"Oh, we're doing great," said Dr. Broker, coughing a little. Belle noticed he looked pale, with dark rings around his eyes that hadn't been there previously. "Nearly every family has given something, and we expect more to trickle in before midnight. I can't wait to see how much we raise tonight!" He coughed again. Maybe he was just sick. It was that time of year, certainly, and he was around germ-infested children all day.

"Second question," said Gabby. Belle wanted her to shut up and leave him alone.

"Did you get any more info about the mentally ill man who was hanging near school? Anything from the police? Some of the moms said he was being paid to stay in the area," said Gabby.

"No, nothing," said Dr. Broker. "Well, actually, they did tell me that he was released on bail and is now in a mental health facility at Weill Cornell."

"On bail?" said Ava. "But how could he afford that? And who's paying for him to be at Weill Cornell? That's where *my* doctors are!"

"I have no idea," said Dr. Broker. He was being a little short with them, which was odd, given Gabby's status as an important donor. "Maybe he had a rich aunt or something. Anyway, ladies, I must make the rounds. I hope you enjoy the party and that, when the auction arrives, you give, give, give." Dr. Broker gave them a charming smile, and Belle felt bile rise in her throat. Then he walked off.

"I love your Salvador Dalí T-shirt!" Ava shouted after him. "Very clever!"

"Guys, I have to find Morgan," said Belle. "Has anyone seen her?"

"Yes, just look for the large white crustacean," said Gabby. "You can't miss her."

Belle took off into the sea of parents, each costume she encountered more disturbing than the next. There were nightmarish animals, weird household objects (someone had dressed up as a toilet brush), monstrous fantasy creatures. She was having a hard time walking in her dress and kept crashing into people and the sides of furniture. She finally saw Morgan in the corner of the room and jumped over to her. She couldn't see Morgan's face inside the big shellfish but could sense from the way she was standing that she was stressed.

"Morgan! What happened? Did you do it? If not, I don't think we should," said Belle, the words tumbling out.

"It's too late," said Morgan. Her voice sounded far away, like she was speaking to Belle through water, which was fitting, given she was dressed as a clam.

Someone tapped a microphone, and the women turned to see Sofia standing on a platform underneath the frame in the middle of her living room, pretty as a picture in her flowy printed dress and veil. "What time is it?" Belle couldn't access her phone, which was hanging on a chain around her neck.

"Five past ten," said Morgan. "Time for the auction. Here we go . . ." Frost sidled up to them, eager to watch the show.

"Hello! *Hola!*" said Sofia. She sounded nervous and parched, like she needed a sip of water. "Welcome to my Surrealist Ball!" Everyone clapped. "Before I introduce our auctioneer, Art Chary, I wanted to make an announcement of my own."

Art always acted as the auctioneer at the Atherton fundraisers; the PA had found that people loved to give money when the handsome, funny, persuasive founder of Welly was at the mic. What was this announcement Sofia was talking about? Sofia cleared her throat loudly. Everyone looked on, waiting.

"First, I wanted to take this opportunity to say thank you for coming to my home. You've all been so welcoming to me, as a new mother to the school, and I appreciate that. I especially want to single out Belle Redness, Morgan Chary, and Frost Trevor for their support and kindness." Belle felt her face burn. The entire room turned to look at them.

"Secondly, I know that many of the other mothers here are entrepreneurs, so what better place to announce my next career move!" There was a smattering of applause. Sofia went on, and Belle died a little inside for her.

"I'm joining a company called Omni Travel group as a luxury travel adviser, specializing in Florida and the Caribbean. So please contact me about planning your next unforgettable family trip!"

"A travel agent? She's becoming a *travel agent*? I thought she was loaded," someone nearby Belle remarked. "Doesn't she live . . . here?"

"You can plan my next trip—and you can come!" yelled Bud Cunningham, who was donning a horned helmet. Trina slapped him on the arm to shut up.

Belle felt like such an idiot. That's what Sofia had been trying to tell them. She did need her own money, but she wasn't going to blackmail them. She was going to ask them to become her clients.

"And please, please, please try my special *postre de natas*—it's a pudding recipe from Colombia that has been in my family for years. I've made enough for everyone to have a taste. *Gracias!*" Belle gave Morgan a look.

"You guys," said Frost now, as Sofia, red-faced, stepped off the podium and Art stepped up. "We are such assholes. Maybe Rodrick is really dangerous—we have to warn Sofia."

"Hey, folks, are you ready to give a LOT of money to Atherton?" said Art, his voice booming though the apartment. "To your sons and daughters? To THE BEST SCHOOL IN MANHATTAN?" Everyone yelped for that one.

They'd been given descriptions of the auction items beforehand—the PA went to great lengths to secure donations, and parents one-upped each other with generous contributions. People gave winter stays in their Aspen ski homes, weeklong trips to Grecian villas, a private dinner at Le Bernardin, cooked by Eric Ripert himself (his daughter attended Atherton), a rival private dinner at BaoFuku, cooked by David Chung, and the showstopper, a soccer scrimmage in Central Park with none other than David Beckham (Brooklyn Beckham had spent a year at Atherton).

Art ticked through each one, couples chatting to each other about what items to bid on, groups forming alliances for items like a sunset dinner cruise ride for twenty in the Hamptons, and a Saturday night rent-out of Torrisi.

The auction always started off with a bang. First up, a private John Legend concert for fifteen people (he and Chrissy were considering Atherton for their children; this was a good way to lock in an acceptance). Impressed murmurs went up in the crowd as couples grouped off, seeing how much money each would be willing to spend for this once-in-a-lifetime experience.

"I'll give everyone five minutes to solidify their bidding plans," said Art, stepping down from the platform. Belle saw him pass by Clara Cain, whose body was covered head to toe in black feathers, and whisper something to her.

Belle looked over at Morgan. She couldn't be sure, given she couldn't really see Morgan's face, but she thought that maybe Morgan had seen the exchange, too. How odd. What could Art be speaking to Clara about?

"What time is it now?" Belle asked Morgan. Her stomach was starting to roil from nerves. She was worried she'd have to go to the bathroom, but her dress rendered the act nearly impossible.

"Ten twenty," said Morgan.

Frost grabbed them both, pulling them into the corner where no one else could hear.

"We're not doing this, right? Please tell me it's called off. It wasn't Sofia. I don't care what you say, Morgan." Morgan shook Frost off. Frost looked as tense as the bird sitting on her head.

Art had gotten back on the podium, the pearl on his head shimmering like a mini disco ball.

"Okay! Let's start. Who's the opening bid?"

Dre Finlay held up the little "A" signs that had been distributed for bidding.

"Ten thousand dollars!" she said, to whoops.

"Fifteen thousand!" shouted someone else.

"Twenty!"

"A hundred thousand!"

"A hundred and twenty!"

"Two hundred thousand!" People were cheering now, everyone drunk on the special punch, a blend of whiskey, some kind of orange liqueur, and copious amounts of maraschino cherries.

"Get more punch," Art kept imploring. "The drunker you are, the more you'll bid!" The benefit always devolved into debauchery—last year's had ended with over a million dollars raised and two moms, Genevieve Thomas and Armena Justice, nearly coming to blows over an auction item for a meet and greet with Anna Wintour (Wintour's daughter, also an Atherton parent, had donated the item).

Things were stacking up to be just as wild this year, and as the auction went on and the bids went even higher, Belle snuck off to see if she could somehow figure out how to pee in this stupid dress. She passed a group of parents enjoying Sofia's *postre de natas*, licking their spoons with delight. Midnight was coming.

Sofia Perez just knew that something awful was going to happen tonight, which is why she'd called in backup. Well, that wasn't the only reason why. She looked over at that extremely handsome backup now, standing behind the bar, pouring premade punch into crystal glasses. Michael caught her gaze and winked, causing Sofia's eyes to water with happiness. She had to actively restrain herself from running over and jumping into his muscled arms, nuzzling into that silly gladiator costume she'd bought for him at Abracadabra on Twenty-First Street. At least he was here with her. At least she had him back. It had taken only one phone call. "I love you," she'd said. "I need you." He'd driven straight to MIA and had landed at LaGuardia three and a half hours later.

But, unfortunately, she still hadn't been able to figure out what was coming. This is what she *had* figured out:

Morgan had been behind her invitation to Atherton. After seeing Morgan with Rodrick, Sofia had done some digging, scrolling through Morgan's social media, back and back and back. Years ago, Morgan had been tagged in a picture at a Welly charity dinner sitting at a table with Sofia's friend, Andrea, the connection that Sofia had been searching for. She'd called Andrea to confirm her findings.

"Sofia Perez! How's NYC? Are you coming down to Miami soon?" Andrea, who had a bit of a drinking thing, already sounded tipsy. It was 3:00 p.m. on a Monday.

"No plans to come to Miami anytime soon. New York is okay. The women here are . . . a lot. But I've made some new friends, including a woman named Morgan Chary. Do you know her?"

"I know Morgan," Andrea had slurred. "We always chat at those Welly events that Harold is involved with. I don't think I've ever met a woman who's more cheerful or energetic. It's like, give it a rest, lady! I leave those dinners feeling like I've run a marathon just by talking with her. She always seemed very interested in you. I'd pointed you out when we were at a dinner at Casa Tua, years ago. I thought she had a girl crush or something."

Sofia had gotten chills.

"Did you ever happen to discuss my, um, marital situation with her?"

Andrea had paused, thinking.

"You know, I can't really remember, but I might have?" That was woman code for: she'd done it.

"I think it was right around the time you and JP had split up, and so maybe that was on my mind."

"Andrea, did you happen to mention Michael to her?" Andrea had paused again, this time for even longer. Sofia had hung up before she'd had a chance to answer, texting her afterward, "Sorry, bad connection! I'll call you in a few days." She'd not spoken to her since.

Morgan had known Sofia needed an out from Miami, and that Atherton would draw her away. So she'd gotten Dr. Broker, her kinky sex buddy, to pull strings in order to secure spots for Carlos and Lucia at the school.

What kind of a game was Morgan playing? Sofia's working theory was that Morgan was behind everything. That she'd lured Sofia up to Atherton to give her cover, then systematically destroyed her friends over these past months. The scooter hit-and-run, The Dress rash, the *New York Post* article, the fake nudes, the lice email! Everything. Sofia had heard a group of women at drop-off the other day tittering about it, how "Belle fell" and "Frost lost." Morgan must have paid Rodrick to work for her—and then exposed him—to convince Belle and Frost that Sofia was the bad guy. All in pursuit of what, exactly? Revenge on Frost for fucking Art; punishing Belle for birthing a "beast," as Morgan had put it at Friendsgiving.

"Why do you think she picked you?" Michael had asked her. They were lying in Sofia's bed the previous night, spooning after sex. Sofia, nuzzling into him, had been happy to be alive. "Ay, who knows," Sofia had said. "I don't understand these women. They have everything they want—healthy children, money, husbands who love them. And they're still miserable."

The only thing that Sofia was certain about was that tonight was when *she* was going to get screwed. In the middle of her party, somehow. That's why she'd made her announcement about her new job; she had to get her narrative out before anything else happened. Morgan was trying to blame her for things that she didn't do! Sofia was a cheater, yes, but she was a good person with good intentions. She hadn't meant to break up her family. She'd just fallen in love. And now she'd fallen in with a bunch of psycho moms.

As the auction raged on, Sofia took a moment to walk around her apartment, checking in with the caterers, making sure the coat attendants were fine. She'd decided to stay sober that night—she needed to be sharp, to watch for any potential pranks or worse. She'd also set up hidden Nest Cams all over the apartment, stashed behind the surrealist decorations. She didn't want to take any chances.

Frost hadn't answered her text from the night of her art show, and Sofia was convinced that Morgan had turned both Frost and Belle against her. The three of them had looked very cozy all evening, as if Sofia hadn't existed for all these months. Sofia wasn't the type to get maudlin, but it did hurt her feelings that Belle and Frost were so quick to think she might be their enemy. The whole thing was like something out of the stories about Colombia her father used to tell her. The gangs, the violence, the allies who turned on each other for money. But this wasn't Bogotá! It was Tribeca, for crying out loud.

Sofia pulled her Schiaparelli veil tightly over her head (the dress was a dupe; she'd found it hanging in a storefront on Canal Street, next to fake Prada purses). The wacky decor was making her paranoid. Would Morgan release rats into her apartment? Would a bomb go off, killing them all? What horrible thing could Morgan think up next?

The auction was popping off. Sofia could hear people bidding hundreds of thousands of dollars on items they didn't need. Being poor again had reminded Sofia of how much *richer* rich people were than the rest of the world imagined.

"Sofia! I'd love to be your first client." It was Armena Justice, in a neon bodysuit, her feet clad in Moon Boots the size of small children.

"Oh, thank you, Armena," said Sofia. She tried to focus, though she was distracted by the noise and the feeling that everything was about to fall apart. But this was important—it was what she'd been working toward this entire time. Becoming a trusted member of the community, someone that the other moms felt good about paying to help them live their best lives.

"We would love to go to a private island for next Christmas break," said Armena. "Just our family. Somewhere out near Aruba—but nicer than Aruba, obviously. I'm thinking a budget of around eighty thousand. Think you could get me some options by next week?"

"Yes, definitely," said Sofia. And she could. She knew of a few places like that; one of her friends in Miami *only* did private islands. Maybe Sofia could really be good at this job! The idea thrilled her.

"And I loved your pudding! So delicious," said Armena, who then walked off. Sofia checked her phone. 11:56. Four minutes until midnight. The plan was for Art, who was now wrapping up the auction—$33,000 for the second grade to sit front row at a Rangers game, donated by a sports agent dad—to do the countdown on the microphone. When the clock hit twelve, a replica of the Times Square New Year's Eve ball would lower dramatically from Sofia's ceiling.

11:57.

"It's almost midnight, folks, and that's the last item gone. By tomorrow, we'll know how much in total we raised for Atherton, and I have a feeling the number is going to big! Huge! All thanks to you, our impressive Atherton community."

Sofia moved toward the center of the room, looking for Morgan, Belle, and Frost, but she didn't see them in the mix. The lights had gone down and the DJ had started up again, playing a very loud version of "Waiting for Tonight," JLo belting as the millennial parents danced like they were in middle school.

11:58.

She then felt a powerful pull, someone dragging her toward who knows where. It was Frost, her pretty face reading total alarm.

"Sofia," she whispered hoarsely. "You didn't have any of your pudding, did you?" Sofia shook her head. Frost was scaring her. What was wrong with the *postre de natas*? She'd slaved over batch after batch last night after the kids had gone to sleep.

"Oh, thank God. Something's going to go down, and I don't want you to be involved."

"What on earth are you talking about, Frost?" said Sofia. Her heart was beating hard in her chest.

"Was it you? Did you vandalize my art show? Did you know Rodrick was at ZZ's?" said Frost now. "Was it you?"

"Are you kidding? I hate Rodrick, you know that," pleaded Sofia. "I do like to follow people around. I even followed you. But it was harmless fun. I was just bored. I'm poor, Frost! I have nothing to do."

Frost seemed to understand this logic.

"I wouldn't ruin Belle's company—she worked so hard on it." Here Sofia lowered her voice. "Though that dress was so ugly, I'm sorry." Frost laughed and Sofia went on. "And I would never hurt Hildy—Hildy is a child! I would never hurt you. You're my best friend." Sofia felt on the verge of breaking down. She saw Tim walking toward them at the same time Frost did. Frost put her finger to her lips and slipped away to her husband. Art could be heard in the background, counting down from thirty.

"It was Morgan! Morgan is the one!" Sofia called after Frost now, but she couldn't tell if she could hear her over the pounding music.

"Ten! Nine! Eight! Seven!"

Sofia ran toward her kitchen, saying a quick thank-you to Jesus that the children were out of the apartment, in Miami with JP. The DJ had turned off the music for the final countdown, and people were pairing off, preparing for their big midnight kisses. Sofia was now standing alone near her stove, looking out at the chaos over her island.

"Three! Two! One!"

Everyone shouted at once, yelling "Cheers to Atherton!" as the ball, a glowing, otherworldly orb, began to lower to the floor, taking them all by happy surprise. The DJ put on Donna Summer's "Last Dance" as couples smooched and swayed. There was Morgan with Art, Morgan's arms tightly holding on to his waist, her face turned so her clam costume could fit into the nook of his chest. She saw Dr. Broker off to the side, watching them, and Belle and Jeff, nearby, Belle eyeing Dr. Broker as she danced with her husband. And there were Frost and Tim, huddled together by the front entrance. Tim tried to pull her onto the dance floor, but Sofia saw Frost resist, saying something to him and then pointing to her stomach. She walked off toward the bathroom, leaving Tim alone.

"Ahhhh!" someone then growled, loud enough to be heard over the music. Sofia couldn't see who it was, so she lifted herself up onto the granite countertop to get a better look, peering over to see Bud Cunningham staggering to the ground, a big lump of a man, not really moving at all. Trina, in a *Game of Thrones*–esque getup, was hovering over him, fanning his face with her hands.

"Bud? Bud? Are you okay?" she kept asking.

Not a moment later, Gemma Corder went down, splayed on the floor next to Bud, and then the same for Julie Klein, and Cat Howell's husband, Charles, and then Gabby Mahler in her polka-dot costume. About fifteen more people crumpled within the span of just a few minutes, stumbling about, unable to stand. "It was the pudding! They all just had the pudding," she heard someone shout. "What did Sofia Perez put in it? She's poisoned us all!"

A person grabbed Sofia from behind, and she swiveled to see Dr. Broker, his handsome face turned gray, his eyes bulging in terror. "*Dios mio*," said Sofia. Was that foam coming out of his mouth? He staggered away and Sofia lost him in the mix.

Sofia felt like she was having an out-of-body experience. Her hands started shaking uncontrollably, and she suddenly felt very cold. She started to curl up behind the kitchen island. Maybe she could shut herself into a kitchen cabinet and disappear.

Then the DJ put on "Believe" by Cher. It was the song Michael played at the beginning of their training sessions, to pump Sofia up before their workouts. "More, Sofia, more! Go, go, go," he'd chant as she lunged and lifted and fantasized about all she'd do to him after it was finished. Just hearing it now created that same surge of endorphins, a kind of instant perk, reminding Sofia that she was a fighter. If she could do twenty lunges, if she could survive on her own in New York, if she could lift herself out of poverty into the highest echelons of society, she could figure this out. She felt a hand slip into hers. Michael was here with her now. He gave her a loving, supportive smile. He was so beautiful. He was hers.

Sofia stood up straight. She hadn't done anything wrong. It was her apartment, but it wasn't her fault. Sofia would beat Morgan. She had to.

## Chapter 15

# Drama!

===

A Note to the Atherton Community

Dear parents,

By now, we're sure you've all heard the tragic news about Dr. Broker. Most of you were there. We know that members of our community are struggling under the weight of the event. Our children also struggle, each in their own ways. We have mobilized our crisis support teams, who've been assisting and supporting those at Atherton throughout this past week.

Tomorrow morning, June 2, a team led by our school psychologist, Sue Grossman, will be available to Atherton students beginning at 8:00 a.m. You and your loved ones are also encouraged to come speak with a mental health professional. Please see a list of resources below on how to communicate with your child about managing grief.

Our goal is to maintain as much normalcy as possible while also being respectful of students' needs and emotions. We will keep you apprised of any changes to Dr. Broker's condition.

All our best,

The Atherton staff and board

Gabby Mahler had only been in the hospital that night for a bit—a couple of hours, maybe, as the nurses had taken vitals and then whatever it was had cleared out of her system. She hadn't even had to drink that disgusting stuff that makes you throw up, like some of the others, as thankfully she'd only eaten a few bites of the pudding instead of the, like, twenty servings that Bud Cunningham had inhaled. But she'd gone down like everyone else. She remembered falling to the floor and thinking to herself: How embarrassing. No life flashing before her eyes. No thoughts of her children or her parents or her horrible, soon-to-be ex-wife, Margo. Just humiliation at being so vulnerable, at being human, something she didn't like to acknowledge but that had been pushing up against her these past few months.

For example, the fact that Margo was leaving her. Had *left* her. For Dr. Fucking Cuddles of West Chelsea Veterinary. Margo had moved out of their family's seven-bedroom on Park and Eighty-Fifth and into his place in Gramercy, and now the kids were spending time between the two homes and there seemed to be nothing that Gabby, with all her wealth and power, could do about it. On top of everything, she missed her Westies, Gus and Van Sant, desperately. They were Margo's dogs, really, so it wasn't like Gabby could have made the case to keep them herself. But they'd grown on her, those little yappy troublemakers, and now she couldn't believe how empty the house was without them.

Gabby was just arriving at pickup, enjoying the perfect June weather, the bright blue sky, the early summer breeze. It was the first day back at school after, well, everything, and it was her turn to have the kids for the night. Three boys with two moms. Now one mom and one mom, apart.

Margo had always been up-front with Gabby about her bisexuality. Before they'd met, Margo had lived with a man, nearly getting engaged to him before breaking it off in pursuit of a more open lifestyle. Gabby, unfairly, had been playing up this "surprise" bisexual thing for the sympathy angle with the other Atherton moms. Whatever. It made Gabby feel better to hear others aghast, the supportive offense on her behalf, the "She left you for a *man*?!" disbelief. And anyway, she'd met this Dr. Cuddles, and he looked more like a middle-aged lesbian than Gabby did, with his Ellen DeGeneres hair and his weirdly full lips. Fucker.

Gabby saw Ava by the door, chatting with Clara Cain and Dre Finlay. There was so much gossip swirling around the incident, and Gabby was happy for the distraction from her pathetic personal life.

"I heard they finally pinpointed what made everyone sick," Clara was saying with an authority that she certainly didn't have. She was in her lawyer workwear—a Hillary Clinton blue pantsuit, her hair like a helmet. "Apparently, it was a very trace amount of potassium hydroxide, the nasty stuff that's found in drain cleaner. That's why Dr. Broker's still in the hospital. He must have been eating a lot of pudding, though no one seems to have seen him doing it. And everyone else recovered just fine."

"Wait, so there were actual chemicals in Sofia's dessert? Who did you hear that from?" said Ava. She was in a black dress and donning large black sunglasses. She looked like a chic spy. "Morgan told me. She told everyone. And she also told me about Sofia's divorce, that she cheated, that she's . . . poor," said Dre, wrinkling her nose in disgust. "I heard she was the one who cut off Belle's hair! I *knew* there was something off about Sofia." Everyone at Atherton was saying they'd always suspected that Sofia was rotten, that she'd been lying to get close to them all, that she was a fraud, a Miami wolf in Tribeca clothing. Gabby held her tongue. She understood what it felt like to not fit in.

Growing up, Gabby had been a loner, knowing she was different from the other girls but not figuring out how until she was deep into high school. It was a different time then—not like today, when everyone under twenty seemed to be queer in one way or another. They, them, X, whatever, though no one wanted to be a boring old lesbian, which made Gabby laugh. She'd been in the closet until after college, dating girls secretly without letting her family in on her lifestyle. How could they have not known? Gabby sometimes wondered, now that she had her own children and was so attuned to their personalities and needs. But it didn't cause a permanent rift, thankfully. Once she was out, her parents embraced her. Gabby now worked for her dad, helping to oversee some of his buildings' management teams. A few weeks ago, he'd said something strange.

"I heard that Jorge Perez's grandchildren are at Atherton. You know that I do business with him in Florida," her dad had said.

"Oh, is that Sofia's ex-father-in-law?" said Gabby. They were sitting at her parents' dining table, a rare, eighteenth-century Louis Seize designed by Claude Messier.

Her father had nodded. "He's a nasty piece of work. I know the grandchildren will be set, but I'm sure he's torturing that woman, Sofia, or whatever her name is. He's a vindictive piece of shit." Gabby had nodded but hadn't added anything. She wondered what Sofia had really been dealing with this year. She didn't strike Gabby as a murderer, that was for sure.

"I'm not sure about any of it," said Gabby now. "At the hospital, they told me it was possibly Ambien combined with the alcohol. Which is why we basically just had to sober up and then go home. I think the people they forced to vomit were just super drunk, anyway. Everyone was so messed up that night."

"Has anyone seen Sofia since?" said Ava. Clara shook her head.

"I heard she's gone back to Florida. The kids are getting looked after by their nanny," said Clara.

Gabby wasn't surprised. Imagine trying to survive in a group of moms who thought you might be homicidal?

"But why would Sofia want to hurt people?" said Gabby. "She wants to plan all our luxury vacations! Plus, she's too hot to be a criminal." Taken as a whole, this was the craziest thing to ever happen at Atherton, and every parent in Manhattan had heard about it, the rumors of a "psycho-mom" pinging back and forth between the poshest neighborhoods. The new mom who'd infiltrated the A-list turned out to be a nutcase. It was glorious. And it was shaping up to be a private school scandal even bigger than the one at Braeburn, when it turned out their headmaster was a total fraud.

The children began to stream out of the doors, down the big stone steps, all elbows and knees in their spring outfits. Sully and Howie emerged with the rest of the lower school, looking around for Gabby. She waved, and they came bounding over, nearly knocking her down with their embraces. Gabby still couldn't believe that her marriage was over and that these little guys would be the children of divorce. It made her sick. You could have all the money in the world, but this could still fuck a kid up.

"Mom, where are we sleeping tonight?" asked Howie, his little five-year-old face slightly sunburned from their Sunday in the Hamptons. Gabby took a deep breath.

"At home, silly, with me! We'll just wait for Mac and then take the car uptown."

Up top, in Dr. Broker's usual spot, stood Mary Margaret, hands behind her back, staring out stoically as each guardian collected her charge. The latest update they'd received was that Dr. Broker was still in the hospital, alive but "incapacitated." The board had already commenced the search for a new headmaster. Everyone felt bad for Dr. Broker, but he was now tainted goods. Some people were saying that he had been sleeping with one of the moms, perhaps even Sofia Perez herself. She was a cheater, after all.

The turnout at Atherton this afternoon had the feel of the first day of drop-off—instead of nannies, it was nearly all moms, and even the working ones like Clara had made time for pickup. Gabby was there herself for that reason, to take the temperature of the school after the disaster of last weekend. Were people thinking of pulling their kids out? Applying elsewhere for next year? She and Ava had discussed it privately. While Gabby was open to sending her kids to a school uptown—that's where she lived, and it might be nice to not have to schlep all the way down every morning—Ava was thinking of using this as an opportunity to switch to public school. Unfortunately, it really did seem like BaoFuku was headed for lights-out, and the Leo-Chungs wouldn't be able to afford the two private school tuitions without that money coming in. Gabby had the crazy impulse to offer to help Ava with her cash flow situation but then remembered herself before saying anything stupid or insulting. Ava wasn't her family, as much as she sometimes felt like she was. But it would be such a shame not to have the kids together, and not to get to see her all the time.

"Mom, look," said Sully, pointing up to the entrance. Lucia and Carlos Perez were standing with Mary Margaret, appearing a little lost as they searched the crowd for their nanny. The entire group was staring at them, the children of the woman who'd been run out of town for possibly trying to kill them all.

Then, as if conjured, Sofia appeared before them, waltzing into pickup as if nothing had happened, as if twenty people hadn't been transported from her party to the ER after eating a South American dessert she'd made by hand. She was in a floral sundress that skimmed her body tastefully, and wearing striking red lipstick and smiling, her teeth looking particularly white. The crowd parted for her as it had on the first day of school, watching in awe as she strode to the front with confidence.

"*Hola, hola,*" Sofia said to them, nearly singing the words. "*Hola.*" Sofia blew a kiss to her children, and they ran down the steps to her, snuggling into her arms with relief. She took each by the hand and then headed directly for Belle, Morgan, and Frost, the three of them standing in a triangle formation, like a flock of well-dressed birds.

Gabby dragged Sully and Howie closer to the encounter, so she could get a good view. Ava did the same with her girls.

"Ladies, long time no see," said Sofia sweetly. No one responded. "I want to make sure you all plan to come to my Atherton Altruist ceremony. I set it for Friday! Mary Margaret is helping me organize it, as Dr. Broker is, well, you all know about Dr. Broker." Gabby couldn't believe what she was hearing. She was loving it. What a pair of balls on that woman.

"We will be there," said Morgan finally, Belle and Frost standing silent, with their mouths hanging open. "Amazing!"

# WhatsApp Chat
## *Atherton Lower School Moms*
### *94 Participants*

**Dre Finlay**

Hiya, Atherton chicas! A couple quick announcements. Spring after-school activities end next week, so remember to adjust your pickup times accordingly.

Secondly, please come out on Friday to celebrate Sofia Perez at her Atherton Altruist ceremony! Details are as follows: Friday, June 4, 4:00 p.m., at Atherton's own auditorium. See you all there!

**Armena Justice**

Hi all! Does anyone have a recommendation for a private piano teacher for summer break? Ours moved back to Russia. Thank you!

**Caroline Press**

Yes, I do, Armena, I'll text it to you.

**Jennifer Smyth**

A quick thought: Should we start a GoFundMe for Dr. Broker?

**Dre Finlay**

I've been in touch with the board, and Atherton is covering all of Dr. Broker's medical bills and then some. But, as head of the PA, that gives me an idea. I'd love to help coordinate a gift for Dr. Broker, something that will brighten his day. If anyone has ideas of what to include, please ping the group!

**Caroline Press**

My company would happily provide Dr. Broker a bound copy of all of the school portraits; that way he can still "see" the students while he recovers.

**Dre Finlay**

Lovely idea, Caroline! And so generous.

**Genevieve Thomas**

We could buy him a summer sweater, something from Loro Piana?

**Lauren Hilderson**

What if we all pitched in and got him a Rolex? Jim's guy on Forty-Seventh Street could get us a good price. It would likely be less than $500 a person.

**Dre Finlay**

I love that, Lauren! If everyone is in agreement, let's get him a handsome watch and a light cashmere sweater.

**Gabby Mahler**

Guys, I don't think Dr. Broker needs a watch or a sweater. He's basically in a coma.

**Kim Berns**

Hi, ladies! For the last time, we're no longer at Atherton, and I'd love to be removed from this chain. I've very sorry for what happened at the school, and must say, this makes us even happier about our decision to move Liam to St. David's this year.

**Gabby Mahler**

We're all *really* happy for you, Kim.

**Sofia Perez**

Hola! I can't wait to see you all on Friday! I have some exciting news to share, and I hope you all can be there to hear it. Especially my good friend Morgan. Besos. Xx


Rodrick Beneto was on a plane back to Miami, sitting on the tarmac about to take off, free at last. He'd spent the last nine months under the thumb of Morgan Chary, and now he was done.

From the beginning, this had been the deal. He'd finish off the job, collect his payment, and then leave New York. She'd said not to worry about the police, that she'd take care of everything, that he could disappear back into his old life. The only promise was that he wasn't to work for the Perez family again; no sadness there, as JP was a complete prick, and Rodrick was sick of dealing with him. There were many rich families in Miami who needed drivers. Rodrick would be fine.

Morgan Chary, however, was a very sick woman. He'd met her a few days after he'd arrived in New York. JP had included a small apartment rental in Murray Hill in their deal. Rodrick, on a walk around his new neighborhood, had been approached by a blond lady in leggings. She'd stood directly in front of him, eyeing him in this creepy way, and then had gotten up in his face. He'd thought maybe she was mentally ill or something and so had tried to ignore her, heading in the other direction, but she'd caught up with him. "Stop, Rodrick. Stop," she'd said to him in a soft voice. Then she'd explained that she wanted him to do some work for her and that she'd pay him well. Rodrick had been confused—he already had a job; what kind of work was she talking about? And how had she known who he was?

They'd gone into a Starbucks and sat down at a table. Her opener had freaked him the fuck out.

"Rodrick, my daughter goes to school with the Perez children, and I'm going to need you to do some very bad things for me." Rodrick had waited for her to go on, but she'd just sat there, silent. She was thin, much thinner than Sofia.

"I don't want a part of that," Rodrick had said warily. And he didn't. In high school, Rodrick had gotten into some trouble, but he'd straightened out, joined his cousin's limo company as a driver, then gotten hired full-time by JP Perez. He was good now. He made decent money, and he had a girlfriend, a teacher.

"What if I said I could help Mirabella?" said Morgan. Rodrick hadn't been sure he'd heard her right. How could this woman know about his niece? Mirabella was his sister's beautiful little girl, and she was sick, really sick, with leukemia. She was in treatment in Miami, but things weren't going great. His sister, a single mom, was struggling. She didn't have the time or the money to deal with it all, and so Rodrick had been stepping in to help, taking Mirabella to appointments when he could. That child was the light of his life. She was why he'd come up to New York in the first place; JP had offered Rodrick additional money on top of his salary to move, all of which was going toward Mirabella's healthcare costs.

"I know people at Memorial Sloan Kettering. It's the best cancer hospital in the world. I could get her in. And she wouldn't have to pay anything." Morgan had leaned close to him. She'd put her cold hand on top of his.

And so, Rodrick had done what she'd asked him to do. He'd had no choice. He'd hit Frost with an e-scooter, one that Morgan had rented. He'd known exactly when to crash into that poor woman—Morgan had timed the whole thing perfectly. He'd gone fast enough to hurt Frost, but not seriously, and had sped away from the scene, his heart racing, knowing his life was now in Morgan Chary's hands.

They'd periodically meet at random locations, discussing logistics for her next scheme, Morgan handing him his payments. Rodrick had robbed Morgan's own spa! Sofia had been there, and she'd nearly recognized his voice. It had rattled him to the point that he'd fled the scene, and Morgan had been super pissed afterward. He was supposed to have "roughed her up" for everyone to see—to have put his hands around Morgan's neck and pretended to strangle her. (Morgan, that crazy bitch, said she already had bruises that would prove he'd really done it.)

Things kept almost going wrong. He'd taken pictures of Frost and Sofia at ZZ's, and this time it had been Frost to recognize him as the man who'd plowed into her. He'd gotten away in time, hiding outside in a nearby awning, taunting the women when they emerged with the lines that Morgan had texted to him. Sofia had then chased him—fast!—all those sessions with her Miami trainer-slash-boyfriend having paid off. Rodrick had barely escaped. If she'd seen his face, he'd have been done for.

He'd dutifully delivered the dead flowers to Belle's apartment, after spending days collecting live lanternflies from the dirty streets of New York. He'd plastered the walls of Frost's art show when Morgan had cut the lights. She'd been behind it all.

At least Morgan had been true to her word about getting Mirabella into MSK. She'd pulled some strings with her friend on the hospital's board, getting Mirabella full financial assistance, plus a housing subsidy. Mirabella and her mom had been up in New York for the past few months, and his niece was getting the best possible care. Her numbers were looking good. *Gracias a dios.*

Rodrick closed his eyes to rest, excited to get back to Miami, to his girlfriend, to the sun. He hoped he'd never have to see or speak to Morgan Chary again. It frightened him that people like that existed in the world—powerful people with horrible intentions. He'd never understood what Morgan was getting out of it all, and he probably never would. The pilot came over the loudspeaker to announce that they were delayed due to a technical issue. Rodrick sighed. He pulled out his phone and started scrolling, bored. A text message popped up. Rodrick braced himself before reading it, tightening his seat belt as if they were about to crash, though they were still safely on the ground.

I know what you've been up to, I saw you with her. If you don't help me, I'll have you arrested. You can try to blame Morgan, but who are they going to believe: a white lady with money or you, a Hispanic driver?

Rodrick bit down on his bottom lip, hard, until he could taste blood. The plane taxied back to the gate, slowly. He'd give her what she needed.

## Chapter 16

# A Meeting at Sofia's!

——

Frost Trevor and Belle Redness were standing outside Sofia's apartment building in Tribeca, taking in the sun before heading inside. A woman with a small white dog walked by, pausing just to their right, allowing the dog to pee so close to them that Frost had to step away to let the stream of urine pass by.

"Uh, we're standing here," scoffed Frost. The woman, who was wearing earbuds, pretended not to hear them, waltzing off without a word.

"Asshole!" Belle yelled after her. "Fucking dog owners are taking over New York. Letting them off-leash in the park, not picking up their poop. Disgusting."

'You've changed, Belle," Frost said, laughing. "You're punk!"

"I guess I just don't give a shit anymore," said Belle, slumping a little.

"I like you better like this," said Frost. She took Belle's hand as they entered, Frost announcing to the doorman who they were there to visit, the women nervously wondering if Sofia would want to see them after everything that had happened. The doorman called up and then, after a short chat, nodded. Relieved, they rode up to Sofia's without speaking. Frost was feeling anxious but determined to make things right.

The door opened, and instead of Sofia stood a good-looking man, with long eyelashes and full lips. This must be the man Sofia had cheated on her husband with, the trainer. Frost had been picturing a meathead-y, gym-rat type, not this gentle beauty, and cursed herself for assuming something, yet again, about which she knew nothing.

"I'm Michael," the man said as he ushered the women into the living area, which, cleared of that horrid surrealist decor, was spacious and spare. They settled in on a loveseat opposite Sofia, who was sitting on the couch in the center of the room, in sweatpants and a tank top, her hair up in a bun. Michael gave Sofia a light kiss on the head before going into another room. Frost was stunned by the interaction, sensing immediately that this wasn't just an affair—it was love. Good for Sofia, she thought.

"So . . ." said Sofia, letting herself trail off, not making it any easier for Frost and Belle. Belle was in one of her many floral dresses, but Frost noticed that with her new haircut, the bob hanging neatly near her chin, everything she wore looked cooler.

"We've come to say we're sorry," said Frost. "We knew that Morgan was going to pull that prank at your party, and we let her. She wanted us to believe that you were out to get us, and she made a pretty convincing case. But we were idiots. She said we were just going to make some people throw up that night, get drunker than usual, and that it would be funny. You'd be embarrassed and maybe leave for Miami. But what happened wasn't funny. Especially Dr. Broker." Frost looked at Belle encouragingly, willing her to say something. Belle was silent for a few seconds longer, but just before

Frost was about to get out of her seat and shake her shoulders, Belle cleared her throat.

"Yes, that's right," said Belle, looking anywhere but at Sofia. "We were wrong to think you were behind anything."

Sofia nodded but didn't add anything.

"Belle found out something," prompted Frost. Belle squirmed a bit.

Michael came into the room and set a steaming cup of tea in front of Sofia, who accepted it with a smile. "Would you ladies like anything? Sparkling water? Coffee?" he asked. They shook their heads and he softly padded out. Of course—the bartender! Frost should have known.

"So, um, Jeff hired this new detective to relook at everything that had happened to us. The Greg guy was pretty useless in the end," said Belle.

"I wonder why," said Sofia, rolling her eyes.

"Oh, shit," said Frost under her breath, inwardly berating herself for her own stupidity.

"Anyway, this new guy went around to all the florists in the city, like every single one. It took him ages, but finally, at a tiny place in the East Village called Sunny's, he found something."

"Wait, I've heard of that place," Sofia interrupted. She was leaning in now, having lost some of her iciness, her eyes lighting up. Frost was pleased to see some of the old Sofia returning.

"Yeah, so had I," said Frost.

"Ask Morgan!" the two women said in unison. Sofia cackled happily.

"Sunny's is the *best* florist in the city, even though it's a hole-in-the-wall and out of the way," said Sofia, doing a shockingly accurate Morgan impression. "The arrangements are amaaaaazzzzing," she trilled. Frost giggled. Belle, who didn't seem to be enjoying the moment at all, went on.

"The owner told the detective that a day before our, er, lanternfly incident, a woman had come in with a strange request—an entire bouquet made from leftover rotting flowers. She'd paid her a thousand dollars cash for it. The owner said the woman was blond, extremely thin, and was wearing workout clothes and a scarf around her neck," said Belle. She sighed.

"Even Jeff knew who it was, at that point. Occasionally, he does look up from his phone." Belle let out a short, bitter laugh. "I still can't believe it was her. Why would she do that to me? We're friends! Or we were."

"She thought Miles was bullying Gertrude," said Frost, looking down at the floor.

"Miles?!" said Belle. "Miles wouldn't hurt anyone. He's just like Jeff—a sweet, dumb puppy," she said.

"We heard her say something about it at the Friendsgiving party," said Sofia.

"Morgan is telling everyone that *you* put chemicals in the dessert, that you wanted them all to get sick. We know that's a lie, but the moms are eating it up," said Frost. "What if someone calls the police? Do you want us to tell the everyone the truth?"

"Not yet," said Sofia. "That's coming."

"What about Rodrick?" said Frost. She was hoping to get out of this conversation without an admission about her affair with Art. So far, Belle was so concerned about herself, and why she'd been targeted, she'd neglected to think about Frost at all.

"I've taken care of Rodrick, don't worry. I saw him with Morgan the night of your itchy party," said Sofia flatly.

"My itchy party? My *itchy* party?" said Belle. She then started to

laugh, an uproarious laugh, doubling over in her seat, tears streaming from her eyes, until Frost and Sofia were compelled to join in,
the three women in utter hysterics, unable to stop, the craziness of
the situation having finally set in.

"You guys, you don't even want to know what Morgan is doing
with Dr. Broker," said Sofia, in between hiccups. "I'm pretty sure
she tried to kill him. Ay, that man did not just ingest a bit of Ambien." Belle's eyes widened. She then took deep breaths to calm
herself down, something sinister coming together in her mind.

"Fuck," Belle said, her face crumpling with the dawning real-
ization that Dr. Broker hadn't pursued her for her good looks or
charm. "What if . . . what if she tells . . . Jeff," she breathed. "He
can't find out. I will kill her. She cut my hair. She cut my hair! And
what she did to Hildy . . . I will fucking murder her skinny ass."

Sofia glanced at Frost, in disbelief that those words had come
out of Belle Redness's mouth.

"I have a plan," said Sofia.

"We're going to help," said Frost. "What can we do?" Belle
nodded, her bob swinging. They'd all gone a little psycho by then.

## Chapter 17

# The Atherton Altruist Ceremony!

═══

Here they all were, at Sofia's Altruist Ceremony, sitting in the plush pews of Atherton's auditorium, a circle of them surrounding the stage. Four chairs were set up in staggered formation, giving everyone a good view of those up top: Sofia, Sofia's adorable children, Lucia and Carlos, and the school secretary, Mary Margaret. The large projector screen used for rainy-day movies was down, likely because of the drizzle earlier that day. The place was full—about a hundred moms gathered to witness the spectacle, to see what Sofia had planned and why she'd called this ceremony in the first place. Atherton had welcomed her in, chewed her up, and spit her out, and they were all excitedly awaiting the resolution of this particular story.

Would Sofia announce she was leaving the school? Double down and stay? Reveal why she'd tried to murder the majority of the PA? (That was an exaggeration: the only one who was even close to dying was Dr. Broker, and the hospital wasn't releasing info about his condition or what had caused it; everyone else had been in and out of the ER in no time.)

The air in the auditorium was stuffy and hot; the landmark ma-
sonry building had been erected in 1860, and as much money as the
school poured into its renovations, it still suffered from under–air
conditioning. The attendees were catching up on weekend plans,
exchanging notes on summer camps, chatting about the TV shows
they were watching, normal mom stuff in a this very abnormal mom
circumstance.

There was an audible buzz as Sofia's three former best friends,
Belle Redness, Frost Trevor, and Morgan Chary, entered the room,
all dressed in black, even Belle, who'd traded her usual girly getups
for a funereal pantsuit. They looked like a trio of sneaky stagehands,
slinking in together right as the play was supposed to start. They
ducked down, trying to go unnoticed, but the combination of their
late entrance plus their out-of-character costumes had the opposite
effect. Heads swiveled to stare, and they sank into three seats in the
back, right at the same time that Mary Margaret stepped up to the
podium and tapped the microphone to start.

"Hello, Atherton! I'm here in place of our dear Dr. Broker,
who's still on the mend. But I know he'd want this to happen in
his absence. Our administration is fully focused on Atherton's four
pillars: Integrity, Peace, Equality, and Simplicity, and this award hits
each one of them. Sitting up here with me today is Sofia Perez and
her children: Lucia, who's in second grade, and Carlos, who's in
fourth. We are here to honor Sofia for what she did on the first day
of school. Better late than never, right?" Mary paused for laughter,
but there was none.

"On September sixth, Sofia, new to Atherton, intervened on behalf of another mother, putting herself in danger to save someone
else. Belle Redness was about to be viciously attacked by a person

experiencing homelessness, and Sofia leaped to her defense, driving away the aggressor by hitting him with her purse. Women are mighty! And here at Atherton we band together to protect one another, friends till the end." There was an uncomfortable amount of throat clearing and a small amount of applause.

"So, let me get to the good part," said Mary, sensing she was losing the audience. "Please, Sofia, will you come here?" Sofia, still sitting, slowly took off the cream blazer she'd been wearing, and then she stood, revealing for the first time what she had on underneath—a teal and orange striped bandage dress, tight enough to be painted on, showing off Sofia's curves, the roundness of her behind, her smooth, tan skin. It was the Sofia of old, the Sofia of September, before she'd morphed into an Atherton clone. Sofia walked over to Mary, taking her place next to her.

"Sofia Perez, will you please accept the Atherton Altruist award for your selfless and brave actions helping another Atherton community member in need?" Sofia nodded and smiled. Then Mary handed Sofia a small jewelry box, which everyone knew contained a gold necklace with an "A" pendant that the PA bought in bulk from Jennifer Meyer, a friend of Ava Leo's.

"Sofia, if you'd like to give a little speech, now's your moment!" said Mary. All the moms held their collective breath. Sofia stepped over to the microphone.

"*Hola*, ladies, and Dreyfuss," she said. Dreyfuss beamed. "And thank you, Mary, for this lovely honor. Our little family feels so lucky to have been welcomed into the Atherton community. My children have made so many new friends, and we've loved getting to know you."

At that moment, the children's nanny, standing near the stage, beckoned the kids to come down to her. The three of them then filed out the side door of the auditorium as Sofia watched, silent, making everyone shift in their seats.

"They're tired, you know?" she said after they'd left. "And they don't need to see this."

The tension in the room had built to the point of near explosion. Moms were gripping their seats, grinding their expensive dental work.

"Get on with it, Sofia!" yelled Gabby Mahler, to some laughter.

"Okay, Gabby, okay," said Sofia slowly, something switching on inside of her, shifting her tone from sweet to sour. "You know, you and Ava have never been very nice to me, especially Ava." Ava shook her head as if to say "Not true," her sharp bangs swaying. "Ava, how's that little shoplifting habit going?" said Sofia. "If we looked in your bag, what would we find?" All hundred attendees turned to look at Ava, whose face had gone from red to white to purple. "It's really too bad your husband's business collapsed, though I'm sure your girls will thrive in public school." Ava slipped down in her seat, trying to hide.

"But we're not here today to talk about Ava," said Sofia. "Or Trina and her drugs, or your messy divorce, Gabby, or how you all try to bribe Dr. Broker with box seats to the Yankees and cases of wine. Is *everyone* sleeping with Dr. Broker? I suppose anyone left over is sleeping with Art Chary. Ay, it's crazy!"

Everyone froze in fear, thinking about their own, closely guarded secrets. What else did Sofia know?

"Today we're going to talk about Morgan Chary," continued Sofia, on a roll now. "Morgan, who vandalized Frost's art show and hired someone to hit Frost with an e-scooter. I have the scooter rental receipt with your name on it!" Sofia waved a piece of paper in the air dramatically. Morgan stood up to leave but was blocked in by the row of other moms, looking at her accusingly. "Morgan?!" said Frost, turning to her friend in feigned surprise. Sofia carried on. "Morgan, who paid a homeless man to attack Belle, and also leaked her private email, *and* ruined Belle's company." Belle then stood up, too, running her hand through her short hair. "It was you!" she said loudly.

"Morgan was the one who slipped drugs into my special pudding, sending you all to the hospital . . . And that's not even the half of it," said Sofia, as Morgan finally pushed through the row and headed toward the exit. The door opened and Mac from the front desk security team entered, blocking Morgan from getting past.

"Mac, move out of the fucking way," said Morgan. But Mac, a former NYPD officer, wasn't having it. He put a hand on her wrist. "Morgan Chary, you have to come with me," he said firmly.

"*Adios*, Morgan," Sofia said into the mic.

"This is ridiculous," said Morgan, repeating herself. "Ridiculous."

Then the lights in auditorium lowered—Mary did this, happily; she'd been watching the whole thing as avidly as she did her Bravo shows, thinking about how this mean mom deserved this and worse. (Mary's friend, Nurse Weiss, had learned that the lice email had come from Dr. Broker's account. It was about time that Atherton's rotten apples were exposed.)

The projector screen lit up. A Nest Cam video came on, and it soon became clear they were watching scenes from Sofia's Surrealist Ball, the viewpoint coming from above the bar. There were the over-the-top costumes, the drunken banter, their faces flashing by one by one. There was Bud Cunningham fondling Julie Klein's butt, Julie smiling at him. (Julie, in a panic, stood up and raced out of the auditorium right then; Trina Cunningham looked as if she might die on the spot.) There were Armena Justice and Jennifer Smyth sharing a passionately sloppy French kiss, thinking no one could see. There was Dave Morehouse taking a big sniff of his ketamine nasal spray bottle. It was sickening in the daylight, the excess even more obscene.

And then Morgan came into view, or a person who everyone knew to be Morgan, as her face wasn't visible beneath the large white clam costume. She was standing in front of the bar, close to the punch bowl. The platters of *postre de natas* expanded before her. She reached into her green Bottega bag (they all knew it was Bottega), and pulled out what appeared to be a vial of liquid, covering her hand with a napkin as she quickly poured the vial's contents into about fifteen of the ramekins. The bartender, the hot one with the abs, walked into the frame. Then it cut to black.

The auditorium was completely quiet as the lights went back on. "Holy shit," whispered Gabby. Sofia stood at the podium proudly as Morgan rolled her eyes and shook her head. "You have no idea what was in that. It could have been sugar, for all you know," she said.

"All right, show's over, let's go," Mac said to Morgan.

"Is she getting arrested?" Trina asked Dre, loudly enough for all to hear.

"How am I supposed to know?" said Dre, who'd been loving it all.

"You're the head of the PA. Duh," said Trina.

"The PA isn't looped in on criminal activity! We plan fund-raisers!" said Dre.

Morgan wasn't actually getting arrested. There were no police involved at all. Sofia hadn't been looking to put Morgan in jail, she'd just wanted her exiled from society. Frost and Belle had pitched in, getting Mac to play his part by utilizing the one thing they had that

Sofia didn't—money. Namely, $20,000 in cash, which Mac had gratefully accepted with a wink. Morgan, ruined, was escorted out of Atherton and sent on her merry way, free to terrorize another group of moms at another private school.

"Thank you all for attending my ceremony!" Sofia concluded, taking a deep bow. The crowd sat in stunned silence. The only person who moved was Clara Cain—she was on her phone, clearly dealing with an emergency.

"I'm sorry, I don't know how Welly's board found out," she was saying as she made her way out of the room. "Obviously I didn't tell anyone! I'm your lawyer, you moron."

Belle and Frost then stood up, whooping and cheering like they were at a Knicks game, the other moms looking on, aghast.

"And remember: I am available to plan your next luxury vacation, courtesy of Omni Travel group. All referrals are much appreciated!" At that, Sofia, triumphant, waltzed off the stage, leaving the rest of Atherton reeling.

## Chapter 18

# Girthy Gertrude!

===

For the past year, Gertrude Chary had been conducting a private experiment. A few times a week, she'd come home from school and cry to Morgan over tales of bullying, stories of torture, episodes of sadness and depression. She'd planted seeds in her mother's brain and then had carefully watered them, waiting for them to grow.

It hadn't been easy to play such a long game. Gertrude knew that she and Morgan had the same illness, had the same drive to hurt. Morgan had tried to hide herself from her daughter, but Gertrude was too smart for that. Little things had tipped her off: Morgan surreptitiously kicking a stray dog when they were in the Caribbean; Morgan lying to people's faces about random, unimportant things only Gertrude knew to be untrue; Morgan's dead-eyed stare in the face of touching tributes. Gertrude had once seen her mother flick a baby in the face when she thought no one was looking.

Perhaps, though, Morgan was too blinded by her love for Gertrude to see the truth about her own daughter. Or maybe she was in on the con, Gertrude fabricating and Morgan purposefully taking the bait. Either way, it had been a fun mother-daughter bonding exercise, Gertrude eagerly waiting to see what her mother would do with this false information. Was this what other girls felt like when they went shopping with their moms or got their nails done together?

Getting Morgan to hate Belle had been easy; Gertrude just painted Miles Redness out to be an asshole. Little, harmless Miles, who'd always been kind to Gertrude. Ha. Girthy Gertrude. Yeah, right. Frost had been a bit more difficult, though Gertrude's opportunity came when she'd found out her idiot father was sleeping with her. He'd barely even tried to conceal the affair; Gertrude saw their emails to each other on her father's Gmail app. What a dummy. Gertrude had been sure her mother would have found out eventually, but she'd hastened the reveal, spraying Blush by Marc Jacobs over a pile of his discarded clothes, knowing Morgan would understand exactly what that meant.

And then Gertrude had watched in awe as her mother had gone to town. Something in Morgan had been unleashed, though it wasn't from the Wegovy (the side effects included nausea and lightheadedness, not "embracing your inner sociopath"). Gertrude had been hearing all the moms talk about perimenopause, so maybe it was a hormonal thing, Morgan going through some kind of "change." Gertrude, for her part, was still waiting desperately for her period to come. She was one of the last girls in her class without it. She and Hildy Redness, of all people. You could orchestrate many things but unfortunately not your own body chemistry.

Gertrude had loved this year, loved witnessing her mother's power. Gertrude had all of Morgan's log-ins and passwords—they were variations on Gertrude's name and birthday—and she would scour her mom's communication while Morgan was at exercise classes. She even had Morgan's phone passcode (it was the date she and Art had met), which is how Gertrude learned about Dr. Broker. He liked to leave Morgan long, er, impassioned voicemails, the likes of which made Gertrude giggle. Morgan sent illuminating email after DM after Signal message after text, leaving Gertrude a trail of delightful terror.

The creativity Morgan had displayed through it all was truly impressive, and Gertrude had made mental notes the entire way. Morgan had dismantled Frost and Belle piece by piece, setting up Sofia, covering her tracks, making it seem as though Morgan, too, was a victim.

Gertrude was in her own room now, sitting on her fluffy bed, an end-of-year slideshow of evil running through her mind. Belle's hair! Frost's accident! It made Gertrude excited to think about it, like how other girls in her grade felt about expensive skin care.

She heard a light knock on her door, and then Morgan peeked her head in.

"Can I come in, sweetie?" said Morgan. Gertrude nodded. Her mother sat next to her. Gertrude knew that her weight bothered Morgan, and so recently she'd been siphoning off doses of Morgan's Wegovy for herself. She'd learned how to administer it on YouTube and had come to enjoy the weekly ritual of sticking herself with that tiny, sharp needle. She'd already lost ten pounds.

"I have some news, and I'm not sure you're going to like it," said Morgan, stroking Gertrude's hair. "You look great, by the way." Gertrude smiled. The school year was over. It was time for the game to end. Gertrude was now ready to share it all with her mom, to have her be as proud of Gertrude as Gertrude was of her.

"We're going to look at other schools for next year," said Morgan, staring out the window instead of at her daughter. "I haven't been thrilled with Atherton, and I think there are places that might be a better fit for you. Maybe one of the all-girls schools uptown. People love Spence and Nightingale."

Gertrude knew that this meant something must have gone wrong. Gertrude didn't care which school she went to, but it hurt her to hear that her mother had somehow failed. To cheer her up, Gertrude said, "And I want you to know that I've been helping you!"

"Oh, how so?" said Morgan.

"First of all, with Hildy. Those nudes?" Gertrude winked. Morgan didn't say anything, but Gertrude thought she saw her mother's lips flirt with a smile.

"Also with Dr. Broker. I mixed some of your special tea into his coffee. I've been doing it for months now. The day of Sofia's party, I gave him quite a lot." Gertrude had thought it would be a nice touch for the celebration, a fun addition to the confusing chaos.

"Okay, honey, I was wondering about that," said Morgan, continuing to pet her only daughter, her face betraying no surprise. "It wasn't the exact timeline I was going for—I was going to have Paul finish out the year, then gradually feel too ill to return to Atherton in the fall. But your way worked, too."

Gertrude glowed with happiness at the compliment. "You've done it all perfectly, Mom. I'm really impressed," said Gertrude, which was true.

"Well, not everything," said Morgan. Gertrude's room was right at the tree line, and the greenery was at its gorgeous West Village peak. They sat there for a few minutes, both thinking about their next moves.

"Mom, I also did something to Dad," said Gertrude.

Morgan frowned.

"What?" Morgan didn't look pleased, and that frightened Gertrude.

"I sent a picture of him with that Tilly girl to a few people at Welly. He's so stupid. I think we're better off without him." Morgan didn't say anything for a minute. "I learned it all from you, Mom!" said Gertrude, a little desperately.

"You are a special girl," said Morgan finally. Then she got up and left, shutting the door behind her.

# Epilogue

Hildy Redness was liking her new school, Brearley, even if it meant she had to wear a uniform: an A-line skirt or khaki pants and a collared shirt. Honestly, wearing a uniform wasn't that bad, though she'd never admit that to her mom, who was *so* happy that Hildy couldn't wear a hoodie to school ever again.

Hildy liked that Brearley was all girls, and she also liked that there were clear rules and grades and stuff like that, unlike Atherton, which had always been loosey-goosey about all those things. She was still getting used to the commute uptown, which was a little annoying, because it meant she had to leave the house super early to get to Eighty-Third Street by 8:00 a.m. She'd been begging her mom to let her take the subway instead of having to sit in traffic with Fred every morning on the FDR. There were other girls at the school who took the train, and Hildy had a phone, so what was the worst that could happen? Her mom said she was "thinking" about it, but Hildy worried that just meant "no." Since last year, after all the stuff with Morgan and Sofia, her mom had been even more overprotective than normal. "Bad people exist," she'd said to Hildy.

She was so effing dramatic. Hildy worried that she'd never really get to do anything on her own. It was so unfair.

If Hildy really thought about it, she supposed she missed Atherton a little. She'd been there since pre-K—it was basically her second home. But this year wouldn't have been the same, even if she'd stayed. For one thing, there was that new headmaster, Dr. Cherry, an old dude who'd replaced Dr. Broker, who'd moved to Boston or something after he'd gotten better. He'd actually been *poisoned*—someone had been dripping drain cleaner into his drinks or something awful like that. But Hildy had heard he wasn't pursuing it legally and had just wanted to leave the city right away. Poor Dr. Broker.

And most of her friends had left Atherton, too, scattering off to other private schools. A couple of Atherton girls were at Brearley with her now, and it was always nice to see a friendly face in the hallway. It was like they all spoke the same language (and had gone through the same traumatic shit with their parents).

It was weird to think that Atherton wasn't, like, Atherton anymore. And sad. But Hildy had moved on. Miles was at St. Bernard's, so their mom could pick them both up on the days they were leaving school around the same time, swinging east from Ninety-Eighth and Fifth with Miles in tow. Her mom wasn't as, like, involved with the Brearley moms as she'd been with that group at Atherton, and that was fine with Hildy—it felt healthier, really. In many ways, her mom seemed better? Like nicer and less focused on herself. Oh, and she'd kept her hair short, if you could believe it. Hildy preferred it that way.

Her mom was also being kinder to Hildy's dad. Rubbing his shoulders when they were watching TV and doing weird shit like that. Hildy had heard them talking about their couples therapist, which, in Hildy's opinion, was a healthy way for married couples to continue communicating (she'd learned that from some therapy TikTok). Plus, Belle was working on a new home design company, which she was calling American Forest. This one had a "The Pillow," or whatever. And that was taking up most of Belle's time.

They still saw Frost and her family occasionally, which was good for Miles, because he seemed to miss Alfred and King. The twins had transferred to St. Paul's and so were living in New Hampshire mostly. Frost kept talking about how much she missed them but how great it was for them to be surrounded by other sporty boys. In hindsight, Frost had said, Atherton probably hadn't been the right choice for their family in the first place.

She'd also heard her mom and Frost speaking about Sofia. Her mom had said something to Frost about the "unexpected success" of Sofia's travel agent business, and that she was hiring people under her and that "all the chic downtown moms were signing up to be her clients." Sofia's kids were now at Friends Seminary, and "Sofia rules the school." Good for Sofia, Hildy thought. She'd always liked her. She was so pretty and fun. Oh, Frost had also mentioned something about Sofia's boyfriend, some guy named Michael, whom all the coolest moms were hiring as their new trainer.

Hildy had never gotten the real story about what happened last year, beyond that Frost and Belle hadn't pressed charges against Morgan for whatever it was she'd done. "I just want to move on with our lives and forget that this year even happened," her mom had said to her dad one night when they thought Hildy was asleep. Honestly, Hildy didn't blame her.

As for Morgan, well . . . Hildy hadn't told anyone this, and she never would, but she'd run into Morgan on the street the other day, uptown, near Brearley, when Hildy was walking to lacrosse in Central Park with a group of friends. She'd thought that Morgan had moved away—Belle had said the family had left for California after Art's embarrassing lawsuit thing. Apparently, Art had been ousted from his own company, which was something Hildy didn't even know could happen! But maybe Morgan was back to take care of some business, or to go to a doctor. Morgan had seen Hildy first, and had approached her, saying something like—"Hildy Redness! Just who I wanted to see! You look amazing!"—which was strange. Hildy's friends had looked at her, like, "Who's this intense blond lady?"

Then Morgan had kind of, like, dragged her aside and interrogated her, asking questions about her mom and Frost and everything else. Hildy answered to the best of her ability, but she just wanted to end the conversation. Morgan was acting a little manic, and she looked super skinny, like too skinny, probably from those weight-loss drugs that everyone was on now. Hildy remembered to ask after Gertrude, which she proud of herself for doing (Morgan said Gertrude was "doing great at her new school," though Hildy didn't believe it; Gertrude was delulu, and not in a cute way). Then Hildy said she had to get back to her friends, and Morgan said something like, "How are your mom and dad? Any news with them?" And Hildy just said nope and shrugged. Morgan looked really pissed about it all. Hildy waved bye and booked it, a little creeped out, and also knowing she'd keep it all a secret from her mom. Belle would *freak* out if she heard, and Hildy just didn't want to deal with that.

Hildy now had her own friend dynamics to survive; she was in eighth grade, and some girls were starting to act crazy. Hildy tried to stay above the fray, and she was pretty good at it, unlike her mom, who definitely got sucked into drama. If Hildy and her mom were the same age, Hildy didn't think they'd be friends. She'd never tell her that, of course. She tried to protect her mom. For example, last year, Hildy had been doing schoolwork on her dad's computer and had flicked over to his Chrome. His Gmail was up, and right before she was about to close the tab, she'd seen a message come in with the subject line: "Your wife is fucking the headmaster." Hildy had clicked on it in a second—what the hell?—and it opened to reveal a series of pictures of Belle, some in that hideous tree costume she'd worn to one of the theme parties, some in that pink suit that Hildy hated. In a few of them, it looked like Belle was kissing Dr. Broker! In one, he was kneeling near her, about to do something nasty.

Hildy had closed the email as quickly as she'd opened it. No kid should have to see her mom like *that*. Hildy had assumed they'd been deepfaked, just like those naked pictures of her had been, maybe even by the same person. Hildy couldn't even imagine the meltdown her mom would have had about it, on top of everything else she'd been going through. So Hildy had deleted the email. And then had deleted it from her dad's deleted folder. Done and done. No one the wiser. What kind of sicko would have faked pictures of her mom and the headmaster, well, Hildy just didn't want to know.

Growing up in New York City was a trip. Everyone was either really rich, like Hildy and her family, or really poor. There didn't seem like there was much in between. Even people with real jobs seemed to be hurting; Hildy had seen that detective guy, Greg Summerly, walking dogs near her school. How funny was that?

Hildy felt lucky for everything she had, she really did, but sometimes she looked at her parents' life, and especially at her mom and her friends, and she'd think to herself: No, not for me. Just no. Maybe Hildy would move to another state, somewhere like Ohio or something. Someplace where people were nice to each other. Was that a thing? She'd find out soon enough. Four more years at Brearley and then she'd be done. Hildy had a bright future ahead of her. She was a good kid.

## Acknowledgments

I would like to thank . . .

My boys, Monty and Sandy, the loves of my life. Monty is now old enough to help me with plot points and Sandy is still young enough to want to cuddle with us in bed. When people say these are the golden years, they're right.

My husband, Charles, for being a lovely partner in life and parenting and everything, and for washing the pots and pans and letting me sleep in on the weekends. You are a hero. Love you, hons.

My dad, for telling everyone he meets that his daughter is an author, and then pressuring them to buy my books on the spot.

My sister, for reading an early version (after I pestered her to do it like five times), and for giving me good notes, including that "Lululemon is lame now." Who knew?

My brother, Ari, for distracting me every day with doomsday articles, giving me that writing break I so desperately didn't need.

Also: Jared Weisfeld and Julie Sasaki, for putting up with those lunatics.

And the cousins: Jude, Olive, Sully, and Kai! And also my wonderful in-laws, Linda and Marcus, and my gorgeous sister-in-law, Alice, and our beautiful nieces, Daisy and Olive.

My forever editor, Megan Lynch, who continues to wow me with her support. Thank you for believing in me and these books. We finally made one with a likable character! Woohoo!

My agent, Alexandra Machinist, the deadpan, brutally honest cheerleader everyone needs in their life. I am so lucky to have you.

Everyone at Flatiron, including Marlena Bittner, Malati Chavali, Kate Keating, Katherine Turro, Claire McLaughlin, Brittany Leddy, and Kara McAndrew. You guys are the best.

The audiobook masters at Macmillan Audio, Elishia Merricks, Drew Kilman, and Emily Dyer.

Christina Lombardi, a PR wizard, for shouting about my books from the rooftops.

My early readers, Amanda Schweitzer, Daily Lambert, and Rebecca Grossman-Cohen. This book would make no sense without your notes. Thank you!

And finally, my (not mean, very nice) mom friends! Please don't ban me from the WhatsApp groups. I love the WhatsApp groups!

## About the Author

**Emma Rosenblum** is the bestselling author of *Bad Summer People* and *Very Bad Company*. Previously, she was the chief content officer of Bustle Digital Group, the executive editor of *Elle*, and, before that, an editor at *Bloomberg Businessweek*, *Glamour*, and *New York* magazine. She lives in New York City with her family.